The Fence My Father Built

The Fence My Father Built

Copyright © 2009 by Linda S. Clare

ISBN-13: 978-1-4267-0073-6

Published by Abingdon Press, P.O. Box 801, Nashville, TN 37202
www.abingdonpress.com

Cover design by Anderson Design Group, Nashville, TN

Library of Congress Cataloging-in-Publication Data

Clare, Linda S.
  The fence my father built / Linda S. Clare.
    p. cm.
  ISBN 978-1-4267-0073-6 (pbk. : alk. paper) 1. Librarians—
Fiction. 2. Fathers and daughters—Fiction. 3. Fathers—Death—
Psychological aspects—Fiction. 4. Oregon—Fiction. I. Title.
  PS3603.L354F46 2009
  813'.6—dc22
                                    2009014618

Printed in the United States of America

1 2 3 4 5 6 7 8 9 10 / 14 13 12 11 10 09

THE FENCE MY FATHER BUILT

by
Linda S. Clare

Abingdon Press fiction
a novel approach to faith

For my brave husband, Brad, and our children,
Nathan, Christian, Alyssa, and Tim.
And for Nova Wilkinson, who became a real angel too soon.

Acknowledgments

This story has reinvented itself many times, but it arose out of the need to know my biological father and to find a place to belong. From discovering my own Native American heritage to facing the addiction and alcoholism so pervasive in my family, this journey has helped me grow. I extend sincerest thanks to both my biological and adoptive families; to my Sisters-In-Ink, Kris Ingram, Kathy Ruckman, Debbie Page, Heather Kopp, and Melody Carlson; to writing buddies Bobbie, Ann, Linda, Sally, John, Jodi, Jennifer, Tamsin, and Deb. My deepest gratitude to wonderful editor Barbara Scott, who said this story deserved a chance.

JOSEPH'S JOURNAL
JUNE 1977

*S*prawled across the bed, you slept facedown, wearing that red cowgirl shirt and the velvet skirt you love. I stood by and watched your breathing. Your hair, so straight and black, reminded me of my people, our people, and I wondered what you dreamed. Years ago, the Nez Perce surrendered to broken treaties, broken dreams. I'm sorry, daughter, but I'm surrendering too.

You're only five, Muri, but you learn fast. In this Oregon desert, the sun beats down hot, and today our tan faces shone with sweat. We walked across the sagebrush and you held the corn snake we found. You held it gently, without fear. I felt as proud as I ever have.

After sunset, we sat on the hill and looked up at the stars. When you got cold I draped my old coat around you and told you all about angels. On the way home, you didn't ask for your mother, not once. It's wrong, I know, but I was pleased.

I had big plans to be your daddy. I was going to read to you every day, teach you the names of all the Civil War battles. I'd teach you how to fish. You'd learn how to listen to the wind and how to skip a stone. Most of all, I'd teach you how to pray.

None of that will happen now.

After your mom called, I broke down and cried, and I couldn't stop. I've lost. Your mother doesn't know our ways but she has the white man's courts on her side. They call it full custody. I cry because I won't see you on your first day of school or when you get your driver's license. My ears won't hear your laughter. You'll learn to climb trees and hold snakes without me. I won't even be able to tell you why I wasn't there.

Maybe when you're grown you'll understand. Or maybe you won't care about the secrets we could have shared, secrets of land and water, secrets of fixing refrigerators. I pray that God, who made all of this for us, will reach your heart in time.

Tonight, I hugged you close, but you held your nose and said, "Daddy, I hate smoking!" I can't seem to get that cigarette smell out *of my clothes. All I smelled right then was the pain of your mother's victory.*

Her car pulled into the driveway, and she leaned on the horn. I waved out the window. She could wait. I shrugged into my suede jacket.

Before I handed you over, I picked up the framed picture I like: the one where you're standing on that wicker chair, holding your ragged blanket. I took the photo out of its frame, careful to hold it by the edges and slipped it into my wallet. When you got sleepy we hunted all over for that grimy blanket.

Your old man has the magic touch with broken appliances too. Just this week I fixed the neighbor lady's old stove. The bottle? Now that's a different story that I've tried to change a hundred times. If you only knew.

Standing by the bed, I watched you sleeping. I stroked your flushed cheek and whispered your name. I carried you to your mother's car, and you opened your eyes and smiled. I saved my tears for later when I opened my wallet. I looked at your photo and weakness ambushed me.

There are days when I feel strong. Those times, nothing can stand between you and me. Most times, though, I'm broken. I'm nothing but an old sinner praying for another chance.

Someday, Muri, come looking for your old dad, will you? Maybe God will light a fire in you and our ancestors will fan the flames. I'll put up a beacon so you'll know where to look.

1

My father left my mother and me when I was five, but back then I didn't hate him for it. He was an angel because he showed me things, told me things, made me see things for the very first time. How to hold a flat stone in order to skip it. The feel of water slipping through my fingers. How to tell the moon's phase.

The last night I saw him alive he took me to the top of a hill to look at the stars. Out where we lived, in Oregon's high desert, there were more stars than black sky. He draped his worn suede coat over my shoulders, and I kept tripping on the bottom, that's how little I was. We walked and walked, and once I fell over a sagebush. When I cried he said, "Sh, angels are watching." Dad pointed to the Milky Way, which took my breath away, and then we shouted out with joy, singing right along with the whole heavenly host. That's how I thought of my father then—as an angel—alive and real and always with a flask of whiskey inside that suede jacket.

Before Mother died she always said he was just an old holy roller. His idea of religion was speaking in tongues while reaching for the bottle. When I was young she mocked him every day.

"Why don't you just take your baby girl on down to the bar with you?" Mother would say. Her words dripped with her special brand of sarcasm. In those days her bitterness only made me feel closer to this father who prayed and this God who loved a sorry man like Joseph Pond.

But by the time I grew up I had come to hate him. Mom did a good job of encouraging my disgust, but I admit that most of my bile came of my own free will. I carefully tended doubts about God the Father, too, and I routinely blamed my troubles on one or both of them.

The day I drove to Murkee, where Joseph Pond had lived and died, I believed that angels didn't exist, at least not on desert highways like this one. My ex-husband Chaz said he and I had simply "grown apart." I tried to make it work for the kids' sake, but after I caught him with that Victoria woman one time too many, I decided enough was enough. Anyway, Chaz admitted he wasn't the daddy type. When he left, I let him go.

The kids and I were alone now, bound for the middle of nowhere. I wondered if angels took assignments out here on Mars.

Mars must be a lot like central Oregon, I decided. I didn't see a drop of water anywhere, and the wind blew hard and constant. Gusts pressed down the grass, leaning it over like a wino who had fallen asleep. Sagebrush, the ugliest plant I've ever seen, was probably the only thing holding down the red dirt. With the way my life was headed, if I didn't find something to hold onto soon, I might blow away too.

At times the kids dozed against the windows, their relaxed mouths jerking shut each time I hit a pothole. They must have been so tired to sleep through all the jouncing. We'd been on the road at least six hours, thanks to my lousy sense of direction and countless sibling quarrels. Nova started complaining as soon as we crossed the Cascade Mountains.

"We're doomed," Nova moaned. Then she argued with Truman over our bottled water supply and how many Milky Ways were left.

"What are you looking at?" I heard Tru yell at his sister. She was probably drilling him with the ultimate weapon—her famous stare. I could see her smoldering gaze in the rearview mirror.

"Everything looks dead." Nova pointed out the window. "Water's probably poison. Acid rain or something." She snapped her gum then, knowing I'd thrown many a student out of the high school library for that very infraction.

"Maybe that's why Grandpa died," Truman volunteered. At nine, Tru, named after my favorite president, was still cheerful most of the time. His sister just groaned and made a face at Tru, then put her earbuds back in place.

I swear she didn't hate everything and everyone last week. Her dyed orange hair, only two inches long on top this week, had been stiffened with Elmer's glue and stood in small peaks.

"Woolly worms," I told her. "Your hair reminds me of fuzzy caterpillars." She attributed her dark mood to my observations and said it was my fault that everything, including the landscape, had died. Sometimes she could be a stereotype of herself.

Maybe stereotypes were all anyone was, including my father. After years of thinking about how I could connect with my roots, Tru had found him on the Internet. He was doing a report for school about Oregon ranchers and accidentally bumped into his own grandfather's name in an article about ongoing feuds over water rights in the desert lands. An address popped up almost instantly, and decades of searching condensed into a few lines on a computer screen.

I'd written to the address that same day, only to learn that Joseph Pond had recently died. His sister, Lutie Pearl, wrote back, "Your daddy was only fifty-five, but liver disease doesn't care who it kills off." He owned a piece of property that was now mine, she said, and coincidentally, the neighbor was threatening to sue their socks off. "Muri," she wrote, "it would bless me if you could come here to clear things up."

Bless her? I wasn't sure I could balance my checkbook, much less clear up a lawsuit. But I wanted more than anything to know my roots, and truth be told, we were temporarily homeless.

As we chugged closer to my father's land, the dust hid deep ruts in the road that could have rolled our VW bus over on its back like a turtle. The kids had named it Homer because it was a camper inside, complete with a miniature stove and a roll of paper towels that came unwound unless held together with rubber bands. Tru kept saying we looked like the Beverly Hillbillies.

That might have been funny if I hadn't piled all our belongings on the roof rack, including a couple of twin mattresses that anchored an assortment of mismatched luggage and cardboard boxes, mostly containing kitchen appliances and old books.

The thought of driving to nowhere looking like characters from *The Grapes of Wrath* made my eye twitch. As if that wasn't enough, Nova was so embarrassed she threatened to bail out of the van and walk all the way back to Portland. My daughter, who was sixteen and therefore knew everything, added, "Your dad's already dead, so what's the point?"

Tru stared at her, with that serious expression he gets. He opened his mouth to say something but closed it again and went back to playing his handheld video game.

I'd told them we were here to settle my father's affairs, but that was only half true and they knew it. Once the school district eliminated my library position, Chaz knew he could pressure me to unload the house. I couldn't stand to live under the neighbors' stares, so I went along with the sale. As soon as the house sold, my ex-husband took his half of the money and ran straight to Victoria. He left his children unable to understand why he wasn't interested in them.

They didn't completely grasp the fact that we had nowhere else to go, and that's why we were driving into the Oregon desert. It was as simple as that. My half of the home proceeds would go for living expenses until I could land another job. I tried to explain that I saw this trip as a means to get my act together and figure out what we should do next. They didn't get it, and I confess, half the time I didn't either. My arms felt numb from gripping the steering wheel; I was a blob of weariness that began behind my eyes and permeated to my fingertips.

"Turn around and find a hotel," my daughter moaned above the chatter of the engine.

"There's not even a Motel 6 out here, Nova," I said.

She sarcastically reminded me that at least motels have swimming pools. I was thinking of letting her test her desert survival skills when we pulled into Murkee and parked in front of the Mucky-Muck Café. The place was as dried up as the rest of the landscape except for a scrub lilac bush straining for shade next to the building.

If we thought this looked like Mars, out here we were the strange ones. At least that's the way the waitress in the café acted. She took one look at Nova's pierced eyebrow (the one I'd forbidden), shook her head slowly, and asked for our order.

"Today's special is the double cheeseburger basket," the waitress said, pointing her pencil at a hand-lettered sign that leaned against a water glass full of cut lilacs, no doubt from the bush outside. She was dressed in one of those old-fashioned uniforms with a Peter Pan collar and a suffocating polyester bodice. A printed name tag said, Dove, and underneath, Welcome to the Mucky-Muck Café. The sign on the front door read, Mucky-Muck is Chinook for Good Food.

"You have GardenBurgers?" Nova wanted to know. She'd declared herself a vegetarian last week. "And a double-skinny hazelnut latte." My daughter had forgotten that we were now on a different planet, one without a Starbucks.

Dove looked at me to translate.

"Pick something," I growled, handing Nova one of those menus where someone had typed in the selections and slipped them inside a thick plastic sleeve.

When lunch arrived, Nova picked at hers and stared, catatonic, out the window. In the light I noticed again that my daughter had Chaz's eyes, a light intense blue that could turn the color of the stormy Pacific when she was angry.

Although most of the time he was mature for his age, Tru made a touchdown by flicking his straw paper between the salt and pepper shakers. I had a sudden urge to hide beneath the table.

Instead, I asked Dove if she knew about the place out on Winchester Road, the estate of the late Joseph Pond.

"Sure, everybody knows the Ponds," Dove said, but I wondered why she was whispering. She gathered up the little wads of paper where Tru missed the field goal. "So sad about his passing. His sister and her husband still live out there, though. Tiny comes in here and hauls off anything we don't want."

"We've been on the road since this morning," I said. "I've gotten lost more times than I can count." I fidgeted with my straw and tried to ignore Nova's grimaces.

One guy at the counter turned around. He was about fifty, his cheeks creased and tanned with the marks of sun and wind. His clothes were standard rancher's attire: plaid western shirt tucked into dark blue jeans and boots with pointed toes and a thick layer of dirt clinging to the heels. A real cowboy instead of the phony environmentalist types I'd put up with in the city. This cowboy sat hunched over the remains of a greasy lunch platter and hadn't eaten the pickle garnish. He stood it straight up in the middle of a half-eaten sandwich and chuckled. He had sharp, deep-set eyes; I couldn't see if they were brown or green. I looked away, hoping he hadn't noticed me staring. Being a librarian, I also hoped he wasn't the type who breaks the spine on a book.

The man stood up and strode over to our booth. "Welcome to Murkee," he said and extended his hand. "Just passing through?"

"No, not exactly," I said. "Nice to meet you. I'm Muri." I shook his hand but felt myself recoil. "And these are my children, Nova and Truman."

"Since the new highway went through we don't get that many tourists," he said. "You got to get off the beaten path to find us, right Dove?"

The waitress nodded. "Way off the path. You got that right, Linc. Unless you're out hunting fossils, that is."

He laughed. "Where are my manners? I meant to say I'm Lincoln Jackson. I know just about everything that goes on around here."

Nova's head popped up from her sulking. "Tell us how to get back to Portland."

I gasped. "Nova! I'm sorry, Mr. Jackson. We've gotten lost a number of times today, and we're a little road weary." I hoped my eyes weren't puffy.

He waved his hand. "Call me Linc, please. And I don't blame—Nova, is it—for being wary of our little town. The sidewalks do roll up pretty early. Not much action here, I'm afraid."

"Linc, then." I nudged Nova under the table.

"Sorry," she said.

Dove broke in. "It's even worse when there's a rodeo over in Prineville. Then we're lucky to serve lunch to the rattlers and jackrabbits." She chuckled at her small joke, and her uniform swished when she moved her arms.

Tru perked up. "Rattlers? Are there rattlesnakes out here?" He pushed up his glasses. Nova rolled her eyes.

Linc patted Tru's arm. "Sure there's snakes, little guy. You ever hold a snake?"

"No, but I want to." Tru sat up taller.

Linc leaned on the back of our booth. "How about roping? You ever roped a steer?"

Tru shook his head. "Like a cowboy?"

Linc laughed. "Shore, pardner. I can teach you all you need to know." Linc brought over his black Stetson and handed it to Tru. "Go ahead, son, try it on."

Tru looked at me for approval, then plunked on the hat. It nearly swallowed his head. "How do I look?"

"Like a doofus," Nova said. "Like this town. Who'd name a town Murkee, anyway?"

I sighed. "Nova, please."

Tru returned the hat, and Linc smoothed the brim. "No offense taken, ma'am," Linc said. "I don't rightly understand it myself, young lady. But my Great-grandmother Ida had the idea. And she insisted on Murkee. She said it sounded like some Indian word."

"So this whole area was settled by your family?" I didn't want to sound nosy, but I was intrigued. I smiled, relieved that these rural folks were so friendly.

Apparently, Dove had been eavesdropping. She came over with our check and said, "Linc here owns just about everything in these parts. Everything but the church and a couple of parcels next to his place."

Tru's eyes got bigger again. "You mean you own the whole town?" He dribbled ketchup down the front of his t-shirt, but I resisted the urge to wipe it off.

Linc seemed to consider Tru's question. "Well, son, I guess so. And when I get access to that creek I'll be a lot happier." Dove shot him a look and resumed scrubbing down tables.

"Why do you need a creek?" Tru looked puzzled. "Does it have lots of fish or something?" He stuffed the last of his french fries into his mouth.

"Tru, use your napkin," I said. I grabbed my purse and dug out money for our lunch, plus a nice tip. "And don't ask so many questions." This was getting embarrassing.

"No problem, ma'am," Linc said. "Let's just say one of my neighbors has been difficult." He sighed. "Then he up and died before we could see eye to eye."

Tru practically shouted, "My grandpa died too! Last week! But I never met him. I just heard about him."

"Sorry to hear that, son." Linc's expression changed, and suddenly, he seemed guarded.

The wind picked up outside, rattling the windows and door. Clouds sped past the restaurant like a stampede, as if they knew there was something wrong here. I shuddered at the thought of getting lost again before the sun set. Now I was anxious to get on with it. Even in death Joseph Pond would complicate my life.

"Mr. Jackson, we're not in Murkee to stay," I said. "But my father, Joseph Pond, passed away recently. We'll be here long enough to set his affairs in order. Maybe you could direct me to his property?" I smoothed a stray hair.

Linc's pleasant demeanor had vanished. His jaw now worked from side to side, and the light in his eyes had turned to sparks.

"Chief Joseph's place isn't hard to find," Linc said. "First eyesore you come to, that's the one." He laughed, but it was a hard laugh. He went back to the counter and straddled the stool.

"Eyesore?" I said aloud. I wondered why he had called my father Chief.

Dove shook her head and gazed up at the ceiling. "Lord, here we go again," she said. "There's a lot of stuff in the yard: bicycle parts, old cars, and that ridiculous fence."

Nova jabbed me with her elbow. "Mom," she hissed. "Let's just go."

"No, I want to hear more," I said. "What did you say about a fence?"

Linc interrupted. "She's talking about that idiotic fence out there. It's, well, you'll have to see for yourself."

The bells on the café door jingled, and another man walked in. He was the opposite of Linc in terms of first impressions. Instead of western attire, he wore a flannel shirt and baggy, worn jeans. A short graying ponytail trailed out the back of his ball cap. He sat at the counter, and I wondered what he was doing in the middle of nowhere.

"Hey Good-looking," he said to Dove.

"Good-looking my foot, Doc. The usual?" Dove grinned when he nodded. She slid behind the counter, poured coffee, and set the cup and saucer in front of him. "It'll be a few minutes for your order."

The man called Doc smiled. "No problem." He was Linc's opposite. His tanned face was easy and relaxed. I liked that, but I quickly reminded myself how foolish I could be about men: giving in, saying yes, and stumbling in, when I ought to be running for my life.

Dove came over to the booth, slapped the check in front of me, and I snapped to attention with a small gasp. She was careful to keep her back to Linc.

"Honey," she whispered to me. "Linc's your next-door neighbor. And he can be a bear, if you get my drift."

I stared at Linc, looking for bear-like signs. Doc wasn't overly friendly with Linc, either, but he did nod his head. Doc's cell phone rang, and he spoke into it in hushed tones, which I appreciated. I was trying to teach Nova a cell phone wasn't the most important accessory on earth.

"Hold the sandwich," Doc said. "Gotta run, Dove. Sorry." He dug around in his jeans pocket.

Dove waved him off. "Get going, Doc. No charge for a measly cup of coffee."

"Thanks, Good-looking." He winked at Dove and rushed outside.

Dove went to the counter, removed Doc's cup, and then turned back to me. "Head straight out to the first gravel road," she said, tossing the dirty dishes into a rubber dishpan, "till you get to the yellow gas company sign."

Linc nursed his coffee. "If you go past the creek, you've gone too far," he called across the room, and Dove nodded. His gaze locked on me. I felt more and more uncomfortable, but I wasn't about to let him intimidate me.

"So we're neighbors." I stood up and approached him. "I'm Joseph Pond's biological daughter. I'm sure this is all a misunderstanding."

Linc looked surprised, but then his eyes narrowed. "Biological, eh? What's that supposed to mean?" He stood up. "You must be the big city girl Lutie's been carrying on about, come to show the country bumpkins a thing or two."

Dove clattered a stack of dishes into the plastic tub.

I stood up taller and cleared my throat. "I'm a librarian, not an attorney."

He rose and reached into his jeans pocket, plunked down a dollar bill, and shook a toothpick from the container. "Well, Miss Librarian, if Lutie thinks I'll back down all because some smart girl from Portland steps in, she's got another think coming."

"That's not why I'm here," I said. "I only want to get things straightened out for my aunt and uncle. That's what my father wanted."

Linc paused and turned to face me. "You think you know your old man?" His neck muscles were beginning to bulge, and he pointed at me with his index finger. "I reckon you're about to find out more than you ever wanted to know."

I couldn't find an answer to that one. Nova and Tru kept giving me anxious looks. "We'll talk soon, Mr. Jackson," I said finally. "I'm sure we can work something out."

"Yeah." Linc threw another bill on the stack. "Here's a little something extra, Dove." He tossed the toothpick into the trash can and picked up his western hat.

Nova muttered, "Hick." I elbowed her in the back.

"I'll look for the sign then," I said as cheerfully as I could. Linc Jackson yanked open the door of the café, and the cluster of little brass bells jingled frantically on the doorknob.

He threw his next remark over one shoulder. "Have a nice day." The door whooshed shut, and a pungent sorrow swept me along with the aroma of lilacs and french fries.

On our way out the bells sounded again, whispering something I couldn't quite hear.

2

My father's place was right off the road near the gas company's warning sign, just like Dove had promised. What she hadn't told me was that the fence had been built from old oven doors. The pink- and aqua-enameled ones, their windows glazed over and dark, probably dated from the fifties. Here and there a white one interrupted the rainbow of color, with a gray-speckled door thrown in for good measure. The oven-door fence stood like a row of teeth, a big smile either welcoming or warning away intruders, standing guard over a creek that was at least six feet across. Hanging from one of the oven doors, a Native American dream catcher, complete with feathers and beads, winked in the sun.

Nova immediately pronounced the yard a junk heap; it was piled six feet high in places and flanked by the remains of at least two old cars. The broken-down, green and white single-wide mobile home, with room additions sticking out in all directions, looked more like a child's homemade fort than a place to live.

Some of the additions were taller than others; made of thin sheet metal, they leaned at dangerous angles. Others were built from ugly grooved paneling, the dark kind you might see in a man's den. A couple of tires were full of dirt and dead petunias, and an empty green bathtub sat near a wooden shed. Several wind chimes, with cherubs and angels blowing heavenly trumpets, tinkled near the trailer door.

Truman's eyes got big, perhaps with the possibilities of dismantling old bicycles and lawn mowers that lay before us. I clutched the steering wheel, wondering why I'd ever thought coming here was a good idea. Two figures from the house approached us.

I pried my skin from the vinyl seat of the van, and the three of us climbed out into the open yard. This was it, I thought. Murkee wasn't going to be bursting with cowboys like Linc Jackson. It was going to be about middle-aged ranchers with oversized silver belt buckles and dirty fingernails, whose wives, with names like Peg and Dotty, would know the names of all the wildflowers and can fruit preserves in one-hundred-degree weather.

The man whom I guessed was my Uncle Tiny stopped a few feet from us, waved, and grinned. He was at least six foot four, dressed in an undershirt and baggy jeans that looked as if they might fall to the ground at any time. No silver belt buckle though. Everything about him was round and smooth: shoulders, multiple chins, and a waistline that explained the need for his red suspenders. A shock of black hair hung in one eye. The gray-haired woman, clothesline thin, wasn't as shy. She walked right up to the van and slapped the sliding door.

"Will you look at this?" she said, wiping her palms across the thighs of her faded jeans. "Will you look . . . at . . . this?" I guessed she was speaking to the air, asking for unseen approval. She turned her head, stared at me, and repeated herself.

I looked back toward the engine compartment of the VW, half expecting it to be on fire. "I'm Muri," I began in a higher voice than I would have liked, "and these are my children, Nova and Truman. You must be my Aunt Lutie."

I waited for her to speak. My first thought was "bag lady." Aunt Lutie looked about sixty, stringy and tough. Her arms stuck out of her blouse at odd angles, skewed like rabbit ears atop a console TV. I decided she must have cataracts.

"So." Aunt Lutie said this as if she were pronouncing someone dead. I caught Nova pursing her lips and rolling her eyes, which told me volumes. She wanted her tongue pierced, and she thought my aunt was strange? I felt like saying, "Sorry ma'am, there's been some mistake."

"You're Joseph's girl, Muri?"

Before I could answer Lutie laughed with a wide-open throaty sound.

Nova looked even more horrified. Tru was too busy checking out the pile of junk to notice. Suddenly, I wished I'd had the foresight to come out here alone first, before dragging my family and my entire life out of civilization.

"Did you get my note?" Once again I felt the annoying eye twitch that no one else can detect. Part of me was afraid to be rejected, and the rest of me would rather be abducted by aliens than stay here. The skin on the backs of my hands felt taut and dry. I fidgeted with my fingers, hoping my new relatives wouldn't swallow us whole. Then Tiny stuck out his hammy hand.

"I guess that makes me your uncle," he said, grinning wide and easy. "Antonio Ramirez, but everyone calls me Tiny. Glad you made it." He reached up and tugged briefly on his hat's brim. There was a certain grace to his movement, a smoothness matched only by the sound of his voice that was low and sure but not threatening.

Truman must have noticed this, because he pushed past Nova into the yard. Normally, my son wouldn't speak to a complete stranger. Not only had I drilled him on "stranger danger," he was usually shy and took longer than most kids to warm up to people. But he didn't dye his hair with Kool-Aid or refuse to go to church. The only thing I worried about was that he'd go blind staring at a computer screen, in spite of those new glasses.

"You got a lot of cool junk over there," he said to Tiny, pointing to a pile of rusty bike wheels and sprockets. "What do you do with it?"

"Sometimes I make new bikes out of the spare parts."

"What happens to the bikes then?"

"You never know who's going to need a bike." Tiny looked a little embarrassed, while Aunt Lutie snorted and tossed back her thin hair, which hung loose and reached just below her bony shoulders.

"Blessed fool's given one to just about every kid around," she said, but I thought I saw her smile at him. "Can't say no." She clasped her hands together briefly and said, "Give me strength, Lord."

From around the corner, squeals and grunts rang out. Several potbellied pigs, the kind people say make good pets and are smarter than dogs, rushed through a small gap beside a shed. They snuffled the ground and jostled each other until they circled Tiny, their snouts turned to the sky.

Tiny spoke to them by name in a high, affected voice. "Now, Jim, you can't push Gordo out of the way like that," he said. "Is it dinnertime already? Dave, you wait your turn."

"Excuse me," he said to us from the middle of the pig gang. "My pigs can tell time." He turned, and they followed him noisily around the corner of the fence. This situation was all too weird for a city girl like me.

We must have looked just as weird to my aunt. With her good eye, Lutie stared at Nova and raised her hands in the direction of heaven. "Lord, send us all the angels," she said and laughed. I felt like crying.

She pointed at Nova's piercing near the upper part of her ear lobe. "That thing hurt you much?" Nova flinched, but Lutie smiled at her anyway.

"Whatever." My daughter had refined her rudeness to this one word; I wanted to tape her pretty mouth shut. Not long ago she'd been optimistic and obedient and still wore her fine ash-blonde hair in ponytail holders and asked for bedtime stories from the original *Wizard of Oz* books. I'd taken her to church, and it was her idea to be baptized in front of the entire congregation.

Even when she was Tru's age she'd smiled a lot and refused to give up her prized stuffed monkey, which she had kept on her bed since she was three. Back then she didn't care if her preteen friends knew about the stuffed animal or her faith. She'd proudly worn a What Would Jesus Do? bracelet.

But sometime during the last few years, she'd thrown her bracelet into a drawer, saying Jesus made life too hard. Her pride turned into bitterness, for which I blamed myself. My Nova had become rigid with anger, a cat backed into a corner.

I was about to defend her, brag about her high grade-point average and talent for designing clothing, when my aunt spoke to me. "Don't worry, honey, she'll grow up eventually, God love her. She's got real family now."

By this time Nova's already pale skin had blanched, and I was getting a headache from the smell of swine and gasoline fumes. Once again Truman saved the day.

"Can I go watch Uncle Tiny feed those pigs?" he said.

"I'll go with you," Nova volunteered, and they escaped to wherever the grunts came from. I never thought I'd see the Queen of Cool move so fast to keep company with farm animals.

Lutie was looking more like Popeye every moment. A lump formed in my throat. I'd always celebrated diversity along with the rest of my educated friends, but I couldn't be this woman's niece. It just wasn't possible.

Lutie smiled and stuck out her scarecrow arms to hug me. "You look so much like Joseph," she whispered. At first I held my breath, because Mother and my stepfather, Benjamin, were never given to signs of affection. Then I relaxed and was surprised when she smelled soothing and mild, like chamomile tea.

"He wanted you to come," she said. "Let me give you a hand with your things." She reached past me into the van and grabbed a grocery sack full of candy wrappers and packages of the mustard pretzels Truman likes. She then draped a stack of dresses on hangers over her shoulder. "Let's get you unpacked."

I nodded, loaded my arms with duffel bags and pillows, and followed her to the door. I tried to picture my father living inside that trailer, doing whatever he did every afternoon.

Linc Jackson had called my dad Chief Joseph, and he got a look on his face, as if they'd been mortal enemies: cowboys against Indians. Their relationship couldn't have been that much of a stereotype, I told myself. At least I hoped not.

A child builds a world to keep the truth in or out, but I'd never bothered to change my perception of who Daddy might have been. Now I was afraid of what lay beyond the oven-door fence I'd just walked through.

3

Aunt Lutie clutched at my arm to lure me inside the house, which looked like a firetrap. The screen door creaked open; it needed a shot of WD-40. I stepped inside, and even though the living room was jammed with stuff, it felt cozy. Lutie hung the dresses on a doorknob and right away asked, "Have trouble finding us? Here, sit down." She motioned to a worn sofa.

I sat down on its edge and expected her to add, "Take your shoes off," like the character Jethro did on that infernal *Beverly Hillbillies* sitcom, which was now stuck in my mind.

"No," I answered. "We stopped back in Murkee at the little café, and I got directions." I didn't mention I'd already met Linc Jackson.

"Oh, you mean the Mucky-Muck. That Dove will help you to death, but she's a hard worker." Lutie perched on the other end of the couch and wove her fingers together as if she were praying.

My aunt was still a stranger, but it made sense to dive right in. I suspected the whole flap was some giant miscommunication or maybe one of those crazy country feuds you read about. I'd had plenty of training in mediation through my work with the teachers union. It wouldn't be difficult to get Linc to drop the lawsuit once I figured out the problem.

"She introduced us to the town's owner too," I said. "Then it came out that he's the neighbor you wrote about. Aunt Lutie, what could possibly make him want to sue?"

Lutie's expression turned to sadness. "I've asked myself that same thing for months now. Linc says he needs the creek for his cattle, but Joe didn't buy it. My brother always said Linc was up to no good." She looked down at her hands. "You might as well know—Joe and Linc couldn't stand each other."

"That much I gathered."

"And Joe always said Linc would do anything to get hold of our place, mostly for the water rights."

"What's so important about water?" I was genuinely puzzled by now.

Lutie's eyes widened in reverence. "It's only just the one thing we haven't got much of out here," she said. "Disputes over the rights have killed folks. They even got a special judge who sorts things out. Water judges, they call 'em."

I'd never heard of such a thing, and I still didn't quite grasp what any of it had to do with me. I decided on a different approach. "What's the lawsuit about?"

Lutie thought for a moment, as if she couldn't locate the right words. Then she took a breath and started in. "First off, you got the right idea about Linc owning nearly everything in this area. A little more than five years ago he up and moved away, left old Ed Johnson to run things. That Ed, he's a piece of work, I tell you."

I tried to coax my aunt back to the subject. "So tell me about why Linc left," I said.

Lutie smiled. "Lord, yes, I sure can get off on a wild goose chase, can't I? Anyway, the creek runs through our land year-round, you know. The water judge said there's a law about water rights so that they always follow the land, not the person. Five years."

"Five years what?"

Again, Lutie snapped to. "If you're gone five years, your rights to the water go away. That's the law. I don't why Linc left. I only know he did."

I scanned the room. "So that means his water rights are—"

Lutie nodded. "Yep, deader than a doornail. Joe and Doc Rubin divided the rights up, so nobody downstream would get shorted. And now Linc's back, saying he wasn't gone but four years and eleven months. He says all the water ought to be his because of some document he filed saying he was back before the five-year deadline. Humph. I remember the day old Linc showed up, and it was well past five years." She sighed.

"If it's so important, why didn't my father try to settle with Linc? Surely Linc knows everybody out here needs adequate water supplies."

Lutie stared out the window for a moment. "There's no reasoning with Linc, I'm afraid. The man hates us. That's the real reason."

I frowned. "But why?"

Lutie sat up tall and drew in a proud deep breath. "Because we're Native people," she said. "Linc Jackson didn't want the likes of us in his town. Pure and simple."

"Good grief, this is the twenty-first century. How can there still be that kind of thing going on? Sounds like the Hatfields and McCoys."

"You're not in the city, anymore, Muri," she said quietly. "Out here there's a whole different set of rules. Joe claimed the creek because artifacts were found there. To him it was sacred ground."

I stood up, feeling my blood surge. "If there are Native artifacts or ruins, aren't they protected?" I glanced at the window to be sure the kids weren't listening.

Lutie got up from the sofa and patted my arm. "What's written in laws and what really happens isn't always the same thing, I'm afraid."

She quickly changed the subject. "Here, you must be tired after your trip. Let's get you settled, and we can talk more later."

Suddenly, I was tired. And confused. I nodded and followed Aunt Lutie down the hall.

"Well, I hope you're planning to stay awhile," she said. Aunt Lutie wanted to give me the grand tour. She led me past the living room down a short hallway to a bedroom. "We got plenty of room if you two girls don't mind doubling up. The little guy can bed down in my sewing room—that's what I call it. Don't worry; I already picked up all the straight pins out of the rug. You can have your daddy's spot. I left his favorite bedspread on." She ran her fingers lightly over a faded chenille coverlet draped across a double bed that took up most of the space. A bureau with a small round mirror above it was the only other piece of furniture in the room. Lutie stood still a moment, as if she were listening for traces of her brother.

I listened, but all I could hear were the pigs outside, still squealing. "It looks very nice," I said. I laid our belongings on the bed, careful not to disturb the smoothness of the spread, and peered out the dinky room's window. "How long did it take Tiny to build the fence?"

Lutie laughed. "Angels in heaven, child. That fence was your daddy's doing, and I was sure we'd soon be seeing the fire marshal. But he knew how to make things sturdy, and he had a way of finding a use for stuff nobody else wanted. Your father loved to build things, just like my Tiny."

The dreams I'd kept in the wallet of my thoughts threatened to dissolve. The educated, intelligent man I'd envisioned began to break down, limp as paper money run through the wash. Joseph Pond couldn't possibly be this ordinary.

"Where'd he get the oven doors?" I asked, although I was almost afraid to hear the answer. What if he was a criminal? Or worse, what if he had been like Mother, compulsive about everything?

Aunt Lutie smiled; the edges of her eyes crinkled in a playful way. "When this appliance store went out of business in Prineville, he snapped up those old doors for next to nothing. By the end of the week we had us a fence. It's pretty crazy-looking, I suppose."

"Very inventive," I said, as she motioned me back toward the front end of the trailer. "How many people would think to use an oven door that way?" It was the most polite thing I could think of to say.

"Time was we didn't need a fence," Lutie said.

"To keep the pigs from escaping?"

"I know what you're thinking." Lutie gazed over our heads, as if the colorful barricade was a member of the family. "What kind of nut uses old stoves to make a fence?"

I must have turned white as library paste. "I didn't mean it that way."

Lutie waved off my apology. "Of course you didn't. Even I thought my brother was odd. But Joe didn't do things for fun. Your daddy put up that fence about five years ago, right after Linc started leaning on us to sell."

"Did he tell you why?"

My aunt crossed her arms and paused a long moment. "I asked that very question. Everybody did. If I brought it up, Joe either got mad or changed the subject. Drove me batty."

I stood there, confused. Why would a dying man build a wall across the desert?

Lutie seemed to hear my thoughts. "Joe never explained his reasons." Her lip quivered. "But just before his passing, he said something I'll never forget. 'We can't let our ancestors down, Lutie,' he told me. 'The fence looks silly, but it's for your protection, to ward off ghosts and grave robbers.'" Her eyes glittered with tears.

"I'm so sorry." I touched her sleeve.

She patted my hand and smiled. "Whatever he meant, Joe built a sturdy fence. I've come to love those old oven doors, and that's reason enough for me. Every time I see that fence, I see your daddy."

I nodded, not realizing how true her words would become.

Aunt Lutie stopped at a small bookshelf crowding the narrow hallway and pointed at the dusty books lining its shelves. "When Joseph took sick," she said softly, "he only wanted to sit and read those history books of his, you know, Civil War and all. At the end I read them out loud to him. He loved history." She paused, and then added, "Come on, honey, let's get the kettle going."

I relaxed some. My dreams began to reconstruct themselves then; they spread themselves out to dry. If my father loved books he couldn't have been ordinary at all. I followed her across the living room to the kitchen area. It was a good five-foot walk.

"Now these are for special occasions," Aunt Lutie said after we'd gotten settled. She reached up into the highest kitchen cupboard and carefully brought down a pair of teacups and saucers. I was ready to be served in Mason jars or glasses cut from old wine bottles. But these were genuine bone china. I picked one up and recognized the Spode trademark.

My stepfather had given Mother a full set of Spode Christmas dishes just before her death. It seemed frivolous to keep an entire set of china to use once a year, but then she had pumpkin plates for Halloween, a horn of plenty soup tureen, and various other occasional dishes. Mom never got around to using any of them. She just took them in and out of the china closet, washing them when they got dusty.

My aunt must have seen me peeking at the marking on the bottom of the cups. "This is a special occasion," she said and smiled. A copper-clad teakettle rattled on the burner. The range, which looked to be from the same era as the oven doors outside, was pink with gray trim, like the rest of the kitchen. It was actually more of a kitchenette, the only nook of the place that wasn't cluttered with knickknacks, piles of magazines, and grocery sacks brimming with aluminum cans.

In fact, it was difficult to tell precisely where the kitchen ended and the living room began, except for a small throw rug, which looked to be woven from women's nylons. I'd always had a problem with claustrophobia and already sensed my chest tightening. It didn't help that the walls were framed in more of the same dark paneling I'd seen outside, or that sacks of empty soda cans were piled everywhere, like a bunch of cats taking over the furniture.

Chaz would have had a field day with the two paintings that hung slightly askew on the wall. One was a small oil painting of pansies that could have been a paint-by-number. The other was a reproduction of Jesus whose eyes followed me across the room. He watched us from atop the Aztec gold sofa. It was threadbare with a Mexican serape draped across the back.

"Can I help with something?" I asked. Mom taught me a great woman does everything with poise and grace, even when she'd rather not. She only said things like this in her more lucid moments, when she wasn't polishing silverware for the fourth time in a week or re-waxing the floors.

Lutie laughed, and I marveled at how relaxed I felt. "Just like your daddy," she said, "forever lending a hand. And you look like him: same black-as-chimney-soot head of hair and lots of it. I'll bet you got the fire of the Holy Ghost the way he did."

I sat at the dinette and started folding napkins in neat tri-angles. The only ghosts I saw came in my nightmares.

She counted out five cups for the saucers and set them on an old metal tray with a hint of rust around the edges. This was more like what I expected. It matched the mound of Oreo cookies and the rest of the decor.

In one corner of the living room sat a green Naugahyde recliner, its footrest stuck out. A wicker basket of yarns, alive with colors from vermilion to a glow-in-the-dark green, rested on the floor next to the chair, as a loyal pet might. Then I noticed the small side table beneath the fluttering lace café curtains in the window.

A gallery of framed photographs crowded the surface. I went closer and peered into faces of strangers that somehow didn't seem all that strange. Several portraits were in sepia tones that made people look softer than perhaps they really were. Most were modern snapshots of men and women, children, and a dog or two. My eyes kept returning to one picture of a dark-skinned, bowlegged man dressed in west-ern clothes.

"We were afraid you wouldn't come," Lutie said softly from behind me. "When Joseph up and died, we didn't know what to do." I heard her voice catch.

I picked up the photo of the man in the cowboy outfit and chuckled.

"Yeah," she said, "Your dad was always horsin' around. He was a real character."

I stared into his eyes then, as if by doing so, I could tell for sure whether I was the daughter of Joseph Pond. When had I ever been accused of horsing around? Perhaps this was what was rolling around inside me like a shaken can of soda.

And what about Benjamin, the man Mom married a few years before she died? My stepfather had a nose that turned red whenever he was angry, which was a lot. He had shiny little hamster eyes and a funny chin that blended into his neck. He was mean when he'd had too much gin.

I saw none of those qualities as I gazed at the man in the picture. Joseph Pond's eyes were dark like mine and held plenty of secrets. That made two of us, I thought. Only I would probably never know what his secrets were.

I held my breath then, thinking for one silly moment that I would hear him whispering to me, explaining how he wanted to rescue me all along. But the only sounds came from Aunt Lutie, rattling the dishes. Suddenly, all I knew for sure was that I could use a shower and some sleep.

Tiny and the kids trooped in then. Tru was starved as usual, and Nova kept silent and clung to the fringes of the room. My uncle occupied a good portion of the living space, so I understood. Perhaps big and tall men weren't meant to fit in subcompact cars or cracker-box trailer homes.

"Oh, my little Pearl, some of that tea would be nice," Tiny said, smiling that same infectious grin. I hadn't smiled much lately, but before I knew it the edges of my mouth curled up too. It felt as soothing as the tea. Tiny poured his from the china cup into a tall plastic tumbler and filled it with ice.

"Where's the TV?" Truman said, pushing his wire-rimmed glasses up on the bridge of his nose. The kid had never been inside a home without cable before.

"We can't get much out here," Tiny said, jiggling his tea so the ice clinked dully against the plastic tumbler. He sat on the couch, and it sagged nearly to the floor under his weight. "The hill behind the creek blocks most of the reception. After that last time when Jim chewed the cord, well, I just never got around to fixing it."

Nova sat in the corner on a kitchen chair with a broken rung. "Couldn't you just get satellite?" Her voice still had an edge of attitude. She picked at her dark blue fingernails, wisely avoiding my gaze.

"Hallelujah, sure. The Clackmans over at the Lazy P Ranch got one last year," Lutie responded, eyeing Nova, but not backing down. "They've got to be mucho expensive, though. People like us got to save up."

"Man, I'd sure love one of them dishes," Tiny said, nudging Tru with his elbow. "Two hundred channels and HBO too."

"Showtime's better," Tru said, and they both nodded. "You surf the Net?"

Uncle Tiny looked puzzled. "No," he said, "we're on a fixed income."

Nova smirked. "He means the Internet, not TV."

"We know all about it," Lutie broke in. "But I guess we'd need a computer."

"Truman brought his Mac," I said, hoping we could get into friendlier conversation soon. "Tru's kind of a computer nut."

"Don't you mean computer *nerd*?" Nova teased. I shot her "The Look." My hands strangled each other, and my left eye twitched like mad.

"Nova, could you help me bring in some of the stuff from the van?" I said this so sweetly even Lutie raised an eyebrow. My daughter let out one of those loud sighs and flounced through the flimsy aluminum door, slamming it on her way out.

I followed her to the far side of the van. "Is it too much to ask you to be civil? I know you're unhappy. This isn't my idea of paradise, either."

"We *have* to go back to Portland."

I tried to make eye contact with my daughter. "Give it a few weeks, will you? I don't plan to stay. But Lutie is my aunt, after all. I think I should try to get my dad's affairs straightened out."

"Why do we have to suffer?" Nova's brows scrunched together. "I mean, why can't Tru and I spend the summer with Dad in Portland? I'm already bored out of my skull." She fingered the little tufts of hair next to her ear, crouching against the van as if she was ready to crawl beneath it.

"If you'll remember," I said, "Your dad is too busy." I didn't add that he was busy with Victoria.

She stared at me. I could practically see her mind processing the odds, weighing her options. She bit her lower lip and sighed again, this time the kind that concedes defeat.

"Fine," she said, but her expression suddenly softened; her jaw got that hangdog look. "How could you? They live in a shack, Mom. A *shack*."

I looked around the back bumper at the house. Nova's eyes watered as if she were going to cry, but then they narrowed again and turned a petrified blue.

I was the one who wanted to cry now. In order to stay tough I thought of Chaz once more. "This is only temporary, hon. I told you that. I had to get away from Portland to figure things out."

"Can't you and Dad figure things out?" Nova asked softly. She pointed at Tiny's junk piles. "All I asked for was a normal life, not a home at the dump." She stood up, paced up and down in the reddish dirt, and then stopped and looked down at her new white canvas shoes. They were covered in dust. "I can't stand it," she shouted, as she yanked each sneaker off and tossed them at my feet. Then she sat down in the dust and cried.

I wanted to be transported back in time, to the place before Chaz had gotten his first big gallery client and before he stopped wanting me. Back to the time when I ran the high school library and drove kids to soccer games on weekends. Streaky clouds drifted as the sunset unfolded, and I waited for Nova's tears to die down.

The horizon was fading; the mountains looked like the backs of dark-robed grieving women, hunched over and still. I took Nova's hand and squeezed it like they do in those support groups where everyone goes by their first name. She looked up at me through smeared mascara and shrugged.

"I'm scared too," I said, pulling her into my arms. She was taller than I was now, by a good two inches. "But I'm not helpless. I'll get a job. Things will work out. You'll see."

"I'd rather be homeless than live here," she growled. I didn't answer.

As I prodded Nova from the rear, we walked back to the house. Tiny and Truman stood at the door, and I could tell they were about to come see what was taking so long. My daughter pulled away when I tried to touch her, but at least she kept quiet.

"Don't worry, kiddo, we'll be okay, I said. "We're strong. We can handle this just fine." I said these things out loud for her benefit, but my voice wavered. She knew the score.

Nobody said much after that. Lutie dragged out examples of the family mail order business: hats made from soft drink cans, strung together with patches of crocheted yarn. I never would have guessed a hat could be that ugly. Tiny fed us tacos and *frijoles con arroz* for supper, and I found out my aunt seldom cooked. Nova and Tru looked as bored as kids at the children's table on Thanksgiving. I couldn't stop thinking about how sticky my skin felt, or how we would manage out here with no phone, TV, ballet, or Library Guild meetings.

But there was no lack of church. In fact, everything in Murkee was connected to the Red Rock Tabernacle in some way or another. Lutie went to services on Wednesdays and twice on Sunday. She met with her church ladies on the other days of the week. How would I explain to my aunt that organized religion wasn't high on my list?

I still believed in God, but most of my views would raise eyebrows in a backwater town like this. Lutie had already spoken about God's love for me and my children. What she didn't know was that I believed in God as Creator, but I wasn't so sure about the Divine's role as my Father. A father was someone who drank too much and wasn't around when you needed a daddy. I wasn't proud of my belief, but I was too hurt to change now. I sat at the table until my eyes stung with private tears and exhaustion.

Around eight-thirty, Tiny nudged Lutie who lay snoring in the green recliner, and she awoke long enough to say good-night and shuffle to the bedroom. Finally, I got Tru bedded down in the sewing room, and Nova stomped off to bed, too, to die of total boredom, she said.

After the lights were out, I sat up in Tiny's miniature living room without so much as a box fan to cool things off. I tried to read but couldn't concentrate. Finally, I tossed aside my book and crept over to the door. I went outside, closing the screen an inch at a time so it wouldn't squeak. I sat on the edge of one of the tire planters, wide awake, wishing I'd brought out some iced tea.

I stared up at the Milky Way's river of stars spilling across the central Oregon sky. It was breathtaking. It had been years since I'd seen a night sky unpolluted by city lights. It had been even longer since I'd taken the time to think of anything but my own survival. Now here I was desperate to work out my little librarian's life in the very place where Joseph Pond had lived and died. Absently, I gouged at the split rubber of the planter with a rusty dog tie-out stake.

Before long I'd filleted the inner rim, scraping out a rage that I didn't fully comprehend. Why had my father left me in the first place? Why hadn't I done more to find him? Now it was too late. I'd never meet him face to face, at least not in this lifetime. Suddenly, it hit me. I was an orphan.

By now, the tire planter looked as if the pigs had chewed on it. I laid down the spike and sagged against the side of the house, watching shooting stars fall from grace.

4

In the morning, after five minutes beneath the trailer's spitting shower, I was barely wet, much less clean. The low water pressure and rust stains streaking down beneath the faucet reminded me of cheap motels, where hard, thin soaps make you sneeze and skimpy plastic curtains leak water on the floor. Still, I was grateful for a shower, and even more thankful for a few minutes of early solitude.

That was one of the things I'd discovered in single life. Aloneness was much different. Since my break up with Chaz, Truman had become clingy. Nova complained about everything or demanded to be driven someplace immediately. Lately, I craved quiet. Constructing a new life required my total concentration.

So I shut my eyes and raised my face up to the fine mist, careful to keep my mouth closed in case the water tasted funny, which I was sure it did. I pretended I was at a day spa, beneath a gold-plated showerhead, listening for Raul, the stylist, to call me to his station. I could practically smell the cappuccino. Just then a raspy voice pierced the steam.

"Muri? That you in there?" Aunt Lutie stuck her head inside the bathroom.

"Almost done, give me a minute." Instinctively, I shielded my body.

"You know it's only five o'clock? The kangaroo rats are just going to bed. I brought you some clean towels." Lutie closed the door and then reopened it. "You figured out that the spigots are on backwards then? Cold is hot and hot is cold."

"I got the idea, yes."

"It's a good thing."

I heard the door close again, so I peeked around the edge of the tropical fish shower curtain to be sure my aunt was gone. When I cranked the faucets off, the pipes made a machine gun sound that startled me. I reached for a towel, worn but fresh, and swiped it across the small medicine cabinet mirror.

Aunt Lutie was right. I did have my father's eyes. I always told myself they were unusual eyes, dark circles notwithstanding. Chaz had said the same thing once—the day I agreed to move in with him. That was back when he was still handing out compliments. I'd ignored the fact that he was full of cheap champagne at the time, compliments of the upstart gallery where we had literally stumbled into one another, eyeing lithographs and experimental mixed media.

It was 1990, just after Mother died. Less than a month later I married Chaz in Vegas, even though I knew both he and my stepfather were too much alike. It was not a good time.

Later, loans and grants had paid for my master's degree in library science, but what had all that education bought me? After all those years, the budget ax had fallen upon the library I'd helped to build. I'd spent long hours of my own time converting the card catalog to computer, entering strings of numbers only a librarian's mind could appreciate, and laminating the bar codes onto the books themselves. I had tenure, but I wasn't about to split my time between three different media centers, checking out videos and repairing broken overhead projectors.

Now what? I was determined not to land in the discard pile but felt as unsure of myself as the last time I'd come home to find Chaz in bed with Victoria again.

Pushing down the memories, I wiped off the fog from the bathroom mirror, slathered on moisturizer, and ran a brush through my wet hair. Jeans and a sweatshirt seemed appropriate for the chilly early morning, and I decided I would walk a mile every day before breakfast . . . starting today. At least it would get me away from everyone for a while longer.

I crept past Lutie, who sat planted in the green recliner with her basket of crochet yarns and what must have been a Bible. After a wave and a whispered explanation, I tiptoed outside.

The air was still and almost icy; my eyes watered from its sting. During the night I'd awakened, shivering, not remembering at first where I was. I'd read somewhere that the desert temperature could go from a daytime sizzle to freezing after sundown, and now I didn't doubt it.

Outside in the yard, mounds of bicycle parts glistened with early morning dew that I'd always heard called angel tears. Broken sprockets stared at me, their gaping eyes rimmed with metal eyelashes. It could have been a postmodern sculpture.

"In New York you'd fetch big bucks," I said.

Walking would warm me. I crossed the rickety bridge that spanned the creek and started off down the road to town. I pumped my arms, striding briskly along the rutted lane, where withered and skeletal evergreens blended into the gray-green of the sagebrush. Tiny had said the trees were infested with a kind of beetle that killed them an inch at a time. That saddened me, and I walked faster.

Sunrise and earth colors inspired my visual senses with their reds and dusty pinks. I carefully avoided little holes in the ground, which I imagined to be rattlesnake hideouts and tarantula dens. I reminded myself that if I left them alone, they'd leave me alone. Still, a hawk's cry overhead startled me. A small rabbit darted back into the brush. I suspected the poor hare wouldn't get far with my "live and let live" attitude.

That philosophy didn't work as well with other areas of life, either, I'd discovered. For the last twenty-four hours I'd gone along with whatever came, tried not to judge, and slept in the corner of a trailer that was so junked out it set my teeth on edge. Nova had immediately stuck her glow-in-the-dark plastic stars to our bedroom ceiling, and their phosphorescence had only kept me awake.

I walked faster, no longer fighting off the urge to get this rundown place in shape. It was the last week in June, and I wasn't used to such bright sunshine. I could barely see without sunglasses. I'd spent five years in the dusty stacks of a high school library, amazed now at how little time I'd spent outdoors. While the rest of Oregon jogged and hiked and canoed and walked to work to save the environment, I'd stayed under the fluorescent lights. I was a mole.

Out here nature was almost shocking. I was hard-pressed to escape the dirt and dust, which permeated everything. It was fine grist, like jeweler's rouge, wearing down the hills as it was transported by the relentless wind.

By the time I reached the gas company's sign at the edge of the property, I knew exactly what I had to do. No doubt Tiny and Lutie would appreciate my ability to solve their problems. Mentally, I plotted out the details of the Pond Ranch remodel. With a little ingenuity and hard work, it might be possible to turn a slum dwelling into something livable.

I was trained to think you needed—no, required—a certain amount of beauty in your surroundings. Both my mother and my husband had an appreciation for the finer things, and I was shocked to discover how much of that had rubbed off on me. Unfortunately, aesthetics was an unknown word to my aunt and uncle.

How would they react to my ideas? Did I have a right to change anything, and was this my house now or what? Suddenly, my enthusiasm shriveled. It took every ounce of energy just to keep walking. I gave into the feeling of deflation and sat down beside a bullet-riddled gas company sign.

Perhaps this rural life would supply the peace I craved. The rolling hills, bucolic and mute, offered me respite. I closed my eyes, relaxing my jaw muscles.

Moments later a slightly off-key whistle startled me. I sucked in my breath at the sound of crunching gravel. A man waved as he neared and called out, "Good morning!"

"You frightened me," I said, brushing dust from my jeans, my heart pounding. "I didn't hear you coming." Suddenly, my still-damp hair felt clumped, and I raked it with my fingers.

"You always this jumpy? I keep birds that don't bolt so easily."

"I wasn't expecting anyone else out here so early. I was out for a walk. I do my best thinking then." I waved back toward the trailer. "I'm staying over there, with my aunt and uncle."

The man just smiled and listened to me babble. The first thing I noticed was his lack of western wear and his scruffy hair trailing out from beneath a baseball cap. His flannel shirtsleeves were rolled up to expose his forearms. I hoped he wasn't a tree-hugging nut.

"Didn't I see you in the Mucky-Muck?" he asked. "Talking to Linc?"

My palms popped sweat at the mention of the name. "Yes, I suppose I was."

"I'm Rubin," he said, sticking out a hand. "Rubin Jonto. I live just over the creek." He pointed with his chin. "You must be Joseph's daughter." His eyes crinkled up at the corners when he smiled.

"Muri. Yes, I'm Joseph's daughter. How did you know?" I shook his hand, determined to remain aloof.

"Be hard not to. You've got Joseph's eyes." Rubin said.

I looked away. "I'm from Portland. Things out here are so different."

He folded his arms across his chest. "That's why I moved here—no secrets. And no city hassles, either."

"Or conveniences," I said, thinking about the crummy shower. "I'm just here for a while to put my dad's affairs in order. He had some legal troubles; you probably know all about that too." I sighed. My head throbbed. I needed my morning coffee. "Mind me asking what kind of doctor you are? I overheard the waitress in the café yesterday calling you Doc."

"Doc? Oh right, Dove. Isn't she a character?" Rubin said. "I'm the local vet, but they all call me Doc. I'm from Portland too."

"You a friend of Linc's?" I asked.

Rubin ignored my question. "Been out here five years. Joseph helped me build the slough over on my place."

"For cattle?"

"Not exactly. Emus are the weirdest animals on earth."

"You raise emus?" I tried not to laugh. These days, it's possible to be politically incorrect about anything. I already wrestled with the discovery that I was part Nez Perce and had grown up watching John Wayne on TV. What if emus were part of this guy's religion?

He shook his head and chuckled softly. "If I had any brains I'd pack up and leave. Yep, I never would have pictured myself with the world's dumbest birds, but here I am."

"I know what you mean—not picturing yourself here." My thoughts swirled with cheap paneling and Lutie's yarn basket. I vowed to keep my mouth shut. I could tell I was entertaining this guy, and it irritated me.

"A friend in Portland, Dennis, told me about another professor he knew who bought the place. The guy had read that emu ranching would make him a millionaire in a year. What a laugh." Rubin shook his head.

"It didn't?"

"Let's just say the poor man had a better chance playing the lottery." He shook his head. "Professors are smart, but some of them don't have much common sense."

"What made you want to get involved?" I couldn't stop myself from asking a personal question . . . so much for vows. I turned one shoulder into the wind, which was gusting now and revving up the way it did everyday.

"At the time I had a pretty solid practice. But after my divorce turned ugly, I needed to start over somewhere else. I bailed out Denny's friend."

"Dennis must be a really good friend."

"He is. Best archaeologist around. But he got hired at Portland State so he had to pass up the offer. Besides, my ex-wife kept leaning on me to patch things up. Murkee looked like a good place to hide."

This time I laughed. "I know what you mean about your ex. Mine drives me crazy too." I wanted to know more about his friend. "Archaeologist, eh? I don't think I've ever seen a real archaeologist, except on TV."

"Denny Moses is one of a kind. He's a Ph.D. *and* the most famous member of the Warm Springs Confederated Tribes."

Rubin gripped the top of the gas company sign. His fingers resembled a surgeon's, even if they were veterinary surgeon's hands. "Sun's going to get hot today." He grinned again.

I looked at my watch; it was nearly six-thirty. "I'd better be getting back. The kids will worry. Nice meeting you, Doctor."

The handshake was one moment longer than necessary, which I imagined to be intentional on his part. I withdrew my hand.

"Out here I'm just Rubin, or Doc, if you like. Say hey to Tiny and Lutie for me," he said. "I'm sure I'll see you around." He turned back toward where he'd first appeared, and I watched him until he was gone. He had a purposeful walk, as if he knew where he was headed.

He seemed anything but a real cowboy. I walked home thinking about Linc Jackson, Rubin Jonto, and John Wayne. If this was the West, it was starting off wild.

"Mother, where *were* you?" Nova stood at the trailer door as I wound my way past Tiny's old tan pickup, parked in the yard with the rest of the junk. Nova didn't call me Mother often, and I sighed. What could have gone wrong in less than an hour?

My daughter didn't wait to hear where I'd been. "I'm like totally dirty, and Tru's been in the bathroom for hours. He's hogged all the hot water, if there ever was any," she said, sticking out her lower lip. "This place stinks. I'm leaving the first chance I get." She glared, but I wondered if her threat was just for show.

I pursed my lips and didn't buy it. "Last time I gave you a driving lesson you couldn't get the van out of first gear.

How far do you think you'll get? I'll speak to your brother." I brushed past her and headed toward the bathroom.

"I'll do it," she said. "Watch me." She plopped down, dressed only in an extra large T-shirt and panties, and glowered at me from the living room sofa. The shirt, one of Chaz's with Grateful Dead dancing bears parading across its front, was so worn it was nearly transparent. I thought I should probably address the subject of modesty after I noticed Lutie's raised eyebrows. I told myself Nova wouldn't really take the van and run off.

"Truman, you almost done?" I rapped lightly on the door. It seemed that just yesterday I was still helping him out of the tub, wrapping him up in a towel, laying out his clean clothes. Now I couldn't remember the last time I'd seen my son naked.

Moments later the door opened and a trail of steam leaked out. "I've only been in here ten minutes, Mom, I swear." He slid on his glasses. "She's such a pain in the—"

"Watch your mouth," I cut in, "even if it's true."

"*Neck*, Mom, I was going to say *neck*."

"Right."

Uncle Tiny poked his head around the corner. "Hungry? I'm baking scones, with plum jelly," he said. Suddenly, I felt starved.

"Somebody help me up," Lutie called from the recliner. "Footrest's stuck."

Nova sighed loudly, helped her aunt, then dashed toward the bathroom. Tru squeezed past me through the narrow hall and sat down at the dinette table. The kitchen sink was tidy and clean. Aunt Lutie had washed the mountain of dirty dishes from the night before.

A sweet aroma wafted through the trailer, so tempting that even Nova might have a hard time resisting. Tiny brought in a platter of his biscuits. "Careful, they're still hot," Tiny said, sliding them onto small plates. He set out a jar of the plum jelly and a tub of margarine, along with a pitcher of orange juice. In his chef's apron he looked as huge as a mainsail. Lutie pulled up a chair, and Tiny ate leaning against the counter.

"Yum," Tru said, crumbs falling from his mouth.

"Yes, they're delicious," I agreed, adding, "Is there coffee? I could make it myself."

"Sorry," Lutie said. "We only drink tea. Herbal tea. Tiny can pick you up some coffee next time he heads into town, can't you Tiny?" I plunged a tea ball into my cup of steaming water, yanking it up and down like a poor soul on a dunking stool.

"Yes, I can see that I'll need to make you a list. And while I think of it, I've got some ideas for sprucing things up," I said. "We could do a lot with the place." I poured myself a cup of orange juice, too, trying not to grimace at the lumpy feel of the pulp. My head, screaming for caffeine, pulsed like a neon sign.

"What do you mean, spruce things up?" Tiny asked. His voice sounded defensive and Lutie was eyeing me. "I know it's not a mansion," he said, waving a spatula expansively. "But it's not done yet. I got a guy in Murkee going to bring down a whole truckload of siding for the sun porch." He folded his arms across his apron.

"I always wanted a sun porch," Lutie said, looking over at Tiny.

"But what about building codes? Permits? If we're going to stay here, the kids really need their own rooms."

"Now you sound like city folk," Lutie said, snorting. "They're mostly the reason why Joseph is dead."

"Why *did* Grandpa die?" Tru asked, reaching for another scone.

"I'll tell you why your granddad died," Tiny said. "He was sick, all right; but I think he just got tired. Tired of fighting. Tired of guarding the ruins."

"Ruins?" Tru said.

Lutie gestured in the general direction of the creek. "Artifacts from the creek bank. It's a sacred place for our people."

Tru wiped his mouth without any prompting and pushed back his chair. "What people?"

Tiny answered. "Native people. Your grandpa and Aunt Lutie here are half Nez Perce. Your granddad was named after their famous chief."

Tru looked incredulous. "You mean I'm partly Indian?"

"A part of you, anyways," Tiny said. "You can be proud."

"Joe always said if we're not careful our heritage will be gone forever," Lutie said and nodded at her husband.

Tru glanced over at me. "Mom, can you learn calf roping even if you're an Indian instead of a cowboy?"

"Of course you can. We don't even know if Mr. Jackson was serious about teaching you to rope."

"He was too! I know it!" Tru was getting anxious, I could tell. "He said he would. I believe him, Mom. Don't you?"

I sat for a few moments, not knowing the best thing to say. "I don't know what to believe yet," I finally said. I picked up crumbs with my forefinger, squishing them like ants. I ate the crumbs one by one and smiled bravely. Before I could explain myself, the pigs squealed outside, and Tiny rushed to see why. Truman jumped up to follow him and I was left with Lutie and the sounds of the water pipes rattling shut.

5

"Oh God, no, come quick!" Tiny's yell had that edge to it that gives you goose bumps—the kind you know instantly is not about some minor inconvenience. Lutie must have known it too. We stared at each other for about two seconds before we jumped up and ran outside. Tiny held in his arms the pig that had caused all the trouble, the one he called Jim.

Sobbing, he cradled the pig like a child. Jim jerked and trembled, his head hung back, exposing a wound in the underside of his piggy neck. "He's bleeding bad," Tiny said, "he just walked up and fell over." He laid the animal on the ground and knelt beside him, stroking the pig's snout.

Tru's eyes were enormous, and he breathed hard. "I heard shots," he said, nearly yelling as if he was afraid no one would hear him. "It sounded like a gun, Mom, just like on TV. *Pop, pop.* Like that."

Some people are efficient and level-headed in emergencies. They're the type who will put their hands inside a man's throat that's been slit open by a chain saw, to keep him from bleeding to death until the paramedics arrive. The whole time they calmly tell the victim everything will be all right. Uncle

Tiny fell into a different category. He looked too scared to move, a wax figure of himself. Truman sat next to him and quietly patted his uncle's shoulders now and then.

Lutie wasn't so paralyzed. She ran inside and brought out clean towels, as well as a confused Nova still wearing a towel turban. My aunt applied pressure to the bleeding, which was getting worse.

"Somebody call 911," Nova said and clasped her hand across her nose and mouth. She sat on the edge of one of the tire planters.

"Who would do this?" I was stunned. There was no telephone here, a fact that made me feel stranded.

"I'll tell you who," Lutie said, pressing the bloody towel harder. "Linc Jackson, that's who. He's threatened us before. Stood right under the bedroom window while my brother's in there dying. Yelled his fool head off about water."

Tiny sighed. "Well, you wouldn't open the door so what was Linc supposed to do?"

Lutie glared at her husband. "I wasn't about to let him in," she said. Lutie's face flushed, even beneath her deep tan.

For a second or two I was hypnotized by the situation, fascinated by the deep red shade of swine blood, which I'd never seen before. I wasn't tempted to stick my hand on a hog's neck, but I did remember the neighbor I'd met just an hour before.

"I'll go get the vet," I said. I started for the van, and then stopped. "This way?" I was getting things mixed up in my mind, and my mental road map suddenly looked upside down.

"No, that's the other side of the creek," Lutie answered.

"Rubin's the vet, right?" The towels were turning crimson now and Lutie's hands were soaked with blood. She gave me a how-do-you-know-him look.

"We met when I was out walking." I reached inside the screen door to grab my keys to the van. "Only I'm not sure exactly where he lives."

"Quicker to get him by following the slough," Lutie said, pointing with her free hand. "Just do something quick, honey. I'm praying for a miracle. Maybe Truman here will fetch him."

Tru stood up, poised to run. I shoved the keys into my pocket and said, "Come on." We jogged off in search of Rubin's place; my son mercifully slowed down to accommodate his mother. A couple of minutes later, we reached the top of a small rise. Below, two houses stood opposite each other.

The one on the right was a ranch-style, with a wraparound porch and some corrals to the side. The other home was a log A-frame, the kind people build themselves from kits. It, too, had corrals and a barn, and it was hard to tell who would live where.

"Lutie said follow the slough," I said, panting. Power walking wasn't anything like running.

"Let's go that way," Tru said, not even breathing hard. He may have been a nerdy kid, but his nine-year-old lungs were in great shape. He pointed to the larger of the two houses, the one that probably looked the most familiar to him.

"I don't know," I said, resting my hands on my knees to get a few extra breaths in. "The vet guy I met didn't sound much like a rancher." I drew in a few more breaths and puffed them out.

A glint of sunlight from a distant peak hurt my eyes. I shielded them with my hand, stared into the brightness too long, and then snapped back to reality. Tru shouted, "Hurry up, Mom." The pig, Muri, I reminded myself. Forget the scenery and get help for the pig.

"There's nobody here," Tru said. He'd already raced to the door of the log house and back to me. "I rang the bell, and I pounded on the door. I yelled real loud but nobody came."

His cheeks were flushed and beads of sweat rolled off his nose. He pushed up his glasses for the umpteenth time. I really should get him one of those safety straps, but wouldn't Nova have fun with that?

"Emus, Tru. The vet said he's got emus." The insides of my thighs stung, where they'd rubbed together. My temper, too, was beginning to chafe. This many things were not supposed to go wrong in two days. If Jim died it would be my fault.

If my son hadn't been standing there I would have asked the sky what was going on, but I kept it in, not wanting to bruise any spiritual leanings the boy might have.

"I'll go, Mom. Stay here."

I let him go, as if I could have kept up anyway. I sank down in a patch of bunch grass that I first carefully inspected for anything that moved and rested my arms across my bent knees. I'd sat on the ground in the middle of nowhere twice in one day—a first. And before noon.

I waited for Tru to return, alternately worrying about my son and Tiny and poor, injured Jim. As ugly as the pig was, black with coarse hairs sprouting here and there, he did have something of a personality. For my uncle, that pig may as well have been the king.

Maybe you did need some kind of savior out here, something to hang onto when God wasn't listening. In the last few months I'd developed this irreverent attitude that perhaps the good Lord was getting on in age and needed a Miracle Ear in order to hear the pleas of this world. I would never say that in front of the kids, though.

Tru came huffing back then, the vet in tow. "Sorry I wasn't home," Rubin said. "Ed had a problem with one of his cows."

I straightened my shoulders a bit and jumped up, brushing the dust from my backside. "I'm so glad we found you. Uncle Tiny's in shock; some horrible person shot his pet pig."

Rubin just stared at me, as if he were about to explain something. Then he looked away for a moment and adjusted his cap, as if he were switching to his veterinary role.

"We'd better hurry," I said, remembering poor Aunt Lutie. I thought we must have been gone for hours, but when I glanced at my watch, a mere ten minutes had slipped by.

"Fortunately, I have my bag with me."

When we'd met before, he'd been friendly and open. Now he averted his gaze like a guilty dog caught chewing the master's slippers. Confusing.

"Just like in the movies, Doc," Tru said. Rubin smiled at my son. We followed Tru, who still hadn't run out of energy, back over the hill. My sides ached, but I trotted as fast as I could.

We sidestepped down the hill and back across the creek. In the distance, mountains jutted upward, still snow-covered in June, looking like frozen giants standing guard. The sun reflected against them as if someone up there signaled with a mirror. Maybe it was a lost hiker; maybe my father wasn't dead after all. I'd forgotten to ask Aunt Lutie where he was buried.

I was always doing this, catching my mind wandering and then chastising myself for it. But if I thought about these lapses in too negative a way, I might end up like Forrest Gump; I'd just keep on running and never stop. Besides, my daydreams kept me going when things got too tough. They were a safety valve. Otherwise, I'd probably have tipped into hysteria at the first sight of pig blood.

"Thank you, sweet Jesus!" Lutie raised her arms to the sky the moment she saw us. "Jim's hurt bad, Dr. Rubin. Real bad. Please do something."

My aunt shook all over then, staring at the blood on her hands like Lady Macbeth. Now that help had arrived she must have given herself permission to fall apart. Tiny's eyes were glazed over, as he sat in the dirt and silently stroked his pet pig. Nova, a towel still on her head, perched on the edge of the tire planter.

Dr. Rubin went to work immediately. He quickly examined the wound and swabbed the area with a strong-smelling disinfectant, casting the used gauze pads into a heap. "Looks like a .22," he said, probing the hole with a pair of long-handled scissors.

That was it for me. I stared in the opposite direction. When he finally said, "Aha! There's the culprit," I peeked. The slug was clenched in the forceps' jaws.

"It's a .22 all right," Rubin said. Tru nodded, as if he saw bullets every day. Lutie talked nonstop, pleading with Rubin to save Jim, praying to the good Lord to have mercy and send all the angels. I wondered if my aunt thought pigs had guardian angels too.

Up to now Tiny had kept quiet. "Of course, he'll do what he can, Pearl, honey," he said, stroking Lutie's shoulder. "If anyone can save ol' Jim, it's Rubin. Why don't you go wash off your hands? Maybe Doc would like some of your iced tea. I know I would." Tiny managed a crooked grin and shifted his weight from one foot to the other.

Rubin glanced up. "Yes, ma'am, iced tea sounds nice. Don't worry. Jim's going to pull through." He tied sutures so deftly, I thought he must have been a tailor at one time. In minutes he'd closed the wound, applied a bandage, and even pulled out of his bag one of those lampshade collars they put on dogs.

"What's that for?" Tru wanted to know. He'd watched the whole procedure carefully, asking so many questions that I'd been tempted to shush him. He had this intense look on his face now, with his brow bunched up and jaw set.

"It's to keep Jim from messing with the bandage," Rubin said.

"Makes him look dorky," Nova said.

"Just like you," Tru countered. The crisis was over.

Lutie called us in for iced tea. Suddenly, my mouth was dry and gritty. My leg muscles reminded me that I hadn't exercised this much since before Nova was born.

We all trooped inside and crowded into the living room. Rubin seemed taller than before. We sat on the sofa, but I stayed as far away from the vet as I could. "I was sure your house was the A-frame," I said.

"Nope, that's Linc's place. I'm just the other side of the fence."

"I knew it," Tru said. He did have a sixth sense about him.

And I was certain my father would have known what to do with the pig crisis too. He would have calmly taken over and handled everything, and I wouldn't have had to run across the desert. Or he would have taught me in a patient, deliberate voice what to do in emergencies, and he would have been proud when I passed this skill on to my children. Joseph Pond would have shielded me from the worst things but taught me to stand on my own. He would have known that violence is useless, but he would have taught me how to deliver a good right hook. I don't know how I knew all that. I just did.

"I thought it would be dull out here, but so far, it's been anything but boring," I said. "First I meet you, and then some wacko shoots a pig. Lutie says it's that neighbor of ours, Linc Jackson."

Rubin was quiet for a moment. Then he stared right at me. The brim of his baseball cap shaded his eyes, but I thought they looked troubled. "Listen. Linc didn't shoot the pig."

"Well, then, who did?"

He sighed. "It was me. I'm the wacko."

"But you just saved its life."

He looked away. "I know, but just before I left to go to Linc's place I was down checking the slough. Something rustled in the bushes, and I thought it was a cow." He looked embarrassed.

"You shot a cow?" Tru said. He plunked himself on the floor next to Rubin. "But it was an accident, right?"

"Course it was," Tiny said. "Accidents happen."

"Thanks, Tiny," Rubin said. "You and I both know Linc's cows are destroying that stream." Rubin turned to me. "Joseph and I worked out a deal. He let me dig the slough to water the emus and my other animals, and I'm responsible for restoring it for bull trout."

I knew it. Another environ-nut.

"Anyway," Rubin said, "cattle get in there. They trample the banks and ruin the shallows."

Lutie brought leftover scones, butter, and jam. "Never mind the water rights or whatever Linc was yelling about." She set down the tray and retreated to her recliner.

"Couldn't you just put up a fence like my dad did?" I said. "I met Linc Jackson. He seems nice enough to me."

"Yeah, Linc's a real nice rattlesnake," Lutie said.

Rubin buttered a scone. "That's the problem. There *is* another fence, one I've repaired more times than I can count. Cows plow through anyway. Besides, we all know what Linc's really after."

"I don't," I said. "In fact, I'm totally confused. What's the big deal about that creek? Somebody strike gold or what?"

Tiny laughed. "Don't I wish."

Rubin's voice took on a bitter edge. "Jackson's been after both of us to sell. He'd love to get back all his water rights. Claims he wasn't gone past the five-year deadline."

"I've heard enough about water rights to last me a lifetime," I said.

Rubin nodded. "Welcome to the other side of Oregon," he said. "But out here water is worth fighting for. Except that even with no rights Linc manages just fine, so there's got to be more to it. Nobody knows what he's up to. Maybe he's hoping I'll go away, but he's in for a fight."

I couldn't believe it. "Killing dumb animals over the environment? Excuse me, but I'd say shooting sounds a little extreme." I wasn't trying to be unfriendly, but I had my limits.

Rubin sighed the way Nova sometimes did. "After you've lived out here awhile, maybe you'll understand. About Linc I mean."

Any other time his explanation wouldn't cut it, but for some reason I was more intrigued than ever by this country vet/environmentalist. "Guess I'm not the only one with a feud going on," I said, unable to think of anything more witty or intelligent.

Tiny stood up. "Thanks again, Doc. I got to tend to the other pigs." He ambled out the door.

When Tiny was gone, I turned back to Rubin. "I believe in settling problems without violence where possible. Don't you?"

"Oh, absolutely," Rubin said. "The Hippocratic Oath is my motto, I swear." I'd seen the way he'd worked to save Tiny's pet. The man couldn't be lying.

"Is that why you were saying you should leave the area?"

"Some days I just get fed up, that's all."

"Can't say I blame you for that."

Finally, he shrugged. "Anyway, I feel terrible about Jim. He'll make it, but I think his voice box is gone. He probably won't be able to squeal or oink, you know. I'll tell Tiny about it later. Sorry."

I smiled. "Accidents happen."

Lutie set two tumblers of her tea on a TV tray. I was dying to figure out this water rights business. Why would Linc Jackson stand outside and yell at my father? Lutie didn't have much to say, though. Every now and then she mumbled prayers and cast a glance up at the picture of Jesus.

Tiny came back inside, fixed Jim a bed from an old play-pen, and set it right next to the TV. Rubin went out and helped carry the pig in.

"Don't hurry off now, Doc," Tiny said. "I figure you better make us out a bill; it being Sunday and all."

"Thanks, but I can't stay. I was tending to a sick steer when Muri came by. You don't owe me anything, except maybe a batch of your scones."

Rubin turned to Tru. "Now you come get me if Jim here has any problems." He handed Tru some extra bandages. "Think you could help your Uncle Tiny change the dressing?"

Tru nodded solemnly. "Yes, sir."

"I'll come back and check on him in a couple of days."

"I'll walk you out," I volunteered. Nova's eyes grew wide. But I was too tired and sore to care, and it had been a long time since I'd had any company. So we strolled out, and I didn't even blush. Well, maybe a little. We stopped at the oven-door fence.

"How far do you think Linc would go?" I asked, thinking about the miniature range war Rubin had described.

Rubin shrugged. "Don't know," he said. "All I know is that Linc Jackson means to get his way. Somehow that creek is just the tip of the iceberg."

Rubin turned and walked toward his place before turning back to face me. "I'm throwing a barbecue next weekend on the Fourth. There'll even be live music. Done this three years running; it's almost a tradition around here. This year the main course is a surprise."

"I'll ask the kids," I stammered, unsure if this was a neighborly invitation or a more personal one.

"Bring the kids and your aunt and uncle too. And extra lawn chairs if you've got any." He held out his hands, palms up. "It's the least I can do, considering."

"Considering what?"

"I did shoot your uncle's pig."

"Right. I'll get back to you about the barbecue."

"All set, then?" He smoothed back the sides of his hair where the wind had turned it loose and jammed his hands in his jeans pockets.

I frowned. "I said I'd get back to you," I said. "But thanks for the invite."

"I'm glad you came to get me," he said. "Really glad."

"See you on the Fourth," I answered, and watched him walk away. Just like the 1970s children's classic by Robert Newton Peck that I was always trying to get kids to read, it was *A Day No Pigs Would Die*.

JOSEPH'S JOURNAL
APRIL 1981

Before I lost you, Muri, you visited one more time. I watched you dance. That velveteen skirt is too short on you now, and you said you were the tallest girl in second grade.

Today, for a few hours, you were mine again. You twirled in your bare feet in front of the recliner where, I suppose, I'd passed out again. I'm sorry. I was out of it until you squealed, "Watch me, Daddy! I'm a ballerina!" I startled awake. I was hung over, feeling like the wrong end of the cow. Even so, I didn't have the heart to tell you that your spins made me dizzy. My head pounded like a jack-hammer, but I had to smile at you, knowing today was good-bye.

When you tipped over my beer, you looked scared, like maybe your mother scolds you for making messes. "It's not important," I said, grinning. You tried to wipe up the spill, and you held your nose and told me you didn't like the beer smell. You stood and saw I was still awake. "Are you watching now?" you asked. "Watch." You held your arms like an arch and twirled until you got dizzy and fell. You sat on the floor and your skirt fanned like a flower around your ankles.

The skirt is getting shiny in the back where the nap's worn down. I bought it for you years ago from a guy in a Prineville bar. He claimed it was Navajo, handmade, with magical powers. I paid too much for it, but you loved it. Your mother says it's too hard to wash velvet.

Daughter, you look so much more like our people than your mother's kin. I told her you must learn the old ways. But your mother won't listen. She's remarried and now I'll see you this last time. I'll tell you why.

You see, the trouble with your mother is that she can't let things go. The binges, a couple of wrecked cars, too many broken promises, she said. I swore to do better, but she kept polishing the tea service, kept shaking her head no. That was the end of your mother and me.

These days, I keep my Bible right here where I can reach it. The Word keeps me going, and I've asked for forgiveness more times than I can count. I tell the Man Upstairs that I'll do better. I repent. I tell Him I'll never touch the stuff again, for your sake. I don't know how far I'll get, but I pray the Lord will deliver me from the bottle for good. When it was time to go, you were still dancing, holding out your arms like angel's wings.

You are an angel—my angel. You smiled, and it reminded me of morning in the desert, when the sun breathes the world alive again. For a moment I thought about not taking you back when the visit was over.

If you stayed, you could learn the flute, the beads, and our dying Native language. You'd make sure no one disturbs the sacred things near the creek. When I'm gone, you could take my place under the cottonwood tree.

Keeping you sounds good, but life is too complicated for that. Even the state says you should be with your mother, although your hair is slick and straight as our ancestors. Only the freckles across your nose set you apart. I've wondered a million times which path you'll take, Native or white. Like the gnarled Manzanita that grows in this desert, there are many directions you could go.

6

All my life I've been a seeker: seeker of truth, seeker of my past, many times seeker of my car keys. I knew I'd have to find the truth about Joseph Pond and untangle this mess over a silly creek. I needed to discover whether Murkee was a good place to raise kids. Chaz, I was sure about. The final papers would come through any time now. Most of all I craved the peace of country life.

I also was aware that breathing country air wasn't going to pay the bills. I would need to apply soon to the unified school district, a tiny district twenty miles away that included three small towns. Library services were probably a luxury, but I could teach history if I had to. If no teaching posts were open, then I would sweep floors, wait tables, or whatever it took to keep us going.

If—no, *when*—I found work, I'd look into finding an apartment. Sharing a bed with a surly teen while my son bunked with a sewing machine wasn't going to work out for long. Much as I appreciated Lutie's hospitality, I wasn't sure I could stand her constant scripture-quoting or Tiny's noisy pigs. Back at the little café, Dove mentioned Mrs. Johnson's duplexes.

That would be a place to start. Perhaps Mrs. Johnson needed a caretaker, a fix-it person. I didn't have the first idea of fixing leaky pipes, but I could learn. A duplex in town would at least be a little quieter. I'd get on it—soon.

I was slowing down gradually to the pace around me, a pace that meant going to town only when necessary, doing whatever came next instead of sitting around in staff meetings writing five-year goals. Here I was on a Saturday morning, babysitting a wounded pig, daydreaming out loud.

After Jim's accident, he could no longer sleep out with the rest of the animals. At least that's what Tru and Tiny told Lutie, although she fussed about converting the space next to the newly repaired TV into a pigpen. Still, she furnished the patient with a ratty blanket and even looked the other way when Tru slipped him table scraps. As I was discovering, her crusty demeanor was a shell for a deep reverence of life, a concern that softened her.

Jim improved every day, and soon he began to wander the house freely. He'd bump into things with the Elizabethan collar and then back up with this surprised look. He couldn't figure out what was different, poor thing, just as he obviously wasn't sure why he could no longer snort and squeal. I sympathized with him. The changes in my life were just as baffling, and I, too, couldn't decide exactly what was different.

"You know, Jim, they need a library in Murkee," I said, straightening his bed while he watched a video on the TV that Tiny had so graciously repaired. "The school has about ten books, and they're all old encyclopedias. No wonder the kids all turn out to be ranch hands and truck drivers."

In fourth grade Loren H. had called me names in the school library, and I'd punched him so hard he knocked the globe off a shelf and split it in two. Mrs. Davis, the librarian, sent me into the hall, and I decided to have my own library some day. After that, I began to categorize and reshelve everything in my life. Here, I thought, was a great opportunity. As soon as the superintendent found out I was available, he would surely hire me.

"I'll have the kids around here begging for John Donne instead of plasma TV," I said aloud to Jim.

The pig stared at the tube. "See what I mean? TV just turns us all into zombies." Jim was as responsive as Nova, although less sullen.

My daughter sat at the dinette table, painting each of her nails a different color. The bottles of polish stood open, brushes atilt, filling the kitchen with the biting smell of acetone. Shades like midnight blue and metallic green suited her; even the bright yellow gloss had a melancholy look to it. She pursed her lips and carefully stroked each fingertip, as if this was the only thing in life worth doing.

"Planning to come with us to the cookout tomorrow?" I asked her so she'd feel more like she was making her own decisions.

"And do what? Hang with geeks? Duh." Nova let out one of her famous sighs and blew lightly on her fingertips. She could be a pretty girl, even beautiful, if she ever gave up hating the world. At least she wasn't wearing all black yet, although I was halfway afraid to praise her for it.

"If you stay here Uncle Tiny and Jim will drive you nuts. You know how they love those *Green Acres* episodes."

"He's not going?" Her breath again hissed out, louder than before. "Fine. I guess I could show for a little while. Teach the losers how to be cool."

"You'll be cool, all right, and don't embarrass the rest of us. You know what I mean."

"My hair? Come on, it's no big deal."

"Wash out that gunk, and I'll forget that you didn't do the dishes yet." I'd insisted the children take over that chore from Aunt Lutie, which was an unpopular decision to say the least.

Nova pushed away from the table and held her fingers up in the air. "My nails are wet. How can I do dishes?"

"Whatever." I smiled. Sometimes I was more like her than I thought.

That afternoon the Tabernacle Ladies, as I called the loosely knit group, assembled at our place for a planning session for the upcoming fall bazaar. Gladys Mason and several others trouped into the living room, where Lutie had set the dinette chairs in a semicircle. They arranged themselves, and I sat next to a large woman named LaDonna Johnson, whose electric blue polyester blouse whooshed with her every move. She was taking notes on a small spiral-bound pad. Aunt Lutie sat in her recliner, holding court and wielding her usual authority.

"Frieda, will you open us in prayer today?" Lutie smiled at Frieda, a mousy shy woman. Frieda looked at her feet. "Come on," Lutie urged, "the Lord perks right up when he hears you praying."

This was going to be a long afternoon. I tried not to look bored and bowed my head politely as dear Frieda started in. The moment she opened her mouth, though, she was transformed from wallflower to warrior. I was impressed, in spite of the God-sized chip I still had on my spiritual shoulder. Somehow, Frieda's prayer lightened me, if only for a moment. I wondered if Nova, who had refused to come out of the bedroom, would feel the sincerity of Frieda's efforts through the trailer's thin walls.

After the "amen," Frieda returned to her quiet self, and Lutie opened the meeting. It was mostly the kind of talk you'd expect from a bunch of church ladies: How many tote tables they'd need and how much to charge for the privilege of selling pies, canned goods, and a myriad of crafts and handiwork. LaDonna was breathless as she outlined her plan for keeping the quilts and the crocheted afghans clean and dry after last year's "*fee-asco*," she said.

"And Linc told me at the end of last season he'll be upping the rent again," LaDonna continued. "Maybe we ought to move the whole kit and caboodle back over to the church." She sighed. "And pray it don't rain."

"But we all agreed that Linc's is the only place big enough," Lutie said.

Gladys broke in, straightening her long legs out into the middle of the room. "That's it right there, LaDonna," she said. "The church is just too crowded, and out in the yard everything is at the mercy of the weather and the dust. We need that hall."

"Suppose we took up a collection beforehand?" A woman named Velma said with a smirk. "Make the menfolk pull their weight." Velma was heavier than La Donna but a lot less cheerful.

The more I listened, the more I was convinced that they were as courageous and fulfilled in their own way as any liberated city woman. The thing that nagged at me was their silence when it came to Linc. I couldn't for the life of me figure out how he managed to run the town and keep these fiercely independent folks in line. Even here, where my outspoken aunt held her own brand of influence, the ladies refused to speak of him except as pertained to the meeting hall they needed.

When the conversation finally sounded more casual—talk of the weather and which animals were doing what, who was attending the county fair this month—I took a chance and asked a question of the group. "I'm curious," I said, suddenly feeling as shy as Frieda. "Why would Linc charge a bunch of church ladies to set up their bazaar in his place?" All the women stared at me as if I'd asked why God made air.

Frieda said, "Linc's only got that way since he's been back." She reached for a cookie and tore a big bite from its side. "He's done so much for all of us. You'd think certain people would be grateful."

Lutie's eyes blazed. "Frieda, if I told you once I told you twice, Linc is up to more than getting his rights back."

Frieda sniffed. "I only meant there are a lot of us who are beholden to him. He never charged us a fee before all this came up with your brother."

I volunteered. "What's the difference between the two venues? Couldn't we just use the church?"

LaDonna chimed in. "At least *someone* has a decent head on her shoulders."

"It's too small, LaDonna." Lutie looked exasperated.

LaDonna rolled her eyes. "It just burns me up to pay to hold a bazaar."

Lutie shrugged. "I know, I know." She sighed. "But how else will we raise enough money for our own hall?"

After a few moments, Frieda spoke in a whisper. "Jesus said to render unto Caesar the things that are Caesar's," she said and looked at the floor once again. The others set their mouths into thin hard lines, and LaDonna's blouse whooshed as she folded her arms over her chest.

Lutie struggled out of the recliner and stood before the group. She looked thinner than usual. "I'll get Muri here straightened out on this later," she said. "Now are we ready for a vote? The hall or the churchyard? A roof over our heads or do we take our chances on the weather?"

"I guess we have no choice," Frieda said with a huff.

"My Dresden Plate quilt was all but ruined two years ago out in the yard," Gladys complained.

"At least the hall's got ceiling fans," LaDonna said, and she fanned herself with her notepad.

"Well, I guess that's it then," Lutie said. "Frieda? What do you say?"

"God is bigger than Linc," she murmured. "Pay the tax and watch what He can do."

After the last Tabernacle Lady said good-bye, Nova stuck her head around the corner and said she was starving. She scavenged the leftover snacks while Aunt Lutie tried to engage her in conversation.

"You're plenty old enough to take part in the bazaar," Lutie said. "Here. Let me fix you up a plate." She piled food on a paper plate, and Nova took it. I nodded at my daughter, and she understood my hint.

"Thanks," she said and pulled a chair from the living room over to the dinette.

"You've got such a way with your outfits," Lutie said, and pointed at the blouse Nova wore, the one my daughter had designed herself. "Bet you and Rhonda Gaye can create a winner," Lutie said.

Nova stared ahead and poked at the food with her fork.

"You might make some new friends." I could hear the wheedling tone in my voice. "Maybe Rhonda is into designing clothes too." Nova groaned, and I let the matter drop.

But I decided it wasn't worth waiting to catch Aunt Lutie alone before asking about Linc again. After all, she'd just said

Nova was plenty old enough for grown-up things. Tiny and Tru would be home again soon, and I needed some answers to questions like why Linc Jackson would bully my father over water in a measly creek? What Linc would need the creek for anyway, except to slake the thirst of a few stray cows? Whether Linc was really King of Murkee?

I laid my hand gently on Lutie's arm. "I need to know what's going on with Linc," I said. Nova looked up briefly and then resumed grazing. "You said all the trouble is over water, right?

Lutie nodded. "Water rights, sure."

"But why? Everyone I've met so far, including Linc, seems so neighborly." I grabbed a basket of paper napkins and began folding them.

"We thought so, too, until a year ago. That's when Linc first asked your daddy to sell. Linc's property doesn't butt up against the creek, but he didn't want a slough like Doc Rubin. Joseph tried to convince Linc, but he wouldn't hear of it."

"That creek isn't exactly the Columbia River," I said. "What's the big deal?"

Lutie rose and grabbed a sponge, wiping counters as she spoke. "It's a year-round creek. Out here water's everything. Anyway, Linc waved a paper in our faces—real official-looking document. Claims that creek belongs to him because of his great-granddad."

"So why would he want to sue us?"

Nova stopped chewing and took a sip of her iced tea. "Maybe he's an evil corporate developer," my daughter said. "Or an alien, breeding little aliens in the creek." She smirked.

"That's enough of that," I said.

Lutie held up her sponge. "Sounds crazy, doesn't it, kiddo? But there've been these rumors—"

"See?" Nova said. "I say let him have the creek. The water stinks." She sniffed her tea and made a face.

"What rumors?" I controlled the urge to scold Nova.

"Just hearsay," Lutie said. "Linc Jackson has kept a lot of families from going under around here." She donned a pair of yellow rubber gloves and filled the double sink with suds and rinse water. "But some say he's bent on putting stick houses all over and some kind of fancy golf course too."

The Tabernacle Ladies had said Linc owned everything in town but the church. "How'd Linc come to own most of Murkee?" I asked.

Lutie clanked dishes around in the sink. "This was Linc's great-granddaddy's town. Ulysses McMurphy bought it in the 1880s for around a thousand dollars, or so the story goes," Lutie said. She looked at Nova. "Back then a thousand dollars went a lot farther than it would today."

I grabbed two flour sack towels and handed one to Nova. She pushed back her chair loudly.

"Hold it," I said. "I need to keep this straight. Linc's King of Murkee, right?"

"You got it."

"He wanted my father to sell this place, which includes that creek out there." I pointed in the general direction of the stream.

"Right."

"Linc claims to have rights to that water. What? From some old document he dug up that says he wasn't gone five years, only four years and some odd months?"

"As the Lord is my witness."

"I'm confused," I said. "Which is more important to Linc—the land or the water rights?"

"To hear Linc tell it, our water rights are what he's really after. Something to do with prior appropriation. Well, anyway, first come-first served. Even though Ulysses was the original owner, your daddy bought this place fair and square."

"So how could Linc sue us, if it's our land?" I opened a cupboard and set a stack of plates inside. So far Nova hadn't dried a single dish.

Lutie clasped her gloved hands together and glanced over at Jesus on the wall. "George says Linc's got proof. But my heart tells me it all comes down to that creek. Water is almost as precious as gold around here."

"I still don't get why Linc won't build a ditch like Rubin did. And who's George?" Now I was completely at sea.

"I heard some men down at the café talking about wet gold," Nova said. "It's like they have more water rights than they have water. Crazy."

"Men do act crazy when it comes to gold," I said. "Even if it is wet gold."

"Amen to that," Lutie said. "Linc's crazy, Muri. And George is the only lawyer around."

"What does Linc's wife have to say about this?" I couldn't believe I asked.

"He's divorced, but his grandson Marvin lives with him."

Nova lay her towel down. "Can I go now?" She gave Lutie a pleading look. "Please?" Her aunt smiled, and Nova scooted over to the sofa.

"To tell you the truth, Lutie, I still don't understand." I dried each Spode teacup carefully. "Linc doesn't seem crazy—far from it. He may own everything, but you said he's pretty generous too. I'll talk to him. This is all a big misunderstanding."

Lutie emptied the sink and stripped off her gloves. "Misunderstanding? Your daddy didn't see it that way. Truth be told, at one time we all thought Linc was an angel. If it weren't for him, Murkee would have dried up and blown away long ago. Agro-biz being what it is, small-timers are barely hanging on."

"What's agro-biz?" Tru asked. He and Tiny banged through the screen door and descended on the platter of cakes and cookies Nova hadn't eaten.

"None of *your* biz," Nova said. She made a face at her brother.

"Enough," I said to both of them. "I'm sure Aunt Lutie has some chores that need doing if you have nothing else to do."

"Why, as a matter of fact—" Lutie began. But by then Nova and Tru had already disappeared out the door.

"Nova can get some ideas for the bazaar from Frieda's girl," Lutie went on as if my daughter hadn't just evaporated at the mention of work. She poured the cookies back into the jar. "Rhonda Gaye is only a year or two younger. Pretty as a picture if she ever gets those braces."

"Nova might not be interested," I said.

"Well, Muri, I wouldn't say this in front of her, but Nova would be downright beautiful if she'd get rid of that eyebrow thing and let her hair grow out some." Lutie had her back to me, but I could tell she was trying to be tactful.

"I'll speak to her if it bothers you that much," I said.

"Folks just talk, that's all. Me, I don't think Jesus gives a hoot what we look like on the outside." She wiped dry the cookie plate and lifted it into the cupboard. "The Lord looks at the heart, and that's a fact."

I wondered what God would see in my heart if he took a peek. Anger? Loneliness? What did it matter? I suspected the community would judge us all by my impending divorce and my daughter's rebellious appearance. I hoped the party at Rubin's place wouldn't turn out to be a "*fee*-asco" as Lutie's friend had put it.

7

The barbecue at Rubin's was a community affair. "Just about anybody who's anybody shows up for his Fourth of July wingding," Lutie said. She was dressed to the nines today, in a skirt and white blouse adorned with studs and shiny beads of fabric paint, the puffy kind in pearlescent shades of red and blue. "Made it myself," she said when I oohed and ahhed over her outfit.

Tiny always stayed home, though, because every year the main course was pork ribs. He said he just couldn't eat ribs and then go home and face the pigs.

"Jim's real sensitive," he added, helping Lutie pack an enormous bowl of his Mexican potato salad and a batch of freshly baked scones into a cardboard box. "I think Doc understands." Tiny laid the scones down gently and hiked up his pants, huge dungarees that slipped if he bent over. Nova said he should have been a plumber.

If he had, the pipes might have been in better working order. As it was, flushing the one toilet in the house was an art, requiring a strict protocol to avoid flooding. The pump that supplied the water for all our needs had to be primed at times, even cajoled, sweet-talked, and prayed over by Lutie.

74

And I'd never thought about it before moving here, but electricity was another luxury city folks took for granted. Out here, the power was off half the time because somebody's tractor backed into a pole, or a bird flew into a transformer, or just because it felt like it, as far as I could tell. Most everyone had a backup generator and plenty of flashlights and lanterns. One good ice storm, Tiny explained, and we might be using that stack of wood to keep warm for a week.

This was life in the outback of Oregon, I reminded myself, the place where all my father's memories were stored. Lutie missed her brother; it was written all over her days. He must have been as good a handyman as she claimed, for poor Tiny had trouble keeping everything in working order.

Lutie frequently dusted all those photos by the window, and once I heard her whispering to his picture. My father had left a hole in her life—that much was clear. She peppered her conversations with stories about how "Joseph did this" or "Joseph loved that." So far, I hadn't the courage to ask her anything painful, like where he was buried or if he'd ever said why he left me behind. But I knew I'd have to find the answer to that question, or I might as well have never come at all.

In the cramped room Nova and I shared, I sorted through the crowded closet looking for something to wear to the barbecue. Our clothes were shoved in with boxes of Lutie's sewing supplies and who knows what else. This would be my first real social outing since we had arrived.

I slid a boot box to one side. It fell over, and its contents tumbled out on the floor. Instead of crochet hooks or balls of yarn, a pile of papers and old photos lay at my feet. Joseph Pond stared up at me from a yellowed photo. He stood on a rise overlooking the creek. Shadows cut across the landscape and highlighted my father's profile.

I picked up the snapshot and smoothed it, running my fingers across his face. I sat on the edge of the bed and tried to pray for the first time since I could remember. I felt awkward and clumsy, but I asked for guidance anyway. Before I could stop it, a tear splashed on the print. I wiped it away and wished I'd come here while he was still alive.

This was what was left of my father: old pictures, newspaper clippings, cocktail napkins scrawled with drawings, and a journal written in a strong upright hand.

My dear daughter, Muriel, the first entry began. What followed was a heartbreaking admission of parental failure but also a life of unbendable faith. My father admitted he was a problem drinker and hadn't been capable of raising his only offspring. One line jumped out and pricked my heart: *The good Lord has been good to this old sinner*, it said, and *I'd die a happy man if I knew you'd joined the fold of our Lord Jesus.*

I still wasn't sure I could enter into his beliefs. I wanted to believe. I just didn't see how God could help me in my situation. I carefully flipped through the entries, which were random but chronicled three decades. I gently laid the other things back into the box and slid it back where I'd found it. I wondered if Aunt Lutie had planted it there for me to find.

Every morning since we had arrived I'd stared at the peeled places in the tiny bedroom's wallpaper, printed like a 1910 Sears and Roebuck catalog. I'd imagine that something of my dad's spirit lay hidden there among the ads for Pears Soap and Dr. Scott's Electric Hair Brush. So far I'd found only a bad photograph. I hoped the cookout would turn up people who had known Joseph Pond better than I and who had loved him at least as well.

We arrived a little late, and I blamed it on Nova. I knew differently, of course; I hadn't been able to make up my mind about what to wear. It felt ridiculous to be concerned about whether I would go with a comfortable denim jumper, or with a more defining outfit. I finally settled for an old white sundress that I'd had forever, so soft it felt like flannel next to my skin. I had no tan to speak of, so I tied a red scarf around the scooped neckline. Simple is better, I decided, and left the scarf behind.

Rubin's veranda-style porch had been draped with red, white, and blue crepe paper, and the wicker furniture was supplemented by folding chairs with *Property of Red Rock Tabernacle Church* stamped on their backs. A makeshift stage filled up a good deal of the yard, and wires for microphones and speakers lay tangled across the sparse grass. Card tables were scattered over the rest of the area, and off to one side three large gas grills had already been fired up.

Men in cowboy hats clustered around metal washtubs full of ice, soda, and beer. Most of the men's faces had deep ruts carved into them, and I wondered if the wind or years of loneliness and hard work had worn them down. Linc Jackson stood in the midst of them.

Women of all shapes and ages hovered over a long table laden with typical picnic fare: cauldrons of baked beans, rows of condiments, potato salad, and watermelons sliced into neat triangles. I recognized all the Tabernacle Ladies and a few more women I hadn't met. Most were softer and rounder than they needed to be, dressed in bright flowery blouses and SAS shoes. Their hairdos were neat cowgirl twists or those short tight perms that only need to be redone once a year.

A couple of the younger ones looked more cosmopolitan, or perhaps they just bought the magazine now and then. Kids zipped in and out of small groups, squealing and guzzling soda.

Nova and Tru hung back until Lutie marched us all off to say hello to some of the Tabernacle Ladies. LaDonna and Velma fussed over the food, and over in a corner Frieda read stories to the younger kids. An emu had nipped one small boy when he stuck his fingers through the fence, and he sat, still howling, on his mother's lap.

Nova and Tru looked bored until Lutie finally said to go "pile some food on a plate." They ran off, leaving me to hold a conversation with Velma, who said she'd canned fifty jars of bread and butter pickles earlier in the day. I listened and nodded at intervals, looking over her head toward the fence where the emus roamed.

Before I could decide where to begin mingling, I spotted Rubin waving at me from his spot near the grill.

"Over here," he mouthed, so after excusing myself, I picked my way across the yard, dodging dogs and kids. I would have been happy to hang back on the edge of things, or at least say hello to Linc.

"I was hoping you'd make it," Rubin said. He laid down the spatula.

I crossed my arms over my middle. "Looks like the whole town's here," I said. I pointed at the crepe paper streamers on the porch. "Who's on the decoration committee?"

"The church ladies take care of me," he said, grinning wide. "Came by yesterday and did all this. They treat me like Doc Hollywood." He winked at me. "How's Jim doing today?"

I wished Rubin wasn't quite so friendly. I wasn't officially divorced yet. "He's fine, but I think the collar is bugging him a lot," I said. "He keeps running into things. Tiny stayed home so they could watch their TV shows. Uncle said you'd understand."

"Sure, I know. Jim might get wind of him eating ribs. But I forgot to tell Tiny that this year it's not pork. We're eating emu." Rubin grabbed a large meaty slab from a tray with tongs and plopped it down on the grill. "Trying out some new seasonings this year too. All the neighbors say it—"

"Tastes like chicken?" I laughed.

Rubin laughed. "Actually emu's more like beef. Very tasty. What a shame Tiny stayed home. He's missing some fine barbecue. Want a sample?"

Before I could say no, a voice rang out. "Hey, Jonto!" A tall, thick man with long black hair and massive arms waved at Rubin.

"My buddy, Denny, from Portland," Rubin whispered.

The big man introduced a petite Asian woman as his wife Gwen. Her hair, blacker than mine, was blunt cut about chin-length. She looked muscular and compact, if a bit long waisted. A baby girl squirmed in her arms. "See how big Leila's gotten since you saw her last? Before you know it you won't recognize your own goddaughter, Rubin Jonto."

"I should get up to Portland more often," Rubin said. He patted the child's head. "Anyway, meet my new neighbor Muri Pond," I stuck out my hand. Gwen handed the baby to Denny and then gave me a hug.

"I'm glad you're here," Gwen said, taking back the infant. "Rubin needs better company than a bunch of emus."

Rubin laughed. "Not easy being an emu rancher, that's for sure. What do you say we get the music going?" He pointed toward the makeshift stage.

"I saw the equipment," I said. "Who's playing?" I imagined real country music, grainy and unfiltered like fresh squeezed cider, complete with fiddlers and a harmonica or two.

"Some of the kids got themselves a band," he said, flipping a charred rib section to its uncooked side. "Linc's grandson, Marvin, and some other boys play a little. Can't say exactly what yet; they've only been at it a few weeks. I let them jam over here after school."

Rubin untied his apron and handed the spatula to a man he called Ed. "Let's go find out what these kids have got. I need another soda, and your hands are empty too."

Denny, Gwen, and I followed Rubin over to the washtub. Rubin's friend plunged his arm into the ice and brought up an orange soda.

I said, "Dr. Moses?"

"Call me Denny."

I asked him to fish me out a 7UP. "Did you know my father, Joseph Pond?"

Denny grabbed another soda and popped it open for his wife. "Course I knew Joe. You remind me of him."

I ducked my eyes. "Thanks." Before I could ask any other questions, Rubin elbowed Denny. "The music's on. Check it out. I brought in a live band this year."

Denny grinned. "Bet they stink."

Rubin said, "I'll pretend I didn't hear that, brother."

We dragged chairs in front of where the boys from the band were adjusting their equipment, sending out feedback squeals on the loudspeaker, and tapping on mics. The leader was a tall, lanky kid with shoulder-length, raven-black hair, straight and hanging in his eyes.

I said, "That Marvin?" Rubin nodded. The kid seemed as full of anger as his grandfather.

Three other boys took their places: a drummer, a bass player, and a chunky kid on a stool plunking out the only three guitar chords he probably knew. Marvin pulled the mic to his mouth. "Hi, folks. We're Road Kill, and we'd like to play some tunes for you."

Someone yelled out, "Know any Hank Williams songs?"

"Sorry. We don't take requests yet," Marvin said, strapping on a battered electric guitar, tossing back that shock of hair that had fallen across his piercing eyes. "This one's called 'In Your Face'."

It was too. "In Your Face" assaulted my ears like a hurricane's roar. Over the thumping bass guitar, Marvin shouted out violent lyrics, something about pushing people around. Leila began to fuss, and Gwen took the baby into the house for a nap, she said. Denny and Rubin yelled to each other over the din, catching up the way friends do.

A few minutes later, Gwen came back outside toting Leila, crying in deep shudders. "I can't take anymore," Gwen said. "She's been teething for a week now. It's driving us nuts."

Denny apologized. "We're going over to Prineville to visit Gwen's folks," he said. "Wish we could have stayed longer."

"Nice meeting you both," I said.

Rubin and I saw them to their car and then came back to where we'd been watching the band.

While Road Kill struggled to keep the beat, Nova stood over to the side. Her eyes fixated on the angry young man with the growling vocals, following his every move. She had a moony look on her face.

Tru and Aunt Lutie sat down beside us. Lutie clamped her hands over her ears. "Dear Lord, I'm glad Tiny's not here for this," she said, grimacing. Then she patted my hand when she saw me staring at Nova, who was all but drooling over the band.

The song must have had ninety-two verses or just the same chorus over and over; it was hard to tell. By the time the last note rang out, most of the people around had pressed themselves against the emu pens. Finally, Rubin stood up and started clapping, knocking over the soda I'd set beside my chair.

"C'mon, let's show a little support here," he said, beckoning to the small groups where most were looking straight at the ground. "These kids have been working hard." He plopped back into the chair, stood the soda can upright, and mumbled, "I'll get you another."

Linc Jackson emerged from one of the groups. He raised his drink and said, "Let's hear it for my grandson." People politely applauded, glancing at each other, as if silently praying for an electrical failure. Marvin and Road Kill then launched into "Louie, Louie," and I amused myself by watching the bass player's hat vibrate with the deafening rendition.

"Excuse me," I shouted to Rubin, "I'm going to mingle." I tapped Lutie on the shoulder. "Keep an eye on the kids, will you?"

I wove through the chairs and around folks with paper plates full of barbecued emu. I wanted to get to know our neighbor and try to smooth things over.

Linc held captive an audience of younger men. I couldn't make out exactly what he was saying, but the rise and fall of his voice made me think of tall tales or the one that got away. As I listened it became obvious that Linc Jackson really was King of Murkee. Men rested their arms on the backs of chairs and spit tobacco juice every which way, careful to avoid the pointy toes of their own boots as Linc spoke. Here and there I caught a few words. In between songs I heard more.

"High time Murkee was put on the map," Linc proclaimed. "How about a real live Oregon dude ranch? Wrangling emus, now wouldn't that be a sight?" The men punctuated his speech with sharp reports of laughter, so loud at times the women at the food tables would look over. I headed over to where the women sat chatting. If they spotted me in Linc's audience I might turn into the subject of gossip. But before I could say hello to LaDonna, I paused. Linc was talking about the creek.

Linc spoke about the necessity for change. "The creek won't take us much farther," he was saying, "and we can't live in the past. We got no other choice." I was ready to sit next to LaDonna when I heard my father's name.

"See, Chief Joseph wasn't interested in progress," Linc said. "He didn't give a hoot about this community or about our future." The crowd murmured. "Chief didn't give a tumbleweed's toenail if he was legal or not."

He turned around and acted surprised that I'd been listening. Every inch of me burned.

"Mr. Jackson," I said. "There's been some sort of misunderstanding. My father's not here to defend himself, but surely there's been some mistake."

Linc's eyes narrowed. "Mistake's all yours, Miss," he said. "Yours and your old man's."

"I'm not even sure what we're talking about. Water, land, what?"

"Goes to show you," Linc said to the men. "City folks don't understand how it is." He turned to me. "I got the papers to prove the rights are mine." He reached into his wallet and produced a document. He waved it at me. "See? This is the original deed to the water in that creek, in perpetuity. That means *forever*, in case you were wondering."

I took a step forward. "I'd like to examine that."

Linc stuffed the paper into his shirt pocket and snorted. "My cattle need that water. And legally, it's mine. I was willing to pay market price, but the old fool turned me down. The way I see it, Chief Joseph owes me."

There was a flurry, and suddenly, Aunt Lutie flew past me. Flashing her puffy paint and fake studs she strode up to Linc, stopping about two inches from his face. Marvin and the Road Kill Band froze in mid-riff as Lutie stared into Linc's eyes.

"My brother never owed you nothing, you jackass," she screeched, shaking a fist and trembling.

The young men chuckled softly. Linc sneered. "I just want what's mine, that's all." He shrugged his shoulders and backed up a little.

"Well, then this is for you," Lutie said and punched him in the stomach. Linc's cowboy hat flew off and landed in the dust. "And don't ever call my brother Chief Joseph again." Linc seemed too stunned to speak. I'd never seen a woman punch anyone so hard. I put my arms around Nova and Tru and gathered them to me.

"Don't tell me you're leaving?" Rubin rushed over and begged us all to stay. I shook my head.

"I think it's best if we go," I said softly.

"Muri, please," Rubin looked hurt.

"I don't want trouble, but thanks for inviting us," I said. "Will you stop by to check on Jim soon?"

Rubin gestured to the guys at the card table to start the hand without him. Then he said, "Jim. Sure, I'll check on Jim."

Linc still hadn't said anything, but he made sure I noticed his long fierce stare. He and the others reminded me of how young boys eye each other, silently daring each other to fight another day. Someone handed Linc his hat. The men gradually drifted back into their conversations, voices starting out subdued and increasing in volume once Marvin's band got going again.

Nova didn't want to leave. She and the leader of Road Kill were already on a first-name basis, planning to watch the fireworks display later on. The fireworks between the two of them worried me at this point.

During a set break Marvin said, "It's cool," peering at me through his hair. "I could drop her off afterwards." Nova pursed her lips at me. Looking at her short cutoffs, I wished she wasn't growing up so fast.

Lutie once again headed off a battle. "I think she'll be okay here, Muri," she said, placing her hand on my shoulder. "I'll ask Doc to keep an eye out."

"Are you sure?" I said, thinking we all should have stayed home with Tiny and Jim. I looked over to Rubin, to make sure he wasn't drinking. Thankfully, he was in control of his faculties, but some of the guests looked blitzed. The tortoiseshell barrette that I thought matched my hair so well began to bite into my scalp.

"This isn't the big city you know," Lutie answered. "Out here everybody looks out for each other. And just because old Linc is cranky, well, Marvin takes after his grandmother's side is all I have to say about that."

"I'd feel better if Rubin brought Nova home instead," I said.

"You can rely on me," Rubin said. "I'll see to it."

"Before midnight?"

"Absolutely. What time is it, anyway?"

"Nova has a watch," Lutie noticed. "She'll let you know, won't you, young lady? Or your Auntie will give you trouble." Nova nodded. She smiled at Marvin, and he announced it was time for the next set.

I was secretly glad we were leaving before I grew to hate "Louie, Louie" even more. I'd found enough truth for one day, and it would be awhile before we would sample barbecued emu.

8

I kept my mouth shut as Tru and I followed Lutie back across the hill. Though it was already nine o'clock, the stars were barely out, watered down against the summer twilight. I've always loved this time of evening when blue-violet colors the breeze, softens the shadows, and tempers the rawness of the day. Even my white cotton dress took on a lavender cast.

Thankfully, Lutie wasn't in a hurry. Tru ran ahead, filled with energy and too many sweets. He waved sparklers and wrote his name in trails of light. I was still a bit jittery.

"All shook up?" my aunt asked. I nodded. She looked calm, as if she socked men like Linc in the gut every day. Looking at her, I felt stronger somehow. I surprised myself that I'd begun to think of a complete stranger as "Dad."

Lutie read my mind, or so I imagined. "Your daddy wasn't perfect, I guess you know," she said, nodding in Tru's direction, acknowledging his wild sparkler circles. "Joseph never could do anything just a little. He played too much, bragged too much, and dreamed too big. But there wasn't a mean bone in his body. He never meant to cheat anyone, not even Linc."

"Linc Jackson really is the king around here."

Lutie laughed. "Bigger than Elvis, I'm sure. At least he thinks he is."

My shoes slid on loose gravel, and I steadied myself against Lutie's shoulder. Someone had worked hard to grade this road. "What kind of work did my father do?" I hadn't even known this about him, whether his hands were smooth or rough, or if his mind held more than the stuff of hard labor.

"Joseph had lots of different jobs. He was a real cowboy for a while, and then he sold office supplies in Tucson. He hated that job. Got work on the dam sites up in Washington, and that's where he lost two of his fingers. Blood poisoning. From the cement, you know."

"How'd he come to Oregon?"

"He got on disability and bought this place with insurance money. The company paid him to go away, you could say. Joseph started drinking too much when he couldn't buy your mother the fancy things she loved. You were born sometime around then, and he and your mom split up."

"To marry Benjamin?" I shivered, although it was a warm evening.

"I suppose. He lost track of you for years. I was back in D.C. until Clinton was elected and hadn't seen Joseph for a couple of years. He wanted to be a history teacher, you know. He finished a couple years of college before he married your mom."

We were at the oven-door fence now, and I stopped. "You worked in Washington? I don't know why, but I thought you'd grown up around here." I had a little trouble imagining her in the high profile setting of federal politics.

Lutie laughed. "I wasn't always a hayseed, young lady," she said, weaving through the piles of discarded bike parts in the yard. "Joseph and I both had big dreams once. I was going to be a senator's wife, and he was going to write history books."

She sighed. "Things don't always turn out the way you think they should."

"Amen to that," Tiny said, holding the screen door open. Jim stuck his snout out to greet us, as wheezy little noises came from where his oinks ought to be. "You're home awful early." My uncle fingered his red suspenders. "No fireworks this year?"

"Oh, there were plenty of those," I assured him, grinning at Lutie.

"Now what's my Pearl gone and done this time?" Tiny wanted to know.

"Nothing that didn't need doing," she said, "and you'll never guess what the Doc had on the menu."

"Nobody you know," Tru said, chuckling. He cast his spent fireworks in the dirt. "Emu. They had barbecued emu."

We trooped inside where I plopped myself on the sofa, suddenly feeling as fizzled as the sparklers. Lutie proceeded to give Tiny a detailed account of the scene with Linc. Tru added sound effects like an old "Batman" episode.

My uncle listened, looking straight at her. Eye contact was something I'd never been able to command from Chaz. When she finished her story, Tiny massaged Lutie's shoulders gently and said he understood. The affection he poured on her was priceless in my view. A vacuum of loneliness threatened to suck the heart right out of me.

Tru didn't want to miss the fireworks show at Rubin's. Tiny offered to let him climb up on the roof to watch the skies, which were by now getting blacker and crowded with a spectacular view of the Milky Way. They found a spot that seemed sturdy, and Tru held the ladder first for his uncle and then scrambled up. I wondered how Tiny would manage to get down, but he said he climbed up there all the time. Aunt Lutie gave me a good-night kiss and a pat, before she went to bed. I lay down in the living room, my spine sagging along with the old sofa, trying not to cry until everyone was out of sight.

It's always easy to navel gaze when nothing is going right and you're looking up at a tacky low ceiling. You can get trapped into feeling that this is the way things will always be, that the planets will always be in some horrible aspect, and that you will always get dumped on by whatever deity you were raised to fear.

With Jim the pig snuffling by my side, and the picture of Jesus avoiding my gaze, I might have sunk into this quagmire myself. I had plenty to feel sorry about, didn't I? My father had gone and died before I could meet him. My husband had dumped me. I was being sued. My daughter was taking up with a wannabe rock singer. And the plumbing was bad.

A tear leaked out. I tried to will it back to where I keep them hidden, but it wouldn't budge. It just rolled down my cheek. I even tried to distract myself with visions of my father, rubbing my mother's shoulders gently, whispering that he understood. That made it worse. Before I could stop I was sobbing in ragged gasps, and Jim was looking at me with piggy eyes, straining to understand. Perhaps he did, since he'd lost something himself.

I was up searching for a Kleenex when Jim ambled over to the door. He sniffed at the air, and then I knew why. I recognized Nova's voice as the door opened.

Rubin had brought her home as promised, but my daughter reeked of alcohol. Nova blurted, "I'm sick," held her hand across her mouth, and ran for the bathroom.

For a moment I stood there. I had to decide whether to punch Rubin for allowing this to happen or follow my daughter. I ran after Nova and found the bathroom door locked. I pleaded with her to let me in.

"You all right?" I whispered through the door, sure that her retching would wake everyone in the house.

"Go away," she moaned in between heaves. I stood outside the door awhile longer and asked her again if she needed anything, the same way I'd done when she had stomach flu as a little girl. I wanted to hold her head and wipe away her tears, but the door stayed locked.

After a few minutes, Nova emerged, brushed by me, and disappeared into the bedroom.

It was senseless to talk; I remembered that from my days with Benjamin and his binges. Best to wait until morning. Nova had never come home drunk before, although she had done plenty of other things to infuriate her parents. This was a first, and I intended to hold Rubin Jonto responsible.

I followed Nova into the room, where she had flopped over the bed sideways, and grabbed my pillow and a lavender crocheted throw. I would have to camp on the sofa all night now, as if I was going to get any sleep with my teeth clenched that way. My daughter and Dr. Jonto would get an earful in the morning. I fumed all the way back to the living room.

"Is she okay?" Rubin was still there, standing in the shadows.

I jumped, gasping like a kid in a haunted house. "I thought you'd gone," I said, clutching the pillow to my chest. Jim had satisfied himself that Rubin wasn't an intruder and had gone back to his spot next to the TV. I wasn't that sure.

Rubin's brows bunched up, and he wouldn't look directly at me. "Sorry about all this," he said. He added a loud sigh. "Everything was fine. Next thing I knew, those kids had all disappeared. I promised I'd watch out for her, and, well, like I said, I'm sorry." He came closer and sat on the edge of the sofa, inviting me to sit next to him.

I shook my head and wrapped the afghan tighter around myself. "This is not acceptable," I said and breathed deeply. "Drunkenness is not okay, especially when it's my daughter. She's sixteen, Rubin. Where I come from that's considered underage."

"I feel like a total fool. She said she was only drinking soda." He had a hangdog look.

"Soda? Rubin, she puked her guts out in there. Anyway, since when will a teenager admit she's drinking? The legal age is still twenty-one." I stood there and shivered, unable to say more.

More retching sounds coming from the bathroom reinforced my point.

Rubin shook his head. "Don't you think she's been punished enough?"

"What would you know about it? You don't even have kids."

"Look, she's making choices. She may not be legal, but she's old enough to make decisions."

"That's the point," I said, aware that my voice sounded shrill. "It's my priority to help her make good choices. So maybe you were right. Move away and my job gets easier."

Rubin froze, as if I'd slapped him. "Fine." He stood up and yanked at the screen door before turning back to me. "You think you wrote the book on living out here? I'll tell you something, lady. Linc Jackson owns this town, and we're the outsiders. Good luck making it past December without a friend or two." He kept his hand on the door.

The fires of regret inched up my cheeks. Since when was I the perfect parent? Here was someone who had the moral fiber to come over and apologize. Wasn't that worth anything?

"I didn't mean that . . . about the moving," I said and extended a hand. "I'm just trying to raise my kids right."

After a few moments he smiled but didn't accept the hand-shake offer. "I know I don't have kids to worry about," he said softly. "I should have watched them more closely. Really, I'm sorry for the trouble I caused."

I could feel my indignation melting, but I resolved to stay clearheaded. He opened the screen again.

"I've got to go," he said, the words slamming me back into reality. Jim looked up from his pig bed. I nodded, and Rubin left.

Aunt Lutie came out from her room then. Her thin knee-length gown fluttered, silhouetting her spare frame. "Everything okay out here?" she asked, looking back toward the bedrooms.

"No, but that's all right."

"Well, you know where to find me if you need to talk."

"I just need some sleep." I exaggerated a yawn.

"Honey, you know your daddy wanted to be here for you, don't you?" Her words poked a hole right through my soul.

I couldn't fight the waver in my voice. "Aunt Lutie, I don't know anything anymore."

"Well, he did. Right up until the day the good Lord took him, he was calling your name. He was too ashamed to find you, but I know he loved you."

"Really?"

"As the Lord is my witness." She sat down on the sofa beside me and put her arms around me. She smelled faintly of talcum powder.

I had too many questions. Did I have brothers or sisters? Had he tried to find me? Did he have my picture? "I want to know everything, Aunt Lutie."

She smiled that closemouthed smile, got up and went down the hall. She brought out the cardboard shoebox—the corners of its lid flayed out like wings—and set it next to me.

I watched her rummage through an odd assortment of papers ad dog-eared photos, until she brought out one snapshot of a toddler standing on a wicker chair.

"Your daddy carried this with him everywhere he went," she said softly, handing me the picture.

I stared at myself, only recognizing a similar smile and the same way I still squinted my eyes when I looked into sunlight. I held it, but I didn't cry at first.

Lutie scrabbled through the contents of the box. "There was something else," she said. She shook her head. "I can't imagine where it's run off to."

"A journal?"

"That's it. He wanted you to have it. Wrote in it just before the Lord took him. Now where could it be?"

"I've got it," I said. I was tearing up again. "It's safe."

"Oh, I'm tickled you found it, honey. He loved you so much, and he wanted to share his faith before he passed away." Lutie looked past me to the table of photos. The lace curtains stirred.

"I'm glad to have it, Aunt Lutie." I didn't say that I was still not ready to leap into Jesus' arms. Not yet.

But I told her everything, about Nova, about Rubin. I even asked her why she'd punched Linc and where my father's grave was.

"Joseph always said expensive funerals were not for him. We scattered him all over the stream on Doc Rubin's place. That's where he went to sit and think. It's where things from our ancestors are buried. "

"The relics? The Nez Perce tribe?"

Lutie shook her head. "The Nez Perce reservation is in Idaho. Around here it's mostly Warm Springs, like Doc Rubin's friend you met."

"Denny's Warm Springs Indian?"

"He's one of the few who escaped the bottle. Started out drinking like so many of the young people, but instead, he went to school and now does a lot to keep our heritage safe."

What I knew of Northwest Native Americans was limited to a few old books I'd read. "Maybe I'll go over to the creek," I said. "I've got plenty to think about."

She patted my shoulder and then stood up. "Listen, honey. Linc tries to make you think he's so big and bad, but I have a secret he doesn't know about." She leaned closer. "Our ancestors and God's angels are looking out for us."

I sighed. Maybe she'd think I was yawning. If she mentioned angels one more time I'd fall apart again.

"Angels, please watch over us," Lutie said.

I was too tired. Something in me snapped. "Stop it," I clamped my hands over my ears. "I don't want to hear about angels," I said and jumped up. "No angels ever helped me." I paced across the rug and avoided glancing at the Jesus picture.

"Only trying to help," Lutie said. She looked sad. I realized that I'd started fights with two people I liked, while Nova, the teen drinker, was in the bathroom sick.

"Oh, Aunt Lutie, I didn't mean—" I squeezed her bony shoulder. "Too many things are happening at once, I guess. I'm sorry."

"No need to apologize, Muri, honey. I'm on your side and so are the—uh, God's messengers. You know what I mean."

"I do." I smiled at my aunt, and she got up to go to bed. "I think I'll sleep on the sofa tonight."

"Night, then. Sweet dreams, Muri." She switched off the light and returned to where I could hear Tiny snoring loudly. I lay down and stared a long time into the still purplish night.

9

If I hadn't witnessed flash floods in Tucson I might have been terrified the Sunday it rained in Murkee. I remembered from my college days the way the weather sneaks up on creatures of the desert. The sky opens, and everything runs for cover. Even the bushes cling to the earth for dear life, while mad waves of brown water rush through arroyos, kangaroo rat dens, and rich people's homes.

No rich people here, unless you counted Linc Jackson. But the deluge poured out in much the same sequence. First came a few fat dusty drops that then invited the masses, pelting the reddish soil; the flicker and jolt of faraway lightning, followed up by its thunderous roll, and little streams flowed down the ruts in the yard and soon formed a shallow lake. Jim's swine siblings begged to come inside too.

"You're dreaming, pigs," Lutie said. The entire roof dripped and leaked. We all rushed around with pots and pans and buckets that filled up too quickly. I scooped as many of the family photos as I could from the table by the window, and Lutie took down the lace curtains she was so fond of.

Tiny and Tru formed a bucket brigade, emptying contain-ers into the kitchen sink. Nova, hung over but useful for once, crammed her clothing into empty trash bags to keep it dry.

"Does the roof always leak like this?" I asked my uncle, already suspecting the answer. He exchanged the full con-tainers for empty ones like someone who'd done this before. I swabbed the floor with a bath towel. The knees of my jeans were soaked.

"Well, last year we didn't get this much rain," he said, tak-ing the sopping towel to the sink for me. He smiled. "At least not all at once." His hands wrung out brownish water, and he handed the soggy towel back to me.

"Let's pray the sanctuary isn't leaking like a sieve," Lutie said. "Tiny, can you drive me into town as soon as we get these leaks under control? I have to show up for Sunday school."

Tiny eyed the roof, which was leaking in more spots by the minute. Outside the rain poured down in sheets. Visibility was probably about ten feet.

"My Pearl, I'd be glad to drive you, but I think we best wait out this storm," he said. "Remember last year? I came close to getting the truck stuck."

Lutie sighed. "Sunday evening will just have to do then. Lord knows we don't need to get stuck in the mud." She rolled up her sleeves and went back to wringing out towels.

I smiled and kept mopping, trying to prevent leaks from penetrating any of the numerous paper sacks that crowded every corner. They were full of Lutie's empty soda cans, but the prospect of the bags turning to a pulpy mess was enough reason to keep them dry.

The rain slammed like marbles against the roof. Aunt Lutie looked up at the ceiling now and then, eyeing the growing wet spot right over her portrait of Jesus. She finally darted over and took the picture down and carefully protected it with plastic wrap, the kind that clings to itself and everything but what you want it to stick to. When she finished it reminded me of a large cocoon.

"Dear Jesus, you going to drown us?" she said to the picture, tucking it beside that crocheted blanket I'd left on the sofa the night before. "You'll be safe over here."

Nova came in and carefully sat next to the afghan. "I need Excedrin—now," she said, fingering her temples gingerly. "Worse . . . splitting . . . headache."

"Careful, missy, you're about to sit on the Lord," Lutie answered, lifting up one corner of the throw. "I'll see what we have in the way of hangover remedies."

Nova winced. "Too loud . . . whisper," she rasped, tacking on "please?" after Lutie clucked her tongue. "A glass of water too?"

My aunt smiled. "I know. You have a mouth full of cotton, poor baby." She went to find a pain reliever while Uncle Tiny explained to Tru the dangers of alcohol. He told him all about the morning-after effects: the dry mouth, the pounding headache, and the aversions to bright lights and the smell of frying bacon. Halfway through the description, Nova pleaded with him to stop talking. "Might . . . hurl . . . again." Tiny obliged and winked at Tru.

"That," he whispered, "is one good reason not to drink." Tru nodded. He always looked serious and intense whenever Uncle Tiny handed out wisdom. I hadn't counted on this little bonus when we moved here; my son, so lost most of the time, had found a friend in his new relative. Chaz had been flaking out on visitation so much that Tiny was the closest thing to a father image my son had. Perhaps this is what it felt like to have family.

The rain let up by late afternoon, allowing all of us to rest. The drips now plunked slowly, as annoying as the leaky faucets in the house. Nova complained incessantly, when she wasn't sleeping, and Tru had that "cabin fever" look that kids get on rainy days. Even my aunt and uncle appeared to be weary of so many bodies crammed into their home. I wished we had somewhere else to go to give them privacy. Truthfully, I would have given almost anything for a few hours by myself.

Next thing I knew, Lutie was wearing a flowered dress and had her Bible tucked under her arm. It was Sunday night, after all. "I'm ready," she said. "Muri, you and the kids want to come along? We have a fiddler and a banjo and can they ever get the gospel rolling. Don't we?" Tiny nodded. He held open the screen and Lutie got up to leave.

"What time is it, anyway?" Bleary-eyed Nova wanted to know. After she had slept on it for so long, her hair looked more electric than usual. It was all bunched up on one side, giving her head a lopsided look.

"Day's nearly over, honey," Aunt Lutie said and stepped back inside the door. "Come join us at services, will you?"

"Services?" I said.

"Red Rock Tabernacle. We'd love to see your sweet faces in the pew."

"Maybe if we had more warning, Aunt Lutie. I'm a mess, and Nova is still nursing her hangover."

"I wouldn't be caught dead in a church," Nova said.

"A polite *no, thank you* will do," I said. I glared at my daughter.

"I'll go." Tru volunteered, and my aunt and uncle accepted him as the delegate from the family. "Come on, dork," he teased his sister. "In church they don't care if you're ugly."

"Leave me alone," Nova moaned and retreated back to bed. She didn't understand how difficult a simple thing like being alone could be.

Lutie wasn't offended, at least that's what she said. "You go on now," she said, "get some rest, Nova. There's plenty of time to get acquainted at church."

Tiny's truck roared outside, and Lutie hustled to join him. "Pastor likes to start at 6:30 P.M. on the dot," she said over her shoulder. "On the dot."

When they were gone my ears filled with silence. I grabbed a Barbara Kingsolver novel and dove in, and then I realized I'd chosen *Pigs In Heaven*. I laughed. In Murkee, truth was stranger than fiction.

The next morning, Tru busied himself floating sticks in the many puddles outside, and Tiny stretched out his huge frame on the sofa. Lutie and I finished cleaning up from the rain. We scrubbed pots and pans and washed soggy towels, while Lutie yakked about church. I admit I wasn't paying attention to anything except the task at hand and the million thoughts streaming through my mind.

Tru came back inside and was the first to notice. "Hasn't Uncle Tiny been sleeping a long time?" he whispered to me. I'd gotten lost in a daydream about buying books for the Murkee Lending Library.

"Uncle won't wake up, Mom," he said, tugging at my arm. "Something's wrong." Lutie always harped at Tiny to watch his "sugar," but most of the time he appeared to eat whatever he pleased.

Until I saw him unconscious on the sofa, I'd conveniently forgotten that he was diabetic. We took turns shaking Tiny, but he didn't respond. I put my ear close to his face and felt small shallow breaths and smelled a fermented odor. His skin, pale and clammy, was a dead giveaway. My uncle was in a diabetic coma.

"Has this ever happened before?" I asked, pulling on my sneakers. My uncle reminded me of a kid who'd keeled over one day in my library. We'd have to act fast.

"It's his sugar again," Lutie whispered. When she said it, sugar had a capital S. "The doctors over in Bend think he needs insulin, but he's stubborn as an old mule. Says needles scare him." Her voice wavered. "They say there's new pills, but he won't listen." She knelt beside her husband. Her hands shook as she stroked his forehead. "Wake up now, honey," she said. "Please, dear Lord Jesus, let him wake up."

The composure she had shown on the day Jim had been wounded wasn't evident now. Instead, she wept and prayed loudly, unwrapping the cocooned portrait of Jesus as she wailed.

"Should I go get Dr. Rubin, Mom?" Tru was visibly upset, but he looked ready to run for help. I wasn't sure why, but right then I pictured my father, taking charge, calmly giving orders.

"I don't think we have that much time, son," I said, and then turned to Lutie. "We've got to get him to the clinic fast. If we can just get him to the door, I can back the van right up."

"Oh, Lord. Oh, Lord. Oh, Lord," was all my aunt could say.

"We could roll him into that big wheelbarrow outside," Tru said. The boy was a genius.

"Go get it."

Even in the absence of my father's direction, I was surprised at how calm I was. My thoughts were crisp and sharp, and I wasn't afraid. We'd get my uncle into the van (later we might laugh about how we'd toted him in the rusted-out

Sears Special with the flat front tire) and I'd send Nova over to Rubin's to call ahead to the Murkee Clinic. Tru would keep an eye on Tiny while I drove to town fast, but not so fast that we got stuck in some mud puddle. I'd make sure that Lutie wore her seat belt and keep her from wigging out altogether.

I'd never tried to lift a three-hundred-pound man before, but sometimes you do things you never thought possible. With Nova and Tru's help we managed to push and shove Tiny, still unconscious, into the van. I put my ear to his face and was relieved to feel his breath again. At least he was still with us.

Lutie and I both prayed, not caring who heard. Lutie was in a dazed state, and her prayers kept getting jumbled up with tears. After making sure Nova was headed to Rubin's, I set off. In my rearview mirror I could see Jim's snout pressed against the window.

All the way to town I shouted back at Tru. "Can you feel his pulse? Is he still breathing?" I mentally rehearsed the CPR I'd retaken last year and instructed Tru to keep his uncle covered.

"How much longer?" he kept shouting back, while Lutie gripped the dash and muttered "Lord, Lord, Lord." I took a deep breath after I nearly hit another pothole still brimming with rain.

The clinic in Murkee turned out to be staffed by Dr. Perkins, who looked to be about five minutes away from retirement. He sat at a desk, working a crossword puzzle. When I explained the situation his boots clunked sharply against the floor, and he moved faster than I thought he could. He grabbed his bag and went outside to where Tiny still lay in the van. I wasn't foolish enough to try to lift my uncle a second time. Besides, Lutie, according to Tru, was "totally sketched out" and sat shivering next to her husband.

"Now Lutie Pearl," Dr. Perkins said softly, "Let me have a look. This young lady here tells me he's forgotten about that diet I put him on." He examined Tiny and then addressed me. "We'll need to call in the Medivac," he said. "Right now."

I nodded. "How much danger is he in?"

"Plenty." He yelled back to his receptionist and instructed her to arrange for the helicopter to airlift my uncle to the hospital in Bend. He added, "Stat."

It took forever for the chopper to arrive. While we waited, the doctor got an IV going and Tiny moved in and out of consciousness. My uncle complained of how thirsty he was and guzzled two sodas, although he said he'd have preferred iced tea. "I'm just itching all over too," he said. His eyes were ringed with dark circles.

"You look like a raccoon," Tru said, trying to keep Uncle Tiny occupied. Tiny laughed, but it was a weak shaky laugh, and he still looked ashen.

Dr. Perkins insisted on giving Lutie a tranquilizer. He also handed sodas to Tru and me and gave directions on the best route to the hospital. We would drive there, and Dr. Perkins would phone Rubin to pass the news along to Nova. I tried to ignore the tired soreness in my back and how much I wished someone else was there to be strong.

Someone like Rubin, I thought, although I was still upset with him about Nova. Maybe it was silly, but suddenly, I wanted someone to take care of me. I wanted to be held and told everything would be okay. Gripping the steering wheel, looking out into faraway clouds and late afternoon shadows, my eyes ached to cry, but I couldn't. Lutie had fallen asleep next to me, but Tru was still awake and singing, "I Know an Old Lady Who Swallowed a Fly." The way things were going, it made more sense to laugh.

10

The hospital only kept Tiny one night, and the rest of us slept in the waiting room on cracked green-vinyl furniture. Lutie snored, and I watched the clock, wondering why I hadn't asked for knock-out pills too. Tru was too tired to stay awake. I thought he looked angelic where he lay crumpled on a small padded bench, a lamp backlighting his hair. At some point, I must have dozed off.

"Are you Mrs. Antonio Ramirez?" The clerk who had shaken me awake wore a shell pink sweater draped around her shoulders, and she smelled of lavender.

"No, I'm Mrs. Ramirez's niece," I said. I sat up. I could imagine how I looked by now but reminded myself that hospital personnel must see disheveled people all the time. We'd dropped everything when the crisis occurred and wore the same clothes we were wearing when we'd mopped up from the rain. Lutie's was one of those polyester outfits with pants and a top that matched: three different shades of blue in a wild geometric pattern.

Aromas only found in these places—a sickening mixture of hurt and healing—made my nose water, the way extra spicy foods can. My stomach felt queasy.

"You can see him now." The clerk's crepe-soled shoes squeaked as she walked away.

We all used the facilities. I dragged a brush through my hair, found some mints at the bottom of my purse, and popped them in my mouth. Lutie washed her face in the ladies' room sink. Then she sat down on the small restroom chair and opened her Bible.

"Aren't you anxious to see him?" I couldn't believe she wanted to hold her devotions at a time like this.

She looked up. "We have an agreement, the Lord and me," she said, smoothing the tissue-thin pages of her *Word*, as she called it. "I start my day with my spiritual food, and he takes care of the rest."

"Breakfast of Champions?" I laughed and opened the restroom door to make sure Tru was all right.

"Gives me all the pep I need." She closed the book. I might have heard her mutter, "Amen."

I got a stab of longing for the faith I'd laid aside long ago, before Chaz and children and some bitterness of my own had shriveled it for lack of tending. One of the only Bible verses I knew echoed in my head: *The Lord bless you and keep you, the Lord make His face to shine upon you, and give you peace. And give you peace.* The singing, in a man's raspy voice, could've been someone I once knew.

Tiny was sitting up in bed, his skinny legs poking out of the hospital gown. In the other beds lay two older men who argued over the TV.

The patient in the next bed couldn't seem to remember how the TV remote worked. Drainage tubes stuck out from beneath the man's sheets. I got the idea he was trying to raise or lower the foot or the head of the bed, but all he did was cut away from an infomercial to an old western. The man laid his head back on the pillow and pulled up his legs so they tented the covers, which partially blocked the second man's view.

That guy, maybe a few years younger, might have been a stroke patient, the way his mouth hung in a permanent scowl on one side of his face. He had the personality to match his predicament, and he glared at his roommate each time the channel switched. Neither of them spoke as they channel surfed and then stared at each other in a silent war.

"Man, am I ever starved," was the first thing Tiny said.

"Me too," Tru said, his eyes still foggy with sleep. "Starved."

"They put you on a special diet," Lutie said. She sat on the bed next to him. She laid her head against Tiny's shoulder, as if to say, *Whew, how close was that?*

"Probably nothing I can eat except rabbit food," Tiny grumbled. "I hate rabbit food." He looked down at the top of his wife's head and kissed it lightly. "Sorry."

An enormous metal cart appeared in the hallway, with trays stacked several layers high. A young man with a moustache and those clear plastic gloves food servers wear attended the cart. After checking the attached card, he brought in Tiny's breakfast tray.

Tiny lifted the stainless steel lid and said, "This it?" He looked like a kid opening up the prize from a cereal box, only to discover how small the toy is compared to the picture.

"You got it." This guy probably heard a similar complaint about every five minutes. You could tell by the way he plopped the tray in front of Tiny.

"Wheat toast, poached egg, oatmeal, an orange. Smells good," I volunteered. I felt twinges of hunger, too, along with a headache. I needed some coffee soon.

"When we visited Grandpa in Portland that time, they had a McDonald's right in the hospital," Tru said. He was referring to Benjamin's latest medical problem with angina. I hated it when he called Benjamin *Grandpa*, but there was no way around it. My stepfather bought the kids lavish presents and took them to fancy restaurants, but he didn't have the foggiest notion of what his grandchildren liked. He didn't care, either, in my opinion.

"I don't think this place has Mickey D's," I said. Tru looked crestfallen. "You'll have to settle for whatever they have."

"Well, I'm not eating anything gross like oatmeal," he said, folding his arms across his chest.

"Amen, buddy. I could go for some bacon and hash browns," Tiny said. He sighed loudly but then dug in. We watched him bolt his food. When the aide came back, Tiny asked for seconds, but the man shook his head no. Before leaving, the guy, who was a bit of a smart aleck, if you ask me, said my uncle was being discharged.

The patient with the drainage tubes sticking out from under the thin covers waved his arms at the aide. His body had slid so far down in the bed that his feet pressed against the foot rail. "Can you help me?" he croaked. But the door had already swung shut.

Lutie took charge. She turned on the call button and adjusted the motorized bed as best she could. The man smiled and thanked her and called her an angel.

A flurry of voices in the hall got Lutie's attention, and she called out, "Praise the Lord, the prayer warriors are here. Tell the ladies to come on in, Frieda." Lutie moved all three chairs against the wall to make room for the group. Six or seven women from Red Rock Tabernacle stood in a semicircle around Tiny's bed. The irascible guy next to him scowled even harder and drooled a little in the process.

I felt like scowling too. Did my aunt really need to make a circus out of this? No wonder Christians got bad reputations. They claimed to be interested in prayer, but I thought they were just plain nosy. Frieda Long would be wagging her tongue, telling all of Murkee about Tiny's emergency. I wasn't eager for Tru to see them in action for fear he'd be influenced and turn into some kind of religious nut.

Lutie held her hands up for silence. "Thank you all for coming," she said. "The good Lord's already working. As you can see, my Tiny's already on the mend."

Tiny smiled and looked a little embarrassed.

Lutie continued, "Let's send up a prayer of thanksgiving."

"Prayer is such a powerful weapon," Gladys Mason chimed in. "Lord, we praise you and we thank you. Thank you, Jesus."

The scowling man cleared his throat and waved his arms around. He tried to get up, but the tangle of wires and tubes kept him tethered to the bed. He was clearly unhappy, but he didn't seem able to speak. His eyes held a mix of terror and rage, and a guttural yell emerged from his throat.

I grabbed Tru and held him close. The man looked as if he might attack. The ladies stopped in mid-prayer and were silent for several seconds. Then, softly at first, a rush of musical whispers filled the room. The ladies lifted their hands and closed their eyes and sang words I'd never heard. The singing in a strange language grew louder and more beautiful with each passing moment.

The angry man who couldn't talk stopped yelling; his face relaxed. He sank back against the pillow and attempted what could have been a smile. Nurses and staff arrived to see what was going on. Before the music died away, the room was packed.

I let go my death grip on my son and remembered the far-away voice I'd heard in my mind. "And give you peace" rang out again, and I had to admit I hadn't felt so calm in a very long time.

The Red Rock ladies filed out as suddenly as they'd come in. What would make them want to drive for an hour just to pray for Tiny? I didn't know the answer, but I wasn't as put off about their Christian zeal. I only knew there was a small opening in my heart that hadn't been there before.

The grouchy aide returned after the call button light had been on for about twenty minutes. Somebody could expire in here, and he'd be off roaming the halls. He yanked the poor guy up in the bed without a drop of visible compassion. But I was being crabby. In the library it's the same thing: all the patrons expect you to be in about a hundred places at once. People look at you as if you've been sitting there doing your nails when you were really running all over the building, trying to find some out-of-print title or calming down an irate parent who thinks great literature is pornography. I remembered the beautiful singing and decided to cut the aide a little slack.

We waited in the hall while they got Tiny ready to leave. After he was settled in a wheelchair we stopped by the hospital cafeteria before leaving. Tru wanted to push the chair even though Tiny barely fit in it. With Tiny's big feet on those metal flaps, his knees hunched up.

Tru guided Tiny's wheelchair down the slick, waxed corridor. Spectral voices paged doctors; the overpowering odors of antiseptic made me dizzy. I'd rather be any place else. These nurses were lucky I'd never been interested in pursuing a medical profession.

We reached the cafeteria and wheeled Tiny up to a table. The smells here were almost as bad: some kind of boiled winter vegetable. But they did have those little boxes of cereal, juice, and thankfully, plenty of strong, brewed coffee. Tiny gazed at the pastry selection. Keeping him on a diet wasn't going to be easy.

"Get used to it, Hon," Aunt Lutie said. I'd never heard her speak so tenderly to her husband. "Guess we'll all need to get used to it."

Fatigue caught up then, and we all appeared comatose for a few moments. I felt much better after the Special K and about three cups of straight black coffee, although I would have given a lot for a Starbucks double mocha today. The cafeteria had filled with nurses and other personnel on an early lunch break. I longed to be where I could stretch out and take a very long nap.

After a while Tiny and Tru chatted. Lutie seemed lost in thought, but her chin trembled.

"What's wrong, my Pearl?" he asked, reaching out to touch her hand.

She looked small and tired now, her cheekbones bonier than ever. She closed her eyes briefly, as if to decide what to say. "It's Joseph," she said. "All this brings everything back." She stared at me then, with a sympathetic yet weary look. "Everything."

"I guess I haven't asked enough questions about Dad's illness," I said. Not that I hadn't wanted to ask, not that I hadn't been aching to know. I just didn't know quite how to ask, and I wasn't sure how to handle the answers."

"We've all been busy," she said. "I didn't know if you'd want to hear about it."

"Why wouldn't I?"

Lutie gathered herself up a bit. Her shoulders reminded me of a shirt hung over a broomstick. "We knew he was dying," she said, eyeing Tru. I knew that meant I might not want him to hear, but I thought he was old enough to hear the facts.

I nodded and she continued. "Liver disease is a terrible way to go. Terrible pain . . . horrible. Kills you off bit by bit." She paused, and Tiny squeezed her hand.

"And I got here too late," I murmured.

"We thought he had a few more months," she said. "We knew it was close, but Doc Perkins said he might have a month or two. That's why I wrote to you about the property and all."

"If only I could've got here in time."

Lutie shook her head. "He caught all of us off guard. One day he was walking around; the next he was on morphine."

Aunt Lutie stopped, and then her face contorted, as if she had inherited his pain. "They said he got enough drugs to kill an elephant."

"Couldn't the doctors do anything?" I was stunned and angry, full of sorrow, wanting to turn back the clock and at the same time rend my clothing and mourn.

"By the time we got him to the hospital, it was too late," she said quietly. "Yesterday I was so scared it would happen all over again." She looked past our heads into the air.

I was afraid too, afraid of how Tru might have reacted if Tiny hadn't made it. Afraid of which of my father's genes might be lurking there to devour my son and my daughter. Plain afraid. "The liver disease," I said, "was caused by alcoholism?"

Tiny spoke up. "Joseph Pond was a good man, Muri," he said. "I knew him probably ten years. He took care of your aunt here, and when I came along he took care of me too. He had a problem with the bottle, but he fought it as well as he could. I don't know why he couldn't kick the habit. I do know he loved the Lord. And he sure loved you."

That was the truth, although in spite I might have wished it had been my stepfather Benjamin whose alcoholism had caught up with him. Then it hit me: all this time I'd assigned perfection to a man I'd never known. I'd judged my stepfather as evil and discounted the fact that he had provided for me. Sure, we clashed; and I wasn't fond of his methods, but would Joseph Pond have done better?

That headache I'd been fighting off threatened again. Being philosophical after a night sleeping on a vinyl chair suddenly seemed like a poor idea. I joined Lutie in staring off into the distance, and then we returned to the room.

The aide rushed in, toting a box full of the stuff Tiny would need now to control his own excesses. The supplies interested Tru, and he rummaged through them while we went out to the discharge counter to sign Tiny out.

"Thank the Lord for Medicare," Lutie said.

My own thoughts still ran more toward the whys of life: why Benjamin survived his abuses of alcohol; while my real father—the one I never met—had lost the battle. Now my headache was full-blown. Instead of dwelling upon life's apparent injustices, I studied the back of the cocky aide's head as he walked us out of the hospital. I hoped I never saw him agan.

11

Uncle Tiny was able to get into the van unassisted for the trip home. He carried a cardboard box filled with everything he'd need: a starter kit of insulin, test strips, a stack of brochures and pamphlets outlining the routine he'd have to follow from now on, packages of gauze pads and Betadine for the sore on his leg, and hypoallergenic paper tape because he was allergic to adhesives. Lutie also made sure he brought home the hospital-issued plastic water pitcher, spit pan, and even the urinal because, she said, "We're paying for this stuff."

Truman had fun with that one. He'd already plotted to sterilize and then try to serve apple juice from it. After I glared back at him, he eventually enticed his uncle into a game of counting road signs. I kept the van pointed home as best I could, praying Nova and the pigs were all right and daydreaming about a long soak in a hot tub.

"Hoo boy," Tiny said, riffling through the stack of American Diabetes Association literature. "It's all so danged complicated. How am I supposed to remember to do all this?"

"That one nurse made us all listen to her speech three times," Tru said. "It didn't seem hard." He pointed at a billboard on the side of the road. "Viva Las Vegas. That's number nine-teen for me."

"Maybe not hard for you," Uncle Tiny said. "She sure did have a lot to say, that nurse." He shook his head. "At least Doc Perkins slows down and uses words I've heard once or twice." Tiny picked up the stack of papers and tossed them in the box. He still looked wan and tired and only halfheartedly pointed out signs on the highway.

"Why don't we stop by the clinic on our way home?" I said. My muscles screamed. "The nurse said we ought to get in to see Dr. Perkins anyway. Maybe we'd all rest easier." Lutie smiled at me, and Tiny perked up a bit, ultimately beating Tru in the sign game.

I passed the time by drilling Aunt Lutie with questions about Dad. Suddenly, it seemed as if the door had been opened for me to be curious. I was careful, though; I didn't want to see her cry again. It might start a chain reaction.

"How many years was he sick?" was the first question on my list.

Lutie folded her hands in her lap and squinched her eyes. "Now let me think on that," she said, "maybe only five years altogether. Could have been longer, only you can't always tell these things. Joseph was never a complainer."

"I see."

"Funny thing was he always had a smile on his face. Bet none of us would have known how sick he was if it hadn't been for Doc Perkins. Your daddy always laughed up a storm." Her face clouded over, and tears welled in her eyes. "Now he's up there laughing with the heavenly hosts."

"I sure hope so." I'd always been a little shaky on my theology, having grown up unchurched, as Lutie would say.

"If anyone makes it to heaven, it'll be your daddy," she said, slapping her hand across her knee, laughing the way she had when we first saw her. Her expression grew serious again. "Joseph died with the Lord's Prayer on his lips."

Tiny heard this from the back seat. "Yeah, my Pearl here was into the third verse of "How Great Thou Art," standing by his bedside." He grinned, but it seemed more from embarrassment than amusement. "I thought Joseph was saying, 'I want water.' Turns out it was 'Our Father.'"

Aunt Lutie rolled her eyes and turned around in her seat to face her husband. "It was an honest mistake, now wasn't it? Lord knew you were trying to help."

I smiled thinking of the scene, wishing I knew the third verse to "How Great Thou Art" or any other hymn.

A half hour later I pulled up to the Murkee Clinic. We all trooped into the office, where Doc Perkins' nurse-receptionist, Clara, sat behind the old metal desk. Clara had been the nurse forever, Dove had told me once, a fact I didn't doubt. I stretched and felt like a pocketknife unfolded for the first time in years. Tiny, Tru, and Lutie sat on waiting room chairs that looked older than all of us combined, with Tiny still hugging his box of diabetic supplies.

Lutie hovered over him like a sweat bee over a cantaloupe. Those two were a piece of work: the pet names and politeness made me think of bad English comedy.

"Comfy? Anything I can get you, Sugar Bean?" Aunt Lutie said. She leaned against his bulk like a tired child, resting her head against his shoulder.

"Why I have everything I need, my little Pearl," Tiny answered, patting her hand, "except a glass of your delicious iced tea." Even Truman rolled his eyes after a while.

I walked over to the desk. "Hi, Clara," I said, "I'd like to make an appointment for a week from now to check on my uncle's progress."

"Feeling better, I hope?" Clara's smoker's voice was coarse as a gravel driveway, but I'd heard she also had a heart of gold. "Everybody in town's been so worried. Several of the ladies want to carry covered dishes out to you. All diabetic menus, of course." She stood up and adjusted her uniform on her considerable hips. "Let me see if the doctor is available. I'll bet he'd want to see you right away." Clara disappeared into the patient area, and I smiled at Tiny.

Doc Perkins did want to examine his patient, as well as to write out prescriptions and dispense a stern lecture about managing diabetes. Doc asked us to come into the examination room. I was amazed that my uncle resisted the idea of insulin therapy.

"This whole business is a big hassle," Tiny grumbled. He sat on the examining table, jiggling one foot against its side. That was the one thing he had in common with Nova—the nervous, jiggling foot syndrome. My daughter did this whenever she acted childish and mule-headed. It wasn't much different for my uncle.

"Well, the bigger hassle," Dr. Perkins replied with a straight face, "is getting your rear end up onto that helicopter when you're half dead. Time you stopped whining and got this under control." He squirted disinfectant onto the sore on Tiny's ankle and applied a fresh bandage. Tiny winced.

"It's stuff like this that'll get you in real trouble," the doctor warned, gesturing at the wound. He turned to Lutie and me. "If that's not healed in two weeks I want him back in here right away." He wheeled around and strode out, his boots echoing across the scarred wood floor.

Before we left I tried to find out how much we owed, but Dr. Perkins just smiled at me. Clara shrugged her shoulders and laughed her sandpaper laugh before returning to her post. I smiled back. I'd joined a new family.

Right then I realized how much I'd been resisting membership. Until now, I'd thought of the characters I'd met as curiosities. As long as I regarded them as cardboard figures in the ghost town of Murkee, they'd remain anonymous and so could I. Somehow, though, they'd sprung to life, complete with hopes and dreams and stories that always made me think of the adage about truth being stranger than fiction. Dr. Perkins and Dove from the café and even Joseph Pond were becoming real to me now. I hoped I wasn't mistaken in my belief that I was the genuine article too.

My immediate family, however, stood at the door waiting when we pulled up. Nova had a look of exasperation I'd never seen before. It was all I could do to keep from chuckling. The moment I stepped out of the van she hit me with a barrage of grievances. Most of them had to do with Jim and friends.

"Totally awful, Muh-ther," she said, running her fingertips through hair that obviously hadn't been gelled, moussed, or spiked in a while. "Two days of torture. No phone, nothing in the fridge, and these disgusting—pigs." She shuddered as Jim pushed past her to greet Tiny. "And that one—" she pointed, "*that* one chewed a hole in my new jeans. So rude."

I tried to stifle my laughter. "You mean the ones with no knees?"

"It's different when you slash them on purpose, Mother."

"Of course. You going to ask if your uncle lived?"

"I can *see* that, Mom."

"So nice of you to notice. Don't plan to leave any time soon, okay? As soon as we get Tiny settled there's something we need to discuss."

"Like what?" The moment she sat down her foot began to jiggle double-time.

"You figure it out while you help Aunt Lutie get lunch. I need a shower."

I hadn't felt this grungy since the time Chaz's Bronco broke down on that campout to Chehalis Falls. The worst part back then had been not shaving my legs for a week; the stubble on my calves had kept me awake at night. Come to think of it, Chaz had kept me awake, and fogging up the windows had no doubt resulted in Truman. At the time we both needed desperately to believe it could still work, but we ended up as totaled as the Ford. Chaz had gotten a trade-in almost immediately; he bought himself a huge SUV and picked up a sweet young thing from Washington.

Today I was just as happy to have smooth legs again as I'd been then, with the added bonus of not expecting a baby or a ten-mile hike to call AAA. I still needed to have the discussion with my daughter, though. I wrapped myself in thick, comfortable sweats and went to find her.

After hearing more protests and choice excuses, I led my daughter out to the van. She fought me all the way, reminding me of a two-year-old who doesn't want a nap. Finally, I slid the door shut. My palms felt clammy, and my heart danced as if I was about to address Congress or talk about sex. Nova slouched against the seat and put her feet up on the dash. Her toes were alternately painted with orange and green, and one foot did all the jiggling.

"We need to talk about what happened on the Fourth of July," I said. I forced her to make eye contact with me.

"What happened?" Nova had a wide innocent look, but I wasn't buying it. Her eyes shrank to a look just a little past "bored."

"You were drunk."

"So?"

I breathed deeply to maintain composure. "First tell me how it got started. The truth, okay?" I wiped my hands on my sweatshirt and realized it was too warm for fleece in July.

Nova shifted in her seat and looked away. After a long pause, she spoke. "I don't know what happened, Mom," she said, her voice suddenly high and small. "After you guys left some guy offered me a beer, that's all. I was only going to have one."

I could feel myself shifting into the "mother grizzly" mode. "I want to know if Rubin was aware of this, and if he was the one offering."

"No, in fact it was Rubin who caught us out behind the house."

"Caught you and who else?"

"A bunch of kids. Marv and a couple of band members. The bass player had stashed a few six-packs back there. We'd go chug a beer or two in between sets and then go back to the party." She gazed out the window toward the creek and shrugged. "I guess Rubin got suspicious after the fourth or fifth time we all disappeared. The other kids took off when he surprised us and left me there to get in trouble. Then Rubin brought me home."

I grabbed Nova's chin and stared into her eyes. "Anything else happen with those boys?"

Her eyes narrowed. "Mother, you really trust me, don't you? Nothing happened, okay?" She jerked her head away from my grasp.

"It's not that I don't trust you," I said softly, "but I have been in that same situation and I had to be sure. You're a young woman now, Nova, and life can get dangerous, especially if drugs or alcohol are involved."

"I can take care of myself," she said.

"I'm sure you can, but it's my job to back you up . . . at least for a little bit longer."

For a moment I thought she'd cry and just become my little girl one more time. My arms ached to hold her, but then her walls slammed back in place.

"There will be consequences, you know," I said finally. "I can't allow drinking, even on the Fourth of July."

"I'm out of here."

"What? You stealing the van and running away again? Give me a break."

"Don't believe me then. You're not—"

"I'm not what? Your mother?"

She stared at me for a moment. Without speaking, she got out of the van and stomped into the house. When I got back inside I had a big red nose and could have sworn I was the one suffering from a hangover.

Joseph's Journal
January 1985

You are my only daughter, Muri. If I had seven sons you would still be my favorite. You're all that's kept me alive on this road that I travel, but I've hung back from contacting you. I wanted to find you, every day, every year. My intentions were good, but I can't trust myself. Every time I think I've got the demon licked, it grabs me and kicks my guts so hard that I wake up right where I passed out. Like old Saint Paul, I pray for God to remove this thorn; but there it is, eating me up. I don't even like the taste anymore, but liquor doesn't care what I like.

Today I stood on the mound and felt the vibrations of the old ones. The soles of my feet grew warmer and warmer, like they knew they touched sacred ground. Atop the burial mound, I tossed a stone into the creek and wondered how much longer I can keep these secrets. The guy next door watches me, and he must be waiting. Waiting for his chance to plunder, waiting for me to break down.

Linc doesn't know it, but I specialize in brokenness. Jesus taught me that being broken is not the same as being weak, although I have more than my fair share of weakness too. Anyway, I once had dreams, little Muri. Big plans. I wanted to enter the ministry, just like my great-great-grandaddy. Maybe I would have been a good preacher. Maybe that way I would have beat the drink.

I never meant to harm anybody, but somehow I took a wrong turn. These things happen, and your life turns out the way you hoped it wouldn't. I thank the Lord for giving me a curiosity for appliances. When I was young I was always the kid who took things apart. I hope you have an urge to fix things, read things, and learn things.

I remember that time you visited. I told you about General Sherman, how he cut a path of destruction across the South, and your eyes grew wider. I laughed so hard when you "emancipated" the bucket of fish we'd caught. I'll be danged if you didn't dump some pan-sized trout back into the river, but I took this to mean you understand the evils of slavery.

I'm glad I taught you what I could, even though you're young. I don't catch much these days. The old hands shake too hard. Truth be told, I keep a line in the water so nobody asks questions. The air is full of our ancestors' artifacts and singing, but we can't tell a soul. Word leaks out, and this place will crawl with traders and collectors and those who'll rob a burial mound for pleasure or fortune. Still, if I land a red side or a native I'll release it. Just to make you happy, Muri, just to keep things free.

When the pain gets to me, I admit I'll take a nip, but it's only because I hurt so bad. I resist the pain but most times, it wins. I read my Bible until I lay aside my pole and fall asleep with the cottonwoods whispering above.

The ancestors come to me then, along with God's angels. They sing and dance and drum and beg me to go with them. I tell them, no, I have to find my daughter first. I can't go until then. God and the angels and the spirits buried beneath me here all smile. Sometimes I dream I have wings.

12

With so many small fires to put out, I almost forgot why we were here. The next day I read the letter from the only attorney in town, a semi-retired man named George Kutzmore. He said he needed to meet because Linc Jackson was threatening to get an injunction. At the bottom of the note was written in ink, "I would have phoned if you had one. Come as soon as you can."

"I need to talk to that George Kutzmore," I told Lutie as I pulled on a navy pleated skirt. I hadn't dressed up this much since I'd been to the ALA Book Awards two years ago. It was still hot outside. Already the waistband of the obligatory pantyhose chafed me. "What's he like?"

She shook her head, laying aside the gold and green crocheted beret she'd been working on. "Smooth operator, that George," she said. "Sweet-talked many a judge into seeing things his way. Could have kept up with any U.S. senator in his prime. Too bad he was only interested in the Oregon desert."

"Whose side is he on?" I stopped short of wearing heels and slipped on black flats.

"George is a good man," Lutie said. "Heaven knows he's tried to find out what Linc's really up to."

"Linc's story about generously providing water for everybody certainly doesn't ring true."

Lutie laughed. "Amen to that. Frieda says he's a wolf in sheep's clothing, and I believe it."

"Forget Frieda," I said. "I'm having a hard time keeping things straight as it is." I didn't add that I never thought I'd ever be interested in water at all.

Lutie came closer and began to speak in a low voice. "Want to know how much artifacts go for on the black market? A few weeks before he died, my brother overheard Linc talking about digging up a fortune near the creek bed and selling his haul to an East Coast collector."

"It's hard to believe all this could be over a bunch of arrowheads," I said.

Lutie sniffed. "It's about a lot more than arrowheads. Joe thought he'd stumbled onto an ancient burial ground."

"A Nez Perce site?"

Lutie picked up her crochet work. "Much older. Maybe ten thousand years."

"How did my dad know? Did he take something and have it dated?" How had a man with limited formal education understood archeology? Out here, we couldn't even get The History Channel.

"I know what you're thinking," Lutie said. "Joe wasn't educated, but he wasn't a dummy either. Just before your father died, he was working with a guy from the university. The professor was convinced the sample predated the Clovis people."

I sat, stunned. "Linc says he's only concerned with sustaining the ranches around here."

"Sure, the neighbors think he's Santa Claus. But I know better and so did your daddy. Linc Jackson is out to own more than every square inch of Murkee. And he's not about to hand out the water to those in need." Lutie sat up straight and folded her scarecrow arms across her chest.

I shook my head, thinking I'd need a lawyer just to untangle this mess. "So how'd George find out about me?"

"Only lawyer around these parts," she said. "Maybe he knows somebody needs to represent us." She was smiling.

"Why would he do that?"

"Around here people have been known to help each other."

I raised my hands in surrender. "I still don't understand this whole thing."

"Well, at least hear the man out before you decide," Lutie said. She picked up her crochet work once more. "I'll be praying like thunder." She smiled again, and her crochet hook wove itself into the yarns and then out again, meshing together the ugliest colors I'd seen since the seventies.

I slammed the screen door on the way out, only partly on accident. It dawned on me as I waited for the van's dual carburetors to warm up, that I was as angry as I'd been in a very long time. I'd gone through my separation from Chaz with hardly a raised voice, and now I was falling apart over a diabetic, a teenage rebel, and a bogus lawsuit. Before I'd ever be able to cry again I thought I might have to scream a little.

So I did, halfway to Murkee. I cursed and shouted and said very mean things about everyone I could think of. I got on the case of all the big problems and every nit-picking little pet peeve. Nova drinking with a bunch of hormonal maniacs. Tiny's refusal to care for himself. Lutie's awful taste in colors. Tru always nagging me about getting a phone.

I felt damp from the heat by the time I got to the part about Tru. The more I thought about it, though, his idea made sense. A phone would be a good thing in case Tiny had another emergency. And since I was required to talk to lawyers, it would be nice for me too. I'd check it out before the day was over.

The day wasn't about to be over yet. I squinted hard because the afternoon sun in Murkee can be blinding, with so few trees around. Every plant looks as if it has fought to be here; even the cultivated ones outside the Murkee General Store appear tough and ready to take on most anything. The area has its own sense of beauty, although I didn't start out thinking it was so. A sky this blue only happens in the high desert; wind is never so alive in the city. Even the twisted low bushes have a story to tell, if you listen.

The very air hung with memories of the settlement days and how the wives would use five-gallon kerosene cans to boil the baby diapers. How they would plant a matrimony vine for shade outside the kitchen and water it with dishwater. How the wells would fail, creating submarginal ranches and feuds and even a few murders. How the men would finally say, "It's sand over the dune" and go on as before.

And I had my own story, didn't I? One that was wagging from the end of just about every resident's tongue, to hear Dove tell it. She told me that Frieda Long, down at the General Store, thought I should allow the sand to pass over the dune by agreeing to Linc's demands. According to dear Frieda, I didn't know the first thing about living out here, where "we all depend on each other." Plus, she said, she'd seen the way Doc Rubin looked at me on the Fourth of July, and we all knew what that meant.

I parked the van but felt as small and alone as I had in grade school, confessing to Mrs. Davis that I'd punched

Loren H. for calling me a half-breed. The law office of George S. Kutzmore was around the corner from the Mucky-Muck Café in a small bungalow in need of paint. It wasn't exactly shabby, but it had none of the big city feel I'd come to expect from attorneys.

Just weeks ago, I'd dragged Chaz to the fifteenth-story office of Schuster, Schuster, and Schuster. I remember feeling so confident that day, as if I really knew what I was doing and how things would turn out. We'd go our separate ways and remain civilized about support and visitation. We'd even exchange Christmas cards, the sort that has a stamped-on signature, but it would be for the children anyway. I'd even worn an outfit similar to what I wore now and had thought I could dress my way past any obstacle.

I felt raw and edgy, and my cordovan leather briefcase didn't help as much as I thought it might in boosting confidence. This meeting with George Kutzmore would be unpleasant at best, and I imagined a potbellied smooth talker in white shoes and matching belt.

I hadn't started out being this suspicious. Before my experiences with my stepfather, Benjamin, and my ex-husband, Chaz, I'd been as open-minded as any child. I'd made it a point to always look for the good in everyone, and back then it had worked as well in the library as on the playground.

Today, I was certain I smelled a rat. I was bracing myself for the worst when he appeared from an inner office.

"You must be Muri." George Kutzmore stuck out his hand.

"Mr. Kutzmore?" I tried not to look surprised. The man was tastefully dressed in slacks and a sport shirt that looked like he bought it at Sears. He was about sixty-five, but he had aged well. This was no used car salesman. Silver distinguished his full head of hair, and when he smiled his steely gray eyes softened. He reminded me of Peter O'Toole riding over the Arabian sands in the movie *Lawrence of Arabia*, but it was only a fleeting resemblance.

"That's Key-utesmore," he said, and laughed a little. "Call me George." He motioned me toward the office and offered me a chair; it wasn't leather, but it wasn't Naughahyde, either.

"Sorry," I mumbled, and sat down.

He sat behind a mahogany desk that took up over half the room. "It's nice to finally meet Joseph's daughter," he said. "I've known your aunt for many, many years."

"Aunt Lutie?"

George cleared his throat. "Your aunt Luticia and I met in Washington a long time ago. She was a Native representative to a Presbyterian Mission Convention. But let's get down to business, shall we?" He pulled open a thick file of papers.

I sat up straighter and tried to appear professional. "I confess. This whole matter seems blown out of proportion. We're more than willing to share the creek water with Linc. I want to be a good neighbor."

George laughed. "Linc's not interested in being neighborly, I'm afraid."

"That much I know." I sighed, and the waistband of my pleated skirt tightened its anaconda grip. I stared out the arched windows, wishing I could simply ignore this problem that had been dumped in my lap.

"Linc claims he filed the paperwork just shy of the five-year cutoff." George Kutzmore shuffled through the papers on his desk and pulled one out. "And then there are the grand-fathered water rights."

"Grandfathered water rights? What does he want now?"

The attorney handed me a sheet of paper. "See for yourself. According to this document, Linc Jackson owns the creek water rights in perpetuity. He's upstream from you and Rubin

127

Jonto, and I'm afraid he doesn't have to share the water . . . legally, that is."

I sagged into the chair. How would we survive without water? According to Lutie, Linc Jackson had no interest in water; he wanted to destroy our heritage. He had already tried to buy out my father; now he wanted to run me off the land too. That my land was a junk pile ringed by an oven-door fence didn't matter. I wasn't going to allow Linc or anyone else to take over a sacred Indian ruin.

George must have read my mind. "Linc and your dad had some bad blood between them," he said. "I know he harassed the devil out of Joe. It's no secret Linc has something against Native Americans."

"Lutie says my dad thought Linc was up to more than hogging the stream and hating Indians," I said.

The attorney nodded. "There's something fishy about this whole thing."

I sat up straighter. "Such as what Linc really wants with that creek?"

"Exactly. All this came up after your dad and the doc wouldn't sell."

"Aunt Lutie told me my father suspected Linc was stealing artifacts and selling them to rich collectors. But she wasn't sure what Linc took from the site."

"You may be on to something, Muri," the attorney said. "Come to think of it Joe once told me he discovered there had been some digging out near the creek. I admit I thought he was exaggerating."

"A lot of people thought my dad had gone round the bend," I said softly. "I guess he did some pretty strange things toward the end."

George leaned back in his chair and looked up at the ceiling. "How much do you know about Linc?"

I looked up at the ceiling, too, half expecting to see one of Lutie's angels floating up there. "Mostly what I've heard from Lutie and her Tabernacle Ladies."

"Tabernacle Ladies? You mean Frieda Long and her friends. Have they mentioned Ulysses McMurphy at all?"

"Linc's great-grandfather, right?"

"Yep. At one time Ulysses—"

"Bought what's now Murkee for a thousand dollars? I heard that part too. And the water rights bit. But why won't Linc work with us?" It flipped my switch that I was still perplexed, even after legal counsel. "What if my dad was right? What if Linc Jackson is making a fortune from ancient artifacts?"

"Bottom line is," George said, "if we find evidence that Linc is dealing in illegal antiquities, none of his 'gone less than five years' argument will hold up." He chuckled. "The Feds will get involved. Besides, we're only a few miles from the Warm Springs reservation. If folks even suspect Linc's desecrating Indian burial sites, people will be furious. Linc Jackson will be history."

"But isn't Linc the town leader?" It didn't make sense that he'd risk enraging the locals.

George shrugged. "Right now I don't have the answer to that. First thing we need to do is a little research. See if Linc's filed any documentation on the artifacts. No reputable collector will touch a piece unless it's documented."

I smiled. "Any research you need done, that's my specialty. Give me an address or phone number, and I'm on it."

George scribbled some information on a scrap of paper and handed it to me. "Gone four years and eleven months my foot. A loophole if ever I saw one." His expression turned serious. "Don't forget, Linc does have documentation on the water rights. But if we can expose what Linc was really up to all those years he was gone and uncover who he's dealing with . . . if we can trace even one illegal arrowhead back to a collector . . ." George closed the folder on his desk. "Or if we locate just one of the artifacts Joe's university guy had catalogued, then we have him. Linc's loophole becomes a noose."

I gathered my briefcase and stood up. "So the first thing I need to do is research. That shouldn't be difficult."

He raised his eyebrows. "Get copies of the photographed items and persuade the professor to sign an affidavit. And look for any documented items Linc may have sold."

I shook George's hand. "Then I'm you're client?"

"Yes, Ms. Pond. I suppose you are."

After my meeting with George Kutzmore, I decided to walk down to the Mucky-Muck Café and thought about the man who was my father and his feud with Linc. This situation was getting more complicated every day. All my life I'd wanted nothing more than to know my father, to understand the where and what and how about myself and my family. Now I was finding out things I wasn't sure I wanted to know. The worst part was that my dad wasn't even around to ask questions of or get mad at or collapse upon in tears when the going got rough. I couldn't look him in the eye to see my own reflection, nor was he around anymore to ask advice about teenagers or legal matters.

Joseph Pond was still a stranger to me.

But I was no longer a stranger in Murkee. The bells on the café door greeted me, as did the smell of Dove's famous cheese fries. She'd set a vase full of gladiolas next to the cash register, which made me smile. I sat down at the counter.

"Good to see you again," she said, tugging down on the bodice of her uniform. I started to ask why she didn't just wear jeans and a t-shirt, but then she got busy delivering armloads of lunch platters. Her business looked profitable, so I decided not to advise her on how to dress.

I nursed a diet root beer for a while and waited until the crowd thinned out. The booths were full of cattlemen and farmers from around the area, and the hat rack was full. I overheard one man say he hadn't been to a better grange meeting in a month of Sundays. I thought they all looked like Linc today, but if he was there I didn't see him. Most of the men tipped their hats and smiled at me when they left. I wondered if they knew who I was.

Finally, Dove's business slowed, and she propped her elbows on the counter near me. I asked her about how to get a phone hooked up.

"No big deal. You can call on mine, and they can get right on it." She handed me a cordless handset. "Shouldn't be any trouble since Doc Rubin had the line strung out there last year. Great idea."

"Since my uncle's crisis—" I thumbed through the skinny local phone book.

"I heard. He's better now?" Dove wiped the counter down and then refilled saltshakers.

"Better." I dialed the number and was surprised at how quickly I arranged for service. Things in Portland were never this easy.

I handed the phone back to Dove. "Thanks," I said. "Now all we need around here is a library. Until I find a job I'd be willing to start one. Can you tell I'm a librarian?"

Dove laughed. Her skin was as smooth and unwrinkled as her polyester outfit. Since she seemed to love pretty things, maybe she'd be interested in literary beauty. I wasn't prepared for her reply.

"Why don't you start one here?" She gestured toward a back room. "We used to hold town meetings back there, but they haven't had one in months now, and the room's gathering dust. You could put in some books if you think it would fly."

"What kind of rent would Linc charge?" I remembered discussion of rent for the church bazaar.

"Linc usually does want rent. But how about I talk to him about a swap? You need work, and I sure could use some help, especially on Sundays after church."

"I waited tables once in college."

"You're in, then. I'll handle Linc. Show up here at eight on Sunday morning, and we'll get you started."

"I can't thank you enough," I said.

"No thanks required. You're part of our little town now." She ushered me to the room, opened the door, and invited me to look around. "Got to get back to the counter," she said, "but feel free. It's not much, but—"

"Oh, no, it's wonderful," I said over my shoulder. "You don't know what this means to me." She was smiling as she worked on the napkin dispensers.

I went inside, and it was cold, the kind of chill a room gets when it hasn't been used in a while. The sweaty places at the back of my neck began to dry. The place was musty and not exactly clean, but a broom stood in a corner so I swept while I surveyed.

In my mind I saw it all: shelves that Tiny could build if they weren't already available, neat boxes of alphabetized cards for check-out purposes, a display of book jackets to steer patrons beyond magazines and into the classics, reading couches arranged here and there, and lines of eager children waiting with stacks of picture books in their arms.

The fiction section would be best to the right of the door, I decided, and magazines must always go next to the check-out counter. I tried to remember if I'd brought all the plastic sleeves to protect the periodicals.

Soon I was humming, something from Mozart, admittedly a bit off-key. I hadn't done that since before I'd left the school library it had taken me years to build. I wouldn't care if this one began with nothing more than a dictionary and some back issues of *Farm Digest*. At least Murkee would have a library.

The prospect of tackling a new project made things like lawsuits and pigs and teenage troubles dissolve into the dust cloud at my feet. It might take some time, but I would convince the townspeople that they needed this and somehow find ways to secure books.

Now how to get people involved? Dove would help there, I realized, with her nonstop chatter to the locals. There was so much to do, but it felt exhilarating, so much so that I didn't hear the footsteps behind me.

"What are you doing back here?" Linc Jackson slouched against the doorjamb. "I hear you been down to see George." He said this as if he had spies all over the town, which he probably did. Suddenly, he seemed more like an outlaw than a hero.

"Dove said you wouldn't mind if I put a few books back here for a town library," I said. I kept sweeping and gave him as much eye contact as I dared, and he stared right back.

He shrugged. "Guess it's all right." He shifted his weight, and I noticed his boots. They were caked with dirt as usual, and chunks of mud tumbled onto the just-swept floor It was all I could do not to scold him.

"If you were to do the right thing about the creek," he said, "we might become real good neighbors. I don't know what Lutie's been telling you, but you need to understand. I got the law on my side."

"I've been informed of your water rights, if that's what you mean." I didn't add that I had suspicions about his real reasons for wanting the creek.

Linc stood up straighter and smiled. "That's what I like about you—besides your pretty face that is. You got a good head on your shoulders. Ready to discuss your selling price?"

"Selling price?" I swept harder and faster.

"For your little slice of heaven. And, of course, the creek, but that's a nonissue."

I stopped and leaned on the broom. "The only thing that's a nonissue," I said, "is that I have no intention of selling my father's land. It may not be paradise, but it's all I have left of him."

"Everybody has a price," he said.

"Excuse me." I pushed my way past him. "You'll be hearing from my attorney."

"Well, la-di-dah," Linc said. He smirked and adjusted his hat.

I stopped at the front counter to thank Dove and tell her the room was perfect for the library. However, I really wanted to cry, and soon. The bells on the door jangled as I dashed for the van.

On the way back home, angry tears streaked my cheeks, and I turned loose, ranting at Linc. Only the sagebrush heard me. At least this time I didn't scream as much.

13

As I drove home, the hills swallowed up the sun inch by inch. Long shadows were thrust across the road like lances barricading my way. It was hard to see. I swerved and nearly ran off the narrow road's shoulder on one of the curves. I glanced back. I'd nearly run over a dead opossum. My hands trembled, and my heart pounded. You can't always avoid road kill.

The association brought back Marvin's Road Kill band, and what he and Nova had been up to lately. I recognized the look she wore—that dizzy, otherworldly gaze. There was no mistaking it, because I'd seen it on my own face too many times. My daughter thought she was in love.

Growing up, my desperate need for love had caused the same moony fantasies and poor judgment; I often jumped headfirst into relationships I should have avoided. Hadn't I won an award in school once for possessing the "Best Imagination"?

Truthfully, since Chaz had left us, I hadn't given the opposite sex much thought. I had more important things on my mind: raising my kids, watching them develop into healthy adults, proving I could make it on my own. And now, protecting my small plot of land and uncovering why Linc Jackson was so interested in a small creek.

What about Rubin? The creek ran through his place too. He depended on the stream's water for those silly emus, so why wasn't Linc suing him? I had to find out, but I didn't want Rubin thinking I was hitting on him. He was a nice guy, but I was only interested in being neighborly. I only hoped he didn't despise me after the way I'd tossed him out the night he brought Nova home.

Nova needed no help from Rubin or anyone else in order to get into trouble. I should have known better, but mothers lose their wits when it comes to protecting their children, even when their offspring sprout face jewelry or dye their heads green.

My daughter claimed I was nosy and nagged too much and didn't have a clue about boys or style. Well, those last two were true enough. Teenage courtships had been dangerous as far back as *Romeo and Juliet*; but these days, the kids called dating "hooking up," which sounded awful to me.

I'd put my foot down about her behavior on the Fourth. I absolutely would not tolerate drugs or alcohol. I also warned her to be cautious about boys, especially the "hooking-up" stuff. She complained that her ten o'clock curfew was better suited to someone Tru's age. When I stood my ground, yelling broke out.

Just then I glanced down at my speedometer. While worrying about Nova, my foot had pressed down on the accelerator, and the van was speeding along at sixty-five on a winding, two-lane road. I eased back on the gas pedal, telling myself to calm down.

In the last two weeks we had argued more about Marvin than we ever did about her appearance. Much more was at stake. I was terrified she'd catch a horrid disease or end up in trouble. Worse, she'd learn the sad truth that boys want to experiment awhile before they settle on one girl. Nova said I wasn't giving her enough respect. There was a fine line between respecting her judgment and making sure she didn't make a mistake she would regret the rest of her life.

My worrying shifted to Rubin. I hadn't treated him fairly, either. Most likely he thought of me as one of those women on the rebound. Still, I rounded every curve in the road fantasizing about a new scenario of our friendship, as if my indecision about him had dissipated.

I have always thought of myself as decisive to a fault. This is true even when I'm edgy and tired of being alone. As tired as I was, though, I would have secretly loved nothing more than to be staring out an open car window, letting the air push against my face, while my true love drove me home.

Was true love a myth? I thought of Chaz, and pain stomped my insides. If we had to break up, why couldn't I be the rejecter instead of the rejectee? None of this was fair. I felt like I didn't have a friend left in the world.

Zoned out thinking about my lonely life, on an impulse I turned at the bullet-riddled sign and drove into Rubin Jonto's front yard.

"I can't believe I'm doing this," I heard myself say. "But I need some answers." I looked up at the porch. Tattered shreds of red, white, and blue crepe paper left over from the July Fourth barbecue still flapped wildly in the stiff breeze. Several large black trash bags, overflowing with empty aluminum cans, sat on the front porch. Folding chairs stood piled against one another, as if the ladies of Rubin's clean-up crew and fan club had abandoned him. Maybe no one was home, and I could turn the van around now that I had regained my senses.

But there he was, looking out of the decrepit screen door. It banged shut behind him as he strode down the porch steps, waving. He had ditched the cowboy shirt and wore a vintage Save the Whales t-shirt.

Rubin strode to the driver's side window and wiped his hands with a very white towel—the sort medical suppliers deliver. "Hey, Muri," he said. His hands were fascinating: big and rugged but with long, tapered fingers like a surgeon's. He folded the towel and jammed it in his back pocket. "Doozy of a morning." He whistled softly.

I cut the engine. "I know what you mean," I said and brushed unruly strands of hair away from my cheeks, but the wind blew them back again. That's the way it was out here. The wind would calm soon, as the colors of evening appeared, but every afternoon it was so windy it would hurl your voice back at you. Then, suddenly, it would give up and die down.

"What brings you over this way?" Rubin asked.

"I was just in the neighborhood," I lied. "Maybe it's not a good time? I could come back later." I started the van's engine, and its chatter filled the air.

Rubin shook his head and smiled. "I was just about to take a break. Come on in, and we'll have tea."

"Really, I could come back." I felt about as obvious as lipstick on one of Tiny's pigs.

Rubin's eyes softened. "You're not in the city anymore, Muri. Out here we consider it bad manners not to offer refreshment when folks come calling."

"Bad manners?" I cut the engine again. "I guess I could stop for—say, do you drink coffee?"

Rubin laughed. "How do you take yours? Cream and sugar?"

"Strong and black." I slid from the driver's seat to the ground, and we walked into his kitchen together. He put on the coffee and apologized for the mess.

The place wasn't messy at all; at least it wasn't cluttered, although dishes poked out of suds in the sink. We sat at the dinette, which wasn't classic or fifties but a Scandinavian design, built with clean lines and possessing an artsy flavor. After a few minutes, Rubin served us both tall steaming mugs full of the best coffee I'd had since leaving Portland.

I blew across the cup and savored the rich aroma. "Neither Tiny nor Lutie drink anything with caffeine," I said. "I've been craving coffee."

Rubin lifted his mug. "Anytime you need a fix, you know where to find me."

I sipped at my drink and, suddenly, realized how tired I was. Rubin's kitchen was cozy, and I felt myself relax.

"You look a little tired," he said. I looked at him hard. "But good," he hastily added. "You look tired, but you look good."

"Thanks," I said. Warmth crept across my cheeks. "Like you said, it's been a doozy of a morning." Then I told him all about my visit to George Kutzmore. I started to tell him about Linc's behavior at the café, but held back. After all, Rubin and I barely knew one another.

When you meet a person who makes you feel at ease, it's so tempting to become transparent—to tell it all. I'm ashamed to say that I'm always looking for that, as if someone out there is waiting for me to unload. But I had learned that a person could be too honest. I'd learned the hard way not to trust any and every man I met. Sitting across from Rubin, I could tell I was falling into the same trap by the way my eyes stung with tears and by the way he paid careful attention.

After a while I stopped talking long enough for him to look thoughtful. Then he got up and rinsed out his empty mug and sat down again. "Muri, it's too bad you had to start out here with so much trouble. George is an old guy, but he's very competent. This business about the water—" Rubin's voice suddenly hardened. "You should know that Linc's dead serious. He's been leaning on me to sell too."

"You're leaving?" I thought of Dr. Rubin, the vet, out taking potshots at what he believed were Linc's cows.

Rubin shook his head. "I tried to negotiate. But he's bullheaded. I tried to get him to see how we all benefit from the creek, but he insists that he's the rightful owner."

"None of this makes sense." I was anxious to get to Linc's true motivation. "I have a feeling there's something about that stream that's worth more than water."

For an instant, Rubin brightened, as if he might know what that something was. Then his face clouded over again. "You've got that right," he said. "If Linc wanted to keep that creek healthy, he'd be a lot more concerned about the pollution. But his livestock damage the stream again and again. That's why I have to shoot if they get in there."

"Can't you fence them out, or scare them off?"

He sighed, as if he'd answered these questions before. "Tried. Didn't do a bit of good. Strays trample the fences, and they don't want to leave where the grazing is good."

"The fence my dad put up is such an eyesore, but I bet it's sturdy." I laughed, thinking of a steer bulldozing through one of the oven doors to get a drink of water. "So Linc is trying to run you off too."

"Sure. I turned his offer down. But I'm the only vet around, so he puts up with me. So far."

"Me too. So far." I wasn't sure this was true. No wonder Rubin thought about moving away.

"Care to see what Linc's up in arms about?" He sounded hopeful now, and I realized it was important for me to see whatever it was, for his sake and for my own. "And what I've been working to restore?"

"Love to," I said. "But I'm not exactly dressed for hiking."

"There's a shed where I keep rubber boots and waders. And work clothes—"

"I'll be fine," I insisted. "Just lend me the boots so I'm not slogging through mud in dress shoes."

At the shed, I slipped on the black, knee-high rubber boots and tried not to think about how they looked with my navy pleated skirt.

We started out for the creek, which Rubin kept calling a "habitat." It had been ages since I'd been around someone who used words like that, and I felt sure Rubin didn't use his environmentalist vocabulary on the ranchers of Murkee.

Rubin and I tromped through the cheatgrass and the rabbit brush, while burrs hitched a ride on our clothes. I'd be relieved if I never had to wear this skirt again. Rubin offered me a hand as we slid down a short embankment. I didn't tell him that to me, the creek looked like nothing more than a muddy trickle. It smelled of rotting fish.

It was nearly twilight, so it was hard to see much. Croaks and chirps filled the air the way they do in summer, and the cottonwoods whispered in the breeze.

"This is it," Rubin said, and he jumped onto a log that lay sideways across the water. "It's taken me a year to get it back to where the fish can breed." He pointed along the edges of the bank. "See all the grass and the shrubs? I've had to replant in order to keep the water cool enough and the banks stable. Once I came out here and found twenty cows having a feast." He crossed back over. I stood on a large boulder, intrigued but not sure what to say.

"What kind of fish?" was all I could think of to ask.

He laughed and sat on a piece of bank that was fairly dry. I picked my way around the rocks, found a half-dry patch, and sat down too.

"Trout. Bull trout, mostly." Rubin's locked his arms around his knees and absentmindedly fiddled with some pulled-up grass.

He told me all about redds per mile and rehabilitating this ecosystem to keep the fish from disappearing completely. His eyes sparked as he fumed about the torn-down fencing and Linc's refusal to keep the cattle penned up, even after he'd gone over to the Jackson place in the middle of the night to help some poor cow birth her calf.

"Linc likes to fish as well as anybody around here. I don't know why he won't cooperate."

"So it's trout against cows?" My remark didn't sound as humorous as I intended.

"Not exactly. But Linc knows as much about ranching as I do about making lace. He doesn't give a hoot about the land or the water, except in some way that helps him make money."

"Maybe he's set on paving paradise," I said, thinking of the old Joni Mitchell song. "You know, put up a parking lot. 'Big Yellow Taxi,' remember?"

Rubin nodded. "I wouldn't put it past Linc to build golf courses in the sand."

I frowned. "I still don't know much about my dad, but I doubt he'd be so upset about development. After all, Lutie says he helped build dams. Sounds like progress to me." I imagined my father at work on the river, pouring concrete or installing reinforcing bar. "Why would he have fought Linc over a stream? Linc says he only wants to protect the water supply for the area," I said. I already had my own ideas, but I wanted to hear what Rubin thought.

"Linc's word is worth less than emus on the hoof," Rubin said. He pointed to the stream bank where deep muddy prints marked where the cows had walked. "Especially when it comes to grazing his livestock."

"I don't know about that," I said, "but it's incredible that he won't keep his animals on his side of the property. Where I came from everyone had tidy fences around their yards."

"How much do you know about open-range policies?" Rubin asked.

"Not much, I'm afraid." I didn't add that I didn't care much, either. I felt myself blush and was thankful for the long shadows of dusk. I shook my head at the thought of ranchers killing each other over irrigation when I'd spent most of my days hating the Portland rain.

Rubin held up a cupped palm full of stream water for me to examine. "Liquid gold. The whole area depends on it. Without access to water, ranchers are out of business. This is life out here."

"I believe you," I said finally. Rubin stared at me for a long while, and I stared back, unaware of the damp ground or the moon, which had risen overhead.

Suddenly feeling awkward, I changed the subject. "Listen, about Nova and the other night." I crossed my arms and took a step back.

Rubin held up a hand. "It was my fault. I should have kept them under surveillance. I'm sorry."

I stepped up onto a soggy mound of earth, but my boots slid sideways. I lost my footing and ended up on my knees. Rubin helped me up, but I was a total mess. "I'm the one who should apologize," I said, wiping at the wet mud on my knees. "I'm her mother." I sat on the mound and rubbed at my dirty shins. "Nova's my responsibility."

Rubin laughed. "Are you kidding? For all practical purposes you're a single mom, right?"

I didn't remember telling him my marital status but I nodded. "So?"

"Teenagers have been known to stretch their parents' patience. Out here we all pitch in—help each other out."

"Lutie said something like that."

"See? From now on Nova won't get away with underage drinking on my watch." He gazed into the early night sky.

I looked up, too, and was stunned. I could actually see the Milky Way without light pollution. I gasped at the stars, their simple beauty hinting at an elegant design.

Rubin flinched. "Something wrong?"

I shook my head. "Sounds kind of corny, but everything's so beautiful." I made a sweeping gesture. "The stars, the sound of the water. Everything." I imagined my father out here, presiding over the landscape the same way I did tonight. "Lutie said my dad loved this place."

Rubin sat beside me. "Joe spent a lot of time sitting right here on this mound."

"I can see why. But did he pile the dirt himself?" I paused, visualizing the oven-doors fence. "My father had some strange hobbies. Was he helping you restore the streambed?"

Rubin stroked at his chin. "Not that I know of. I'd come out here in the evenings—on steer patrol—and there'd be Joe, sitting on this mound, looking up into the sky. Sometimes he'd have a bottle; sometimes he'd sing Native songs. Sometimes he'd read or look as if he were praying. I tried not to disturb him."

I pictured what Rubin described. Somehow it comforted me to sit on the very place my father had touched. The stillness, the stars, and the sound of water playing over the creek's stones converged in my mind, and I felt a peace I hadn't known in ages. Before I knew what had happened, my shoulders brushed Rubin's.

"Sorry," I said, pulling back.

"No apologies necessary," he said. "You probably think I tricked you into coming out here, anyway." He stood up.

"No." I got up, too, no longer worried if the back of my skirt was muddy. "I'm impressed. You've done a great job out here."

Rubin stuffed his hands into his pockets. "I try. But I'm telling you, Muri. Even if you manage to prove Linc's up to something, he won't quit so easy. That's another reason I'm looking into getting out of here. You'd be wise to have a back-up plan yourself."

"Right now we don't really have anywhere else to go." I hadn't meant to say this and instantly regretted my honesty.

"Just thought I'd warn you."

I appreciated the advice, but I remained quiet for a moment, long enough to let the touchy subject slip away with the onset of evening.

Finally, Rubin spoke. "Guess we both ought to be getting back. Tongues will start wagging."

"We're friends, right?"

He nodded.

"Then there's nothing to talk about. Come over tomorrow? For dinner I mean? Tiny's lasagna night." I added this last part in case my company wasn't enough.

I hoped it was. "Tiny's lasagna?" he said, facing me again, laughing. "Wouldn't miss it. Everyone in Murkee has tried to pry that recipe out of him."

My knees ached as we trudged back to Rubin's house. He had to help me yank off the mucky rubber boots before I could slip my shoes back on. I enjoyed Rubin's company, but I was glad he wasn't pushing me for more.

145

He stood outside the van as I started Homer up again. "Thanks for stopping by," he said. "Nice to chat with someone who knows a thing or two about ecosystems."

"Ecosystems? Don't let that get around or Murkee will think I'm a tree-hugger too."

"You mean you aren't?"

I glanced at my muddy skirt. "Not dressed like this, I'm not. See you later."

When I pulled into the yard I saw that someone had left the porch light on for me, but the house was dark. I checked my watch; I was shocked to see it was so late. The pigs lay in a huddle by the front door and only raised their snouts briefly when I tiptoed past them.

In the bedroom Nova was asleep or pretending to sleep as I let my soiled skirt drop on the floor and shimmied into a thin nightie. That night I dreamed of cattle and trout warring, each trying to consume the other, and once again I dreamed of Joseph Pond.

14

The next week my final divorce decree arrived in the mail. It was official now. I hoped Lutie's Tabernacle Ladies wouldn't brand me as some kind of loose woman. The mere thought of explaining my ex's abandonment tired me.

For days I felt lost and found myself daydreaming a lot. Every time I thought of trout I'd get this crazy mental picture of a little kid dumping a bucket of fish back into a creek. I couldn't stop thinking of my father or of Rubin for that matter.

Yet somehow I sensed a connection between the two men, one that ran beyond the knowledge that Joseph Pond used to fish and sit on a dirt mound out by the creek. It occurred to me that I really didn't understand enough of the land and water disputes that both Rubin and my father waged against Linc Jackson. I decided to make good on my promise to George Kutzmore and do a little research into that issue, as well as Native artifacts.

That afternoon, I gathered all the information I could: every deed, title, and a pile of Joseph's paid bills that Lutie had kept, along with his Acme Boot box full of stuff. She

gave me a puzzled look as I surfed the Internet on Tru's computer. (I had to pay for dial-up connection, but it was worth
it.) I browsed for water and land use laws and left the photo
albums out in case I needed them. I placed the legal papers
and all the other items in neat stacks on the bed.

One thing was becoming clear. Dad was no accountant.
He had no obvious system for his affairs, just scraps of paper
thrown together with some letters and some cocktail napkins
scribbled with notes and diagrams. I forced myself to save the
personal things for later and tried to organize the rest.

He hadn't left much in the way of savings. But neither did
there appear to be debts. He'd paid for the land outright and
had developed the electrical and water hookups years ago.
The only problem seemed to be the house itself, which had
started out as a trailer and even now barely rated as a permanent dwelling, as Tiny kept building on.

At the bottom of the box lay a few photos of Indian
artifacts, arrowheads and potsherds, mostly, but also a few
ceremonial beads, a grinding stone, and a smooth stick with
a pointed end. Beneath each object my father had written a
title and its use. One caption read, *The "kap'n," or pointed
stick, was used by tribes such as the Warm Springs and Paiute
for digging roots.*

I brushed my fingers across the faded words. Warm
Springs? Paiute? Dad was a member of the Nez Perce. I knew
their range had been mainly in Montana, Idaho, and Eastern
Oregon. The Nez Perce reservation was located in Idaho. I
stared at the photo. Where had these artifacts come from and
where were they now?

The urge came over me to sit on what I'd come to think
of as Joseph Pond's mound. I need to examine that spot by
the creek more closely. I wasn't sure what I'd do if I found
anything like an arrowhead. I thought about taking it to be

analyzed by an expert, but out of respect for my father and his people, I'd probably just set it back where it belonged.

I shoved the papers back into the boot box and then changed from my ratty shorts into a pair of khakis and a blouse with colors that flattered my winter-pale complexion. I twisted my hair up into a large claw clip and spritzed on a pear-scented body spray. Gathering up the box, I headed for Rubin's place once again.

The sign on his door said he was out on a call. I tore off a scrap from a blank page of Dad's journal and penned a short note asking Rubin to get in touch. As I wedged the note into the corner of the screen, the inner door suddenly opened. Startled, I dropped the box and then knelt down to pick up the papers before they blew away.

"May I help you?" A willowy woman stood there. She was maybe thirty, with reddish hair cut boy-short and big lips, the plumped-up kind people pay for. I thought I'd met every single person in Murkee, but I was wrong.

"I was leaving a note for Rub—I mean the doctor," I said, suddenly much too warm. "Will you see that he gets this?" The faint sound of a computer printer hummed in the background.

"Of course," she said, smiling without showing her teeth. "He'll be a while. An emergency came up. Ed Johnson's mare got into trouble early this morning."

"I thought I'd met everybody around here," I said, hoping I sounded casual. "I'm Muri. I live next door."

She ran her hand through her hair the way my daughter would. In fact, on closer inspection, this woman couldn't be much older than Nova. "I'm Kristin. I come up here from

Prineville once a month to make some sense out of Rubin's books. He's way disorganized, you know?"

"Will you let him know I'm down at the creek? He'll know where I'm talking about." This time I smiled.

Kristin shrugged. "If he gets back any time soon, I'll let him know." The screen door creaked closed, and she disappeared into a back room. I was relieved that she was from Prineville and told myself that pouty, collagen lips weren't that attractive.

The stream would be a good place to study the journal and photos in Dad's box, as well as check out the land better. After all, when Rubin and I slogged over there I'd been more interested in the ecosystem and watching out for stray cattle. This time I tramped through the grasses and sagebrush, eager to explore.

I climbed back onto the dirt mound near a cottonwood, close as I could to the bank without getting soaked. The trickling water soothed me. I could see where Rubin had planted native vegetation. The barbwire fence separating his land from Linc's drooped in spots and leaned inward in others. It definitely was not as sturdy as oven doors. The muddied, trampled grass proved livestock had forged paths down to the water from Linc's place.

At a sandy spot on the bank I kicked off my shoes and then dipped my toes in the clear, cold shallows, running the bottoms of my feet over smooth stones. Shy fingerlings darted into crevices as I disturbed the silt. Just like in songs and old corny poems, the stream spoke and sang, and I closed my eyes to hear what it was saying.

The power is in the water. I'd heard this once in a documentary about the Colorado River. Here in Murkee, Oregon, on a forgotten strip of land, it seemed all too true. Linc Jackson's motive must be power in the form of antiquities that would make him a wealthy man. And my father had refused to hand over his creek and its artifacts.

And yet, if power was in the water, wisdom must be there too. Chief Joseph: the only thing I knew about the great Nez Perce chief was his famous line, "From where the sun now stands, I will fight no more forever." I knew my father's side of the family had Nez Perce blood and held sacred all ruins and archaeological sites. Dad also had the unfortunate alcohol addiction that stereotypes many Native people.

Linc was a bigot and a bully . . . and maybe a thief. But Joseph Pond had met his enemies with the same passive resistance as his ancestors. If my daddy was anything like Chief Joseph, it might make up for other things—like dying before I had a chance to meet him. If power was in the water, I certainly didn't feel much of it just then.

"Too late, is more like it," I said to the minnows that nibbled at my red toenail polish. "Guess he can't call to say he's coming home."

Feeling powerless, I sat stock-still. Somehow in searching for my roots I'd discovered myself as a single mom, a rural librarian, and an unlikely protector of this creek cutting through the desert. How could I do it all? For an instant I wished I had some of Aunt Lutie's faith. She seemed to think God gave her enough strength to face anything. But I quickly shoved those thoughts aside. The weeks since I'd left Portland had proven that in this life, you were on your own.

Tumbling over boulders and fallen logs, the water had power; it seemed to disagree with my spiritual views. There was something more, the ripples insisted. "God is everything," I thought I heard it whisper. "These banks are sacred, like a watered garden."

I drew a deep breath, held it briefly, and then sighed. The last words sounded familiar, yet I had no idea where I'd heard them before. Besides, what was sacred about trout habitat and dirt mounds? Snowy puffs from the cottonwood trees blew across my vision, but no answers came as I watched them bounce along in the breeze.

I thumbed once again through the photos in the shoebox. On the back of the first one, my father had scrawled additional notes: *kap'n stick, found April 2005, burial mound on east side of creek*. The other photo, showing three arrowheads, was dog-eared and creased. I turned it over. In the same shaky hand it read, *University guy says one of these may be pre-Clovis*.

I stared at the photo and tried to remember what I knew about ancient peoples. *Clovis* referred to Clovis, New Mexico, where some of the oldest North American ruins had been discovered. I vaguely recalled reading about an archaeological find in Oregon, a site that was more than ten thousand years old. If Dad had found artifacts that predated any Northwestern Indian tribe, they had to be rare and priceless. Although Lutie suspected Linc was after the creek's water rights, I was convinced our neighbor was more interested in selling what he'd stolen from the stream's banks.

I stood up and brushed off the seat of my pants. Maybe I hadn't been paying attention to the right things. I stepped off the mound and scanned the red ground, looking for what I didn't know. I'd know it when I saw it though.

Moments later, I caught a glint. What looked like a shiny tapered rock protruded from the soil near the mound's base. I plucked the object from the dirt and sucked in my breath. In my palm I held a reddish, pointed rock, with delicate fluted edges.

"He found a burial site and tried to keep it sacred," I murmured. The rock looked hand hewn; it had to be an arrowhead.

The water seemed to flow a bit faster then, sparkling light dancing its way past me as I stood in this peaceful place. *Like a watered garden.* Just like this stream, things were becoming clear. I wrapped the arrowhead in a napkin from Dad's box and nestled it under his journal.

My pulse raced. First, I'd need to prove that Linc had removed artifacts from the site. What was he doing with them? Selling them on the black market? If I could locate even one stolen or illegally traded artifact, his argument about being away less than five full years wouldn't hold so much as a cap-ful of water. I stuffed everything back into the box, cradled it under one arm, and jammed my still-wet feet into my shoes. I was excited and anxious all at once, thinking of settling this matter for good. Too bad I wasn't paying much attention to my surroundings. Before I knew it, I came face-to-face with one of Linc's fence crashers.

Cows don't usually scare me, but this one caught me off guard. Plus, she had foot-long horns and was no doubt really thirsty. A calf bawled beside her. Mama made for the stream, checking me out the way cows will, one eye at a time. Her baby trotted at her side.

I reacted like a city girl. I couldn't shinny up a tree, but I knew enough to hide behind a scrubby bush. I watched them approach the water with true bovine grace, trampling bushes and crushing wildflowers. The bank crumbled under their hooves as they drank, and the mama left a fresh cow pie as well.

Now I could see why Rubin was so mad. I came out from behind the bush, hollering and waving my arms, yelling inane things like "Shoo!" "Get lost!" and "Go home, Elsie."

"Elsie" looked at me over her massive shoulder and lowed. The calf edged closer to her side, and then they both went back to drinking. Cattle are not known for their smarts, and these seemed slower-witted than most.

I tried again to divert the cattle back across the divide to Linc's property, but all I got were more stares and a couple of bored moos. I finally picked up the boot box and started back to Rubin's at a slow jog. I'd let him know I'd caught Linc's cows red-handed. Finally, Linc's motives seemed crystal clear.

This fight wasn't over water. It was about the priceless things buried near the water. My father knew it. Linc knew it. Even those dumb cows must know it. I tripped on a gnarled manzanita branch and fell to my knees. Somehow the box stayed upright. Burrs, seedpods, and mud clung to what had been brand new khaki pants just a few hours ago. The branch had ripped through the fabric and left an angry scratch on my shin. Out of breath, I slowed down and walked.

I imagined Joseph Pond striding across his own land, although the photos showed him sort of short and bowlegged. He'd have looked out across the horizon to the creek, toward the distant pinkish hills, and he would have longed for me to be there, too, or at least come to visit two weeks out of the year. He would have shown me how to repair a stove and described his future plans. And he would have told me over and over how much he loved his only daughter.

"What happened to you?" Rubin was getting out of his truck as I hobbled toward him. My shin had bled more than I realized and stained the khakis, which were now a lost cause. He looked puzzled but smiled as he hauled his medical supplies from the pickup bed, which smelled of straw and manure and some kind of antiseptic.

"I fell." I pulled up my pant leg, and he insisted on tending to the scratch. I tried not to wince. "It's Linc. I mean his cows.

I tried to get them back on the other side, but they won't budge. They're eating up the camas you put in."

"Confounded cattle." Rubin flung down a pile of used gauze, crusty with blood. He strode over near the emu pen and entered a small shed, leaving me to wonder what I'd started. When he emerged he was carrying a shotgun.

I laid the box on the hood of his truck and quickly caught up with him, already headed toward the stream. "Is that really necessary?" My stomach dropped as I saw his expression. "They're only dumb animals, Rubin. Please." I huffed and puffed as I tried to keep pace; the cut on my leg throbbed. I shuddered. What if he'd lied about accidentally shooting Jim?

He just kept going. Finally he spoke. "You think I enjoy this? I'm a *vet*, remember? Anyway, I'm only going to fire into the air to scare them off."

"Well, that's good. If you're shooting cows, you're liable to scare *me* off."

Rubin smiled wide, melting my suspicions. "Don't want that," he said. "Definitely don't want that."

When we got there Elsie and her youngster were grazing just inside Linc's side of the property. Apparently, they knew enough to get back to home base or else they were simply finished mauling the stream. After much waving and yelling and Rubin's ear-splitting whistle, they meandered off. I was thankful that no shots had been fired.

Rubin was less enthusiastic. "Fence is trashed," he said, pulling a downed post to its upright position. "Got a mind to string razor wire this time. See how Linc likes *that*." He let go, and the stake nearly touched the ground, held back only by drooping cross wires.

I pointed downstream. "Maybe you should get some used oven doors yourself. It would take a bulldozer to tear down those things."

"Or a bull," Rubin said.

"Good grief, he doesn't have bulls wandering around does he?"

Rubin turned his attention to the stream, and I nodded sympathetically as he vented about the damage. The camas lilies were broken off at ground level. Places where he'd worked to keep the bank from crumbling wore telltale hoof marks. I sat down by the cottonwood again. The mound had become a friend. The air hung still and heavy, busy with the drone of insects and the gurgle of the stream.

"What do we do now?" I asked. He was knee deep in creek water, shoring up the bank with his bare hands.

These were the same hands that earlier in the day had no doubt helped deliver a foal, saving its mother from something awful. He'd probably been up since before dawn, and now the long shadows of late afternoon shaded his face. Suddenly, he looked very tired and beaten.

I stood up and waded out into the water. "Show me what to do." He smiled at me, and I knew I'd said the right thing.

We piled up river rocks and scooped gravel. I slid a piece of bark under the still-moist cow pie and dumped it on Linc's side. I felt better putting his mess back where it belonged. The mosquitoes came out and feasted on my arms, but I was happy anyway. I heaved a bowling ball-sized stone into the water, just to hear the belly flop sound it made. The water smelled muddy but refreshing.

"Ever get tired of all the hassles?" I asked him, thinking of the ongoing argument with Linc and of my own troubles that threatened to wash me away. "Some days I think I'm drowning."

Rubin stopped and rinsed off his arms. We stood next to my cottonwood tree. "Yeah," he said, "I've been close to throwing in the towel."

"Over cows?" I gathered some flat stones and tried to skip one across a still pool in the water. The pebble sank.

He smiled. "If cows were my biggest problem, I'd be lucky. Here," he said, picking up another rock, "hold it flat like this." He sailed a pebble out and it danced on the surface.

"I thought I was coming to Murkee to think and get my dad's affairs in order—a couple of weeks, a month tops. But the way things are going, I'm stuck here." I hurled another stone. This one skipped perfectly to the other side. "Linc ever say anything about selling or collecting Indian artifacts?" I studied Rubin's expression for a reaction.

He seemed genuinely surprised. "No, he never mentioned anything, but I've heard talk. One of my clients claims she saw a ton of stuff in one room of his house."

"Let me guess," I said, chuckling. "Is the client Frieda Long?"

Rubin nodded. "That Frieda, she's an original. We never know what to believe. But what makes you think Jackson's moving Native American relics?" Rubin eyed me as if he thought I'd done something wrong.

"Just a feeling," I said. "And don't worry; I haven't broken into his place. But I am checking into it. I'm not sure, of course." I blew out my breath. "I'm not sure about a lot of things anymore." I bent and scooped up a few more pebbles from the bank. In the shallows, a smooth heart-shaped, palm-sized rock caught my eye. "This one's lovely." I rinsed off the silt and held it out for him to see.

He turned the heart stone over in his hand and pointed to a crease that formed the top "vee" of the heart. "The tribes would look for this sort of rock. See how the edges look worn?" He ran his fingers over the crease. "This notch might anchor a haft of some sort. Tie it to a stick and voila! You have yourself a fine ax."

"Do you think this could be an actual artifact?"

Rubin weighed the piece in his hand. "Hard to say. It's a little small, but maybe." He handed it back. "I'm no expert."

I was no expert, either. "Should I even remove a rock from this place?"

Rubin shrugged. "Maybe you could have somebody look at it."

"Great idea." I pocketed my treasure. "Know anybody?" Later, I'd put it in the box with the arrowhead.

Rubin squinted into the sun. "Denny Moses. You met him and Gwen on the Fourth."

"Think he'd be willing?"

"Denny? He's Warm Springs himself, remember? He'll jump at the chance. Especially when I tell him how Linc is out to get the both of us."

"And ruin my father's reputation in the process," I said. "But Linc doesn't know who he's dealing with."

Rubin tossed a pebble into the water. "At least we have something in common. That goat isn't used to anyone standing up to him, and Joseph knew how to get him going."

"How well did you know him? Joseph, I mean?" It felt odd to say my father's name. I wanted to know everything about him, but I got the feeling I'd learn something I didn't want to know.

Rubin moved a little closer. My heart jackhammered. I didn't know what he'd say.

"Your old man was a piece of work," he began, closing his eyes briefly, as if to conjure up Dad's image. "I never knew anyone who could fix things like he could—refrigerators, toasters, any appliance really. He kept my GMC running. Wouldn't ever take a dime."

"Aunt Lutie says he couldn't say no, either." Tears stung my eyes.

"Well, temperance wasn't one of his virtues. But the man had a heart of gold, and he loved to talk about Christ. Everybody said so."

I listened for my father's voice, but I only heard cows lowing.

Rubin wiped off a tear from my cheek. "We were all sad to see him go so sudden."

"They said he had a few more months, and that's why no one got hold of me sooner." A lump exploded in my throat. "I just hope he wasn't mean when he was drunk."

Benjamin's face came into full view in my mind, his nose swollen with gin and spite. Where had my mother come up with these guys, anyway? My stepfather's lip had curled up slightly every time he'd pronounced sentence on an aspect of my life. I was pierced with the thought that Joseph Pond had been cruel and critical as well.

"No, Muri, Joseph may have hit the sauce too much, but he was never a brawler," Rubin said quietly. "He defended himself but he never started things. In fact, that's why Linc hung that nickname on him. Your dad refused to step outside one night—they were arguing over selling your place again—and Linc started taunting him, calling him Chief Joseph."

"I will fight no more forever," I murmured.

"What?"

"Nothing."

Joseph's Journal
April 1989

When we build a dam we work from sunup to sundown. First we set the rebar, so the dam will be sturdy. Then we pour concrete—miles and miles of concrete. I don't mind the work, but the concrete lime is eating up my hands and spreading up my forearms. Every day I look for red streaks on my ash-gray fingers. I look for signs of concrete poisoning. Here on the dam, if the rebar doesn't get a man, the concrete will.

Dam-building's serious business, even when it's only repair work. Chief Joseph Dam was once a grand sight, and now we're putting it up ten feet higher than before. Men have always tried to break the Columbia, to steal the river's power. Here we are again, fools every last one of us. Old Man River will make us pay. Sooner or later, the Columbia wins.

I've already seen three guys pay with their lives. Lew, a new guy, left behind a wife and a tow-headed baby boy. And a teen-age daughter, Susan. She must be about the same age as you are, Muri.

Susan's skinny. She wears too much makeup. Her outfits are too skimpy. I try to picture you, daughter, and I pray you don't wear high-top basketball shoes with your skirts the way Susan does. She listens to a singer called Madonna and used to fat mouth her daddy before he died.

I hope you have the sense to eat properly. Remember how you'd only eat peanut butter and graham crackers when you were little? You'd clamp your mouth shut or just scream and scream when your mother tried to force you to eat any other food. Your mother said you were spoiled and difficult, but I thought you were strong and brave.

Susan used to argue with Lew about her curfew, about boys and parties, about getting her ears pierced. She'd stand out in the street, so it wasn't really eavesdropping. I can imagine you being that stubborn.

That last day I worked with Lew he shook his head and told me, "That Susan—she never gives up. The younger generation is all going to the devil."

We old-timers liked to scare new guys with stories of how a man could get impaled on the rebar up here if he happened to lose his footing, if he forgot to tie off. That's what we were doing, Lew and I, setting rebar. I always secured my line, but Lew didn't. Said he couldn't do his job tied up like a mule.

That day, the river was backed up against the sunset. I could almost feel the water bearing down on the concrete, millions of acre-feet boiling. It was as if the river thirsted for human sacrifice. That's when Lew fell, and his screams quieted everything for a time. Then we turned our attention back to the concrete because we had to get paid; we had a deadline. On the pour line, some grumbled that Lew shouldn't have got the river mad. I pray for all the workers, especially new guys. Sometimes they die anyway.

Lew has been replaced by a guy from Oklahoma. Says he's got nine kids, none of them girls. Not a one. The Oklahoma guy drinks Everclear in the dark and says if something happens to him, well, he's got nine boys to take care of the wife. We talk about these things while we set the concrete forms, and at night we drink until we sleep.

Every day the Columbia bows down a little more, and I bow down right along with it. Don't want to, but I do. I look to heaven and pray I'll last long enough to see you, to tell you how I love my baby girl. Don't give up on me, Muri. Don't give up.

15

Back at Rubin's, my father's box sat waiting on the hood of the truck. It was already past five-thirty. Kristin was just sliding into her metallic red Accord. I was tired and hungry and needed to know where she fit into Rubin's life.

"So who's Kristin?" I picked up the box in case I didn't like the answer.

He laughed. I looked into his eyes, which were a toasty light brown. "Books," he said. "She does the books. Have dinner with me?"

"I didn't let anyone at home know where I was going," I stammered. Even in the twilight I could see the sparks in his gaze, hopeful, anticipating. Since when had I been so coy? Back in Portland no one knew your name. No one cared if you were hurting, or needy, or knew you'd driven your own father away at an early age. I wanted to believe that here, with emus clamoring in the pens, things *did* matter, that Rubin did care.

Rubin took a step back. "Look, I'm not trying to push you. Call home if you want. You have a phone now, remember?" He spoke as if he were calming a nervous mare. "Invite Tru and Nova over, too, if it makes you more comfortable."

I looked down at my soggy shoes and torn trousers. "I'm a mess, that's all. And, really, you don't want to get involved with—"

"With what?" He frowned a little.

"With me," I said. "I'll be honest. I'm on the rebound. My divorce only became final a few days ago."

"Can we at least be friends? I know. That sounds like a come on, but I really enjoy your company."

"You'll be sorry." My voice had shrunk to a whisper.

"We've all got stuff we deal with. I like to think God sees the glass half full. I'm an optimist too."

I relaxed my death grip on the boot box. "All right, I'll have dinner with you this once. But first I'm going home to clean up." As if I could shower away the glow I was sure I now wore. If I weren't careful, before long this guy would have me believing in miracles too.

I showed up back at Rubin's an hour later. I'd dressed in a white gauze top and faded jeans, fervently hoping we wouldn't need to return to the stream tonight. Smells coming from the kitchen reminded me that I hadn't eaten in hours.

Three dogs and two cats greeted me at the door, but none of them was impolite: Rusty, a Welsh Corgi; Stone, a black lab, and Speed Bump, an enormous stray he'd taken in recently, wagged and slobbered their helloes. The cats were a bit more aloof. At Rubin's command the dogs went back to their rugs and lay down, and the cats kept on being cats. Rubin wore a white chef's apron that said, *2007 Emus Barbecue Cook-Off*. I hoped we weren't in for another rack of bird ribs.

Celtic music played softly in the background, alternating between joyous and melancholy. Rubin had cleaned up too. He handed me a stemmed glass of sparkling cider and invited me into the kitchen.

"Pasta," he said, waving one of those spoons with wooden tines for grabbing noodles. "Quickest thing I could think of." A pot of marinara bubbled on the stovetop, and I set to work arranging refrigerated breadstick dough on a cookie sheet. I'd already noticed how well we worked together back at the stream, anticipating each other's moves. Every accidental brush of our arms, every slight bump of our bodies in the cramped kitchen made my stomach flutter.

"Everything smells delicious," I said.

He stopped stirring the sauce. "You look nice tonight," he said. My legs wobbled in spite of my mental command to be still, yet I kept up my casual act. I was enjoying the vet more than I wanted to, more than I knew was a good idea.

"What temperature do I set the oven on?" I asked, and slipped the breadsticks in.

"Three seventy-five, ten minutes. If you can trust the fine print."

When the oven timer chimed later we both jumped.

We loaded our plates and Rubin refilled our glasses. We drank cider, not wine; but I felt buzzy, a little like those Dali paintings where everything drips.

At first I didn't even feel like eating, knowing it would be impossible to eat angel hair pasta with red sauce in any dignified way. But the sweet mingling of fresh basil and elephant garlic was too tempting to resist. When my first bite splattered droplets across the white blouse, I said forget it and dug in. I tried to remember we were only friends, but I felt flushed and clumsy.

After dinner we headed outside to the porch. We sat cross-legged on the wicker settee and sucked on after-dinner mints. We both loved fresh basil. "What a coincidence," I said.

"I don't believe in coincidences," he said. "Everything happens for a reason. You included." He looked serious now and gave me that kind of stare that made my breath catch.

When he moved closer, I gasped and pressed myself as far against the back of settee as I could manage.

"You all right?" Rubin looked confused but backed away.

"You don't understand," I said. A hot tingling crept across my cheeks. "I like you—really. It's just too soon. I told you. I'm not ready. Yet. Maybe never. Besides, I've got kids to think about."

Rubin stood up. "No hard feelings?"

"None. I'm sorry. I shouldn't have given you the wrong signal."

"At least you're honest. I like that." He smiled. "Friends?"

"Sure. Friends."

It was too soon. A jumble of emotions and thoughts swirled in my head. If I was this uncomfortable, I wasn't ready for a relationship. I told myself to slow down, that I'd only been out here in nowhere land a short while. There was plenty of time to sort out my life. I scolded myself to quit obsessing about my new neighbor.

Yet I continued to think about this unlikely veterinarian turned conservationist, whose manners both surprised and pleased me. Here was someone special, I concluded, someone worthy of friendship. What could be wrong with that? We sat back down a little farther apart and time flew by as we shared our pasts.

Sometime after midnight I fluttered back to my senses. I stood up and stretched. "Walk me home, will you?" My heart pounded at the thought of Nova waiting up, grilling me with a bunch of questions for which I had no easy answers.

Rubin switched on the porchlight and smiled at me. "You okay?"

"I feel like a teenager that busted curfew." I leaned against the porch railing and slid back into my sandals.

He laughed and then placed his jacket around my shoulders. "We'll just say we were watching the stars, right?"

"The stars, right."

We strolled across the hill back to the trailer. The moon was nearly full and spilled light across the creek. The only sounds came from distant cows and the crunch of the dry grass beneath our feet. The night sky was spectacular. I was glad I didn't have to count the stars. Whoever said there are a certain number of them was guessing.

We lingered along the way, but I said I'd better get home. I took deep breaths, tried to steady myself, and then stopped short. "You smell that?" Smoke. I was sure of it.

Rubin nodded and stared in the direction of the trailer. "Over there," he said, and broke into a run. "Your place is on fire!"

I ran after him, and a few seconds later we barreled around the oven door fence and into the yard. Flames licked the nearby shed room. I dashed for the trailer door and nearly yanked the screen from its hinges.

"I'll get the hose!" Rubin yelled. He cranked the spigot open and sprayed the roof of the trailer. "Sparks landing on the house," he shouted. "It's liable to catch any minute!"

"Fire!" I screamed and dashed through the smoke. I tripped over a video game controller in my son's room as I tried to shake him awake. He roused, and I steered him into the hallway.

"Hurry, Truman."

"Nova! Aunt Lutie! Tiny! We've got to get out now," I shouted, and they emerged from their bedrooms with startled sleepy looks.

"Are we going to die?" Tru mumbled.

"No, son, nobody's going to die," Tiny said. Jim the pig awoke from his spot next to the TV, and we all stumbled out into the yard.

The small storage shed next to the trailer shot orange embers into the air; some of the cinders swirled onto the roof of the house. Rubin aimed the garden hose at the blaze, but the flames edged closer to the house every minute. It was plain we didn't have enough water pressure to make a dent. Then I saw the van through the haze.

Decrepit as it was, it was the only thing of value I had left. Flames poured out the cracked, blackened windows, and a burned-rubber smell bit into my eyes and nose as the engine compartment sizzled and popped.

"The van!" I grabbed a bucket.

"The pigs!" Tiny screamed, squeals coming from inside their wooden pen. He ran as fast as I'd ever seen my uncle move; and when he got the door unstuck, Dave, Gordo and the others raced into the open. Nova jumped out of their way. "Oh, Mom," she said. "The van's totaled." She buried her face in her hands.

Lutie disappeared into the house and emerged with an armload of pots, pans, and Tupperware bowls. She dropped the load beside a utility sink on the side of the house and proceeded to fill them. "Let's go kids," was all she said, and even Nova obeyed. Tru threw water against the trailer walls as fast as he could, while Nova seemed intent on saving the van. Lutie muttered prayers as she filled empty containers.

The water from the hose was little more than a trickle now. "There's no pressure," Rubin shouted above the crackling roar. "Get Linc on the phone."

"What for?" I asked. Linc was the last person I wanted to see.

"He's got the water truck at his place," Rubin explained. He dialed the number and tossed his cell to me. A man answered, and I quickly told the hired hand about the fire.

"We're on it," he said, and the phone went dead.

Please let him show up, I prayed.

The pigs huddled next to Tiny and kept getting tangled in the hoses. They looked as forlorn as Nova, and all except Jim whimpered like small children. Tru had decided he belonged with the men and directed them where to point the hoses.

The only thing I could think to do was to fill up a bucket I'd found. Out here there was no such thing as fire departments or 911. Out here you had to rely on your neighbors—neighbors who might be trying to force you out or siphon off your water for themselves.

I managed to slosh most of the bucket's water down my shins. When I tossed what was left on the burning engine of the van, the fire practically laughed out loud at me. Nova sat at the farthest edge of the yard, staring at the ground. Rubin saw what I was doing and shook his head. "It's a lost cause," he said.

"Isn't anyone coming?" I pressed the empty bucket against my abdomen. I wasn't giving up.

"Linc should be here any minute." He shook the hose as if to coax more from it. "Pressure always like this?"

"Been that way awhile," Tiny said. "Pipes rusted."

Nova yelled, "Can somebody get these pigs away from me?" They had bunched themselves around her.

Tiny led his pets away from Nova. "They won't hurt you," he said.

When the water truck showed up, Linc took his time getting out of the cab. "Good thing I was close by," was all he said. The men got to work getting the fire under control, and I kept the bucket brigade going just so I wouldn't be tempted to break down and cry. Linc worked as hard as any of them to put out the blaze. Maybe he wasn't so bad; after all, he did show up with the water truck.

My fingers ached from hauling water. It was nearly light now; the first tinges of red and pink brushed the horizon. The air was still thick with smoke, but the noise had died down. The pigs slept in a knot next to a heap of old machinery. The scene appeared sad and ghostlike. Even Lutie and Tiny stood silently, as if there wasn't much left to say.

Linc drove off as soon as the fire was out. He'd been a good neighbor, and it bothered me that I still didn't trust him. I couldn't allow myself to trust him. I couldn't trust anybody.

Then Rubin got a call from a nearby ranch. "Got to get going," he said, flipping the phone shut. "Yearling over at the Long's got a problem." He placed his hand on my shoulder. "Let me know if there's anything you need."

"I'm so glad you were here," I said. "So glad." I felt like hugging him but saw Nova eyeing us so I folded my arms across my chest. He strode over the hill, and I breathed a sigh of thanks that we had all survived.

The trailer suffered only a few burnt shingles, but the shed and van weren't so lucky. Both had been reduced to shells. The heavy smell of charred wetness permeated the air. I surveyed the piles of bike parts and junk. Anyone could see Tiny's clutter was a fire hazard. I'd seen the mess of wiring in that shed. It was overloaded and dangerous. And what about a spark from an exhaust pipe? The stubble of dry grass surrounding the van could easily have ignited. I narrowed my eyes at Nova, remembering her vow to leave even if she had to steal a car. She looked at me and asked, "Can I go back to bed now?" I was too tired to argue with her, so I nodded, and she followed Lutie and Tiny inside. Tru took the bucket from me and wanted to help with the van, but the engine was shot.

"Daddy won't like this," he said.

"Daddy won't find out about this," I said.

16

The sharp smell of burned-out wiring lingered for days. Nova stormed around, blaming me for the whole mess. She'd never become a famous fashion designer. She was stranded on Mars, she said about every ten minutes, because the van was a total wreck. Her escape route was foiled, and it was my fault. The sad truth was, so far the only thing we'd found that might have started the fire was that tangle of wiring in the shed. I'd never seen my uncle so sad.

I found it impossible to sleep much because I got up several times a night to make sure things were unplugged. The rest of the time I lay next to Nova and listened to her breathing or tried to count the glow-in-the-dark stars she'd plastered all over the ceiling. Inside a week I was exhausted, and when I finally slept, it was hard and deep and difficult to wake up.

In fact, the border between sleep and waking felt perfect, a paradise I didn't wish to leave. Perhaps it was the dreaming; perhaps it was just that I still needed more rest. Sleep felt so pain-free and soft that I didn't want to come back.

In my dreams Rubin popped up where I least expected: at the beach, where I miraculously didn't sunburn and the sand was as fine as sugar; in the new Murkee Library, checking out veterinary magazines, or sitting beside his stream.

He had come over regularly the last few days. He wasn't an eco-nut; he was a caring and compassionate friend. Okay, I had to admit, more than a friend. The whole town was talking about us, but I hadn't been listening. I was a grown-up, and it was none of their business, now was it?

This morning I didn't feel so grown-up. Perhaps it was childishness that kept me clinging to sleep, trying in vain to return to where Rubin and I had left off. Finally, Nova woke me up, rummaging through her backpack.

I raised my head. "What are you doing?" I wanted to add that perhaps they couldn't hear her in Cleveland, but I didn't. I can be a real bear in the morning.

"Nothing." She continued to rattle papers. I rubbed my eyes and sat up, pulling on the green cotton robe I'd worn for fourteen summers and sliding my feet into scuffs.

Nova was already dressed in those baggy cargo pants she loves and a too-tight tank top. Her hair was purple this week, Marvin's favorite color, I guessed. Those two were as much a topic of gossip as Rubin and I were these days, and it was all I could do to stand parental watch.

"What on earth are you looking for?" This time I sounded grouchy and in need of coffee.

"I need to find Dad's phone number. You know, the one at the gallery."

"Why? What's going on?"

"I just need to talk to him."

"You swore you never wanted to speak to your father again. That was last week, I believe."

I dragged a brush through my tangled hair with quick, sharp strokes, and then banged the brush down on the dilapidated bureau. The picture of my father that I'd set there jumped a bit, but I may have imagined it.

"Mo-ther." Her forehead scrunched up. "Is it a crime for me to say hello to my dad?"

"No, not a crime," I said, preparing for battle. "But it's not like you. Is anything wrong?"

"Of course not," she said, and then added, "Yes!" It wasn't an admission, just the way kids say, "Aha!" She waved a scrap of paper from the pack, and then paused. For a moment I thought it was true, that she simply wanted to check in with Daddy. Then she shot me a look and blew out through her nostrils like an angry bull. Her bottom lip quivered. "You want to know? You really want to know?"

"Of course I do," I said as calmly as I could. I caught my reflection in the small round mirror above the dresser. Places where the silver had worn away from the back made me appear transparent in spots.

"Why can't you go ahead and sell? Everywhere I go I hear about how our family came out here just to stir up trouble. *Your* dad's dead, Mom. Face it. And all he left you was a bro-ken-down trailer and a bunch of junk." My daughter was red-faced now, but she didn't stop there. "If it wasn't for Marvin I would have moved back with Dad a long time ago." Her chin jutted defiantly. "Just drop it, Mom. Please. It's so embarrass-ing. Everybody says Linc deserves the water."

"Everybody? Everybody on his payroll, you mean. Besides, it's much more complicated than that." I decided not to explain what I'd found at the creek bed. Employing one of Nova's favorite avoidance tactics, I changed the subject abruptly. "By the way, what's going on with you and Marvin?" I felt the prickles of motherly protection rise along the back of my neck. "Well?"

"We're just friends," she insisted. "That's all." I thought of my new friendship with Rubin and doubted it.

"What about you and Rubin?" she asked. "Everyone says you guys are together." Nova had backed up now; she stood at the doorway. I'd backed myself into doorways plenty of times as a child. Sarcastic remarks like these were hit-and-run insults.

"It's none of your business, young lady," I said, feeling my own face flush. "I'm an adult. Well? Are you two, well, you know?"

"How could I be? Linc watches Marvin like a hawk too. I still need to call Dad." She left, and I wondered why her eye twitched slightly.

When I finished dressing and walked out to the living room Nova was already on the phone. Lutie sat in her recliner, crocheting a harvest gold soda can hat, and Tiny was cooking something over in the kitchenette. Tru must be outside with Jim, I guessed, playing with the bike parts and junk. Suddenly, the place seemed even drearier and the word *kitsch* came to mind. A wave of loneliness smacked me from behind, and I remembered how once I had been the wife of an up-and-coming art gallery owner.

"Daddy," Nova yelled into the new cordless phone louder than necessary, "I miss you so much."

Chaz had never been more than mildly interested in fatherhood and hated being called at work. But he must have been sympathetic today, because Nova jumped right in.

"I can't stand it here," she said, turning her back to me. "There's nothing to do and everyone wears Wranglers and the school is a joke. And," she paused dramatically, "and Mom's getting us all in trouble."

After a few minutes, Nova turned and handed me the phone. "Here, he wants to talk to you." She folded her arms and pouted.

I took it reluctantly, partly because it was the first contact we'd made in a while, and partly because I didn't want to feel sorry for him. Aunt Lutie had warned me about this, so I said a terse, "Hello."

Chaz's voice was equally cool. He didn't even ask about Tru. "What's up?" he demanded to know. I could just see him standing there in the gallery, pursing his lips, doodling away on the phone book the way he always did. He was probably dressed in a black turtleneck and designer jeans, like that proved he was an *artiste*.

"Nova's exaggerating again," I said. My eye twitched. "This is all about water rights. It's really about the whole creek area—the land around it." There, I felt better throwing in a bit of truth.

"Water? Hold on, will you?" Chaz spoke to someone in the background. I heard a high thin female voice, and I hoped it wasn't Victoria, the bimbo he'd moved in with. Actually, I knew little about the poor girl, but it was fun to trash her for hooking up with such a loser.

Finally, Chaz spoke into the phone again. "Muri? How much you think that property's worth?"

His question caught me off guard. It wasn't like him to think in terms of money. He'd confessed to me once that the gallery only ran in the black after he'd hired dear Victoria.

"What difference does that make?" I felt defensive and suddenly wished George Kutzmore was here.

"For one thing, you need cash, not a junkyard in the middle of nowhere. Sell the place and get the kids out of that hole. Whatever you get from the property, just remember:

your stepfather, Benjamin, wants that loan cleared up." Chaz conferred with the phantom voice in the background again.

"My name was never on that loan," I said. "Legally *you* owe him the money."

Now he turned on the charm; that was his style. He always alternated between making nice and twisting your arm.

"Hey, we were in all that together. You said—" Chaz was a weasel of the first degree.

"You got that in writing anywhere?" I was shaking by now, and the cup of tea Tiny handed me sloshed about in the mug.

"You obviously don't care about your children," Chaz said, throwing in a curse word or two. "The gallery's their future. If you insist on raising them in that slum, then I guess I can't stop you. But you're dragging them down with you." Then he hung up.

I stood there, listening dumbly to the "If you'd like to make a call" recording before I pushed the off button. The only call I really wanted to make was to my father, but that was impossible. Instead, I stared out the window at the brilliant sunshine. It made my eyes water; that's what I told Aunt Lutie.

She was up now, scrabbling in a paper sack full of aluminum cans. When I looked around she was bent over at the waist and her skeletal fingers raked through the bag's contents. But she turned and smiled as she sifted through the Dr. Pepper, Squirt, Bud, and Coors empties. I was just glad she always rinsed them before she brought them in the house.

Nova stomped around and demanded to know what that awful racket was, which of course was totally different than the noise she was making. When she learned that Chaz had cut off the conversation, she automatically blamed me. Her purple hair spikes turned my stomach. It would serve Victoria right if my daughter showed up on their doorstep.

"Sit down," I said, giving Nova the "or else" look. "It wouldn't kill you to act like you're part of the family."

"This stinks," she said and perched on a chair at the edge of the room nearest the door.

Aunt Lutie smiled at her anyway. "You're as stubborn as your grandpa," she told Nova, who clucked her tongue and stared at the ceiling. "And Joseph had the magic touch. He could fix anything that needed fixing," Lutie said. "Something that was beyond mending, he'd just invent a new one. Like you, Nova, with your beautiful creations."

"My creations?" Nova asked. She looked disgusted. "My creations are doomed, like we are." A black cloud parked itself above my daughter's head.

Tru came in, with Jim trailing behind him. Tru sat on the floor next to the recliner, where Lutie had stationed herself. I sat with Tiny on the sofa, and we all listened, as if we were about to learn the family secrets, which I was certain we were.

"Take engines." Lutie cleared her throat. Tiny got up and headed toward the kitchen, returning momentarily with a glass of water. She smiled at him and took a sip. "Joseph could get a motor to obey him no matter what was wrong. Just sweet-talked it until it purred, I always thought. That was before I took a basic auto repair class down at the Prineville Senior Center."

She looked at Tru. "Your grandpa owned as much junk as your uncle here." Tiny glanced over sharply and then broke into a sheepish grin.

"Watch what you call junk, my Pearl," he said.

Nova rolled her eyes and stood up. "A pile of garbage is more like it," she said. "I'm going out." She started toward the door. I blocked her exit, glowered at her, and she flopped back down with an exaggerated sigh.

Lutie smiled at my daughter. "Don't forget, Rhonda Gaye is coming over to help you get started on an ensemble for the bazaar."

Nova let out a sigh of exasperation and folded her arms over her chest.

"Now these soda can hats were Joseph's idea," Lutie continued, carefully staring down at one of them, all hooked together in avocado green and a hideous brown. "He said he knew how we could recycle and make a buck too. Before we knew it we had more orders than we could fill. Sell out every year at the bazaar."

"Think what you could do with a web page," Tru practically shouted. "I know how to design them—piece of cake." He jumped up, and Jim, who must have been dreaming, jerked awake with the only kind of snort he could muster. "We'll all be rich," Tru proclaimed. He pushed his glasses up on his nose and for a moment I imagined the next computer magnate. Well, at least he looked the part.

"You want to hear about your grandpa or not?" Tiny said, patting Jim back into sleep. Then he added, "Teach me about your computer real soon, okay?" That was my uncle's way, I thought. He disciplined Tru without shaming him. Plus Tiny's nose didn't turn red, which was a big thing in his favor.

Nova stood up again and began to walk out. "Where do you think you're going?" I demanded. I couldn't believe her manners were so poor.

She whirled around. "I can't stand it here," she said. "I'm going out."

"Out? Out where?"

"Just out."

"Probably going to meet that Marvin guy," Tru said.

"Shut up, you little menace. It's none of your business."

"Nova Irene, I'm warning you—"

Nova gave me a hard, cold look. "You can't tell me what to do," she said. "You're afraid Daddy will come out here and rescue me."

"What about poor Rhonda Gaye?" Lutie asked.

"Rhonda Gaye can shove it," Nova said.

Tiny and Lutie's mouths dropped open.

"Apologize," I said, standing up again to block her exit. "And I forbid you to leave."

Nova and I proceeded to have it out. Tiny escaped outside with Tru and Jim, and Lutie crocheted, occasionally getting up to sort through the cans for new material, quietly ignoring us. But when Nova picked up an empty Diet Coke can and chucked it at me, I lost my head. She had definitely stepped over the line.

"If you weren't so selfish, we'd still be in Portland with Daddy," she said, flinging another empty can my way. Either she wasn't trying to hit me or she was a really bad throw.

I picked up the can and gripped it so hard it caved in on one side. "Selfish? *I'm* selfish?" On impulse I heaved the dented can at her feet.

"Well, let's see," my daughter continued, kicking the can aside. "First you lose your job."

"That wasn't my fault you know. And don't *ever* throw anything at me again, young lady, or—"

"Or what?" Nova had grabbed another can and started toward me. Lutie still sat in her recliner. She glanced up at me now with the kind of eyes you know will dissolve you if you look too long, but I was past defusing the situation.

"I'm still your mother. Show some respect." How lame. Words I swore I'd never say, and here they were, flying out of me. I stepped back.

"Well, how do I respect that you're divorced? Wow, what a coincidence that you don't care what happens to us." I hate it when kids lay guilt on you that way, but I couldn't back down.

"Wipe that smirk off your face. And the divorce wasn't my idea." There. Now she would know I was serious. "I don't know what to do with you," I said. Tears stung the edges of my eyes. "I hate watching you destroy yourself. You have so much going for you. So much potential."

She made an ugly face. "So that's why you ripped us away from our friends, and let's face it—civilization as we know it—to come live in a hole. Who cares if Tru and I would rather be anywhere else on the planet? Mom's got dead relatives to visit." Her face was crimson now, and she hurled another empty can at me. It missed me but struck poor Lutie's leg.

Lutie stared up at the ceiling, mumbling, "Oh, sweet Jesus—"

"That does it. Apologize for hitting your aunt this instant," I said, picking up the can. "Do it now."

Nova just stood there.

"I'm at the end of my rope," I screamed in a new octave. "You leave me no choice." I shook harder than ever, but I took a deep breath as we stared into each other's faces. "Apologize or pack a bag."

"You kicking me out? Fine, I'm outta here." Nova stormed off into the bedroom, emerging a few moments later with her backpack. She was crying, but she kept her eyes down and didn't speak. The sleeve of my favorite silk blouse hung from one of the open zippers on her pack. As she left, the door slammed and then bounced open again, inviting me to follow her the way I'd always done before.

Before I could run after her, I felt a hand on my shoulder. Lutie's touch felt gentle and at the same time firm. "She'll be back," my aunt said softly. "Let her go." Her eyes were foggy with tears, softening the harsh angles of her cheekbones into a comforting expression.

I took the tissue she offered me, dabbing at my eyes and blowing my nose. Tru came inside wearing a puzzled look, and I was about to cry all over again, but Lutie offered him a simple, straightforward explanation.

"Your sister needs to cool off, son. I wouldn't worry too much. When she gets hungry, she'll be back."

Tru nodded as if Nova left home every day, which wasn't that far off. She had run away before, usually after a similar argument. Once she'd stayed away for two weeks, which scared me to death. We had the police out looking for her. Even after I found out she was staying three blocks away with a friend, I had trouble sleeping, imagining my precious girl out on the streets of Portland. A mother's worst fears always run to the dramatic—she was some kind of dope addict or sleeping on the streets—so that if the truth is any better, you automatically feel relief.

That time she'd come home after everyone was in bed. It had been after midnight when I'd discovered Nova rummaging through the fridge, shoving leftovers in her mouth as if she hadn't eaten in days. And she hadn't, which is why she'd decided home wasn't so bad after all.

But now home wasn't all that great. Even I thought so. My heart ached at the prospect that this time she might be serious.

Lutie shooed Tru outside to fetch Tiny and took me by the hand. "Sit down," she said, and we perched on the edge of the sofa. I kept my back to the Jesus portrait so I wouldn't blubber.

"I'm so sorry for creating such a scene," I began, still sniffling. "I've tried just about everything with that child."

"Hush, now," she said. "It's fine. We can't hide the truth from each other. We're *family*, after all." She smiled at me and then up at her picture of the Lord.

"Why don't we pray?" she said.

That was all I could stand. I collapsed into her shoulder—just folded up like a TV tray with a broken hinge. I sobbed while she prayed with a strange authority, her sharp clean smell soothing the kind of pain that only parents of lost children comprehend. After a while she said, "In Jesus' name we pray, Amen." I sat up straighter and felt oddly relieved. The cap of her sleeve was dark with my tears.

"I know it hurts," she said, still holding my hand. "Losing a child is the worst sort of pain."

"I thought you and Tiny didn't have children. Sorry, I didn't mean to blurt that out."

"We didn't," she said. "But I remember how it was for Joseph when your mom left with you. He never really did get over it. And not many people know it, but once I lost a baby."

"I'm so sorry. What happened?"

Lutie smiled. "Sometime I'll tell you that story."

17

My ears roared with Nova's angry words and the slapping sound of the screen door. I was numb. By dusk I wasn't feeling much like practicing tough love. She should have come back by now. The daylight had faded, and I imagined the harsh desert swallowing her whole. Coyotes, snakes, even Linc Jackson were some of the dangers that raced through my mind. But what could I do? We'd already alerted the sheriff's office, where a female deputy had told me not to worry, that Nova would show up when she cooled off. Finally I went to the bedroom, where I gazed at the portrait of my father, smiling in his cowboy outfit.

Once I'd read somewhere, "Stand in the middle of the pain." So I did this until, like some warrior being tested to the limits of his strength, I sank down to my knees. I fell back upon the chenille bedspread, stared up at Nova's plastic stars and hoped Tru didn't come looking for me soon.

My dreams must have pitied me, because I didn't remember any of them in the morning. After getting dressed, I concentrated on how Nova would show up any minute, pouting, hungry, and impossible as always. I went to the window, looking for signs of movement. Her hair, I thought, pulling on a light jacket. Purple hair would be easy to spot. I rushed out the door, and I heard whispers of my own thoughts. *Where are you, Nova? Please come back to me. To us.*

I went as far out as I dared, stopping on top of a berm next to the creek. I scanned the horizon. The water was as dark and immutable as it had been the day we arrived, and gurgling sounds near the banks taunted me. I was a hypocrite—a horrible mother. Last week I'd allowed dinner at Rubin's to go way past my intentions. When I should have been watching my daughter, I'd been caught up in an infatuation with the guy next door. If I'd been paying attention, I might have prevented the fire.

Nova would probably agree with my miserable assessment. But she wasn't here. Suddenly, I missed her constant stream of sighs and "whatevers," her doomsday predictions, and sarcastic remarks. I ached to stroke her woolly hair—orange or purple—watch her paint rainbows on her nails, and kiss her nose. I called her name until my throat ached, but there was no reply. Even after I'd gone back home and phoned every soul for miles around, I sat up late, on the edge of hysteria. I was too exhausted to cry, so I tried my own brand of prayers. God seemed far away. Unlike the authority my aunt had when she called upon the Almighty, I felt as if I were speaking to a frightening and distant deity. Most of my efforts at intercession came out as "please, please." In between prayer and pleading I listened for Nova's familiar sounds, hoping the screen door would creak open in the middle of the night.

For three days I thought of little except my missing daughter. Nothing else mattered, although I had to act quickly on what I knew about the burial mound. I'd called the Warm Springs

Tribal Council to find out about laws against selling artifacts and learned about the NAGPRA law. The initials stood for Native American Graves Protection and Repatriation Act. It was a federal law passed in 1990. Apparently, the FBI routinely investigated stolen pieces, and there were stiff penalties for dealing in Native American grave goods. But I also learned that East Coast and European collectors paid top dollar for rare or ancient finds—the older the better.

Later, Lutie and I sat close together on the sofa and opened her photo albums. The faces of people I didn't recognize stared back at me. Beneath each photo, handwritten in a neat script, a caption listed names and places and the occasional date. The earliest one was undated. It was a picture of a brave, yet sad, great-grandmother of obvious Native American heritage. Anna, her name had been, and the caption said she had died at age twenty-six of a tumor.

The photography made it difficult to see too much detail. In some the lighting was poor or the shot had been taken from so far away that I couldn't make out features. Others were torn or faded or fragmented in some way—a little like the Ponds in general.

Especially my father. Was Joseph Pond the real daddy I never knew, the one who should have watched me grow? I'd asked myself this so many times. One day, probably next week I used to think, he'd call me on the phone and beg me to forgive him. He died before I had the chance.

I flipped through the album, running my fingers across the photos. Now I'd found what was left of him, and in the process, I had lost my own daughter. I began to sob once more.

Lutie patted my shoulder. "He'd get to feeling bad about losing you, and he'd call us in the middle of the night, just to see if I'd heard from your mom."

I sniffled and wiped my eyes.

Lutie handed me a tissue. "Stay tough, now, and the Lord won't let us down."

Through all of this my mind kept straying back to Nova. Linc's threats didn't matter until I found her. I'd called everyone we'd ever known, but so far she hadn't surfaced. I reported her as a runaway, and Lutie prayed with the church ladies. By now, Murkee would be awash in gossip, but I didn't care.

Tru didn't say much. He was as quiet as Jim, who now nuzzled up against me at the oddest times. If the phone rang, I started with dread and joy. I'd combed the area on foot as far as I could walk. Nothing.

My vision narrowed until I saw my daughter in everything. Once I could have sworn I heard her voice over the rattle of the shower pipes, but it turned out to be Tru, asking for five dollars through the bathroom door. I was so shaken that I'd rinsed again to shower away the sharp smell of disappointment.

"So do I get the money?" When I emerged Tru still stood there, a large claw hammer hanging from a too-big tool belt, hanging around his waist. I was wrapped in my green robe with a shell pink towel wound around my hair. He smiled and said I looked like a giant ice cream cone.

"Ice cream?" I said, trying to sound normal through the catch in my throat. "You want five bucks for ice cream?"

Tru pushed up his glasses. "No, Mom, it's for nails. Tiny says we're going to need more nails."

"Nails? What are you two up to this time?"

"We're building Aunt Lutie's sun porch. I drew the plans from some pictures we pulled off the Web. Tiny's got these rolls of screen out in the yard—had them forever, he says. That's where he got the idea in the first place."

He followed me to the bedroom where I fished a bill out of my wallet. "Here," I said, "But be careful. You ever swung a hammer before?"

"Aw, Mom."

"Try not to smash your fingers, okay?"

He dashed off with the money, probably to avoid any further mothering. I couldn't help it, though. He was my baby, and I wasn't about to let this one get away. There is a place in every mom's heart, I imagine, where she keeps her offspring forever as children, innocent and eager to be nurtured. I was no different. Both my children could grow up all they wanted, but I would best remember their formative years. Someday I'd tell stories to their children, and I'd remember only what was true: that they were the greatest kids in the world.

Still in my robe and turban, I sat on the edge of the bed and longed to haul out the baby pictures and the school photos that I knew were here somewhere, most likely in the bottom of one of the packing boxes Tiny had stored for me. Chaz tried to get away with more than his share of our albums, but I'd discovered his plan and rescued my half. Dividing up family portraits gets ugly. Who wants to look at people with their heads neatly snipped out of the picture?

I'd kept most of the milestone photos—shots of first steps and first bikes, rationalizing that Chaz had usually been off at some gallery gala. Now I thought of Nova and her fourth-grade ballet recital, the sea foam green tutu and tiara and satin toe shoes, although they weren't really on toe yet. She'd worn an angelic smile, and in those days I would have bet on her future sainthood.

My daughter, the one who had pasted dandelions on scraps of construction paper to present to me on Mother's Day, was missing. The bed we'd had to share here, lately so sharply divided, had once been a sanctuary, where she'd cuddled next to me after a bad dream.

I jerked back to reality; time was running out. I dressed hurriedly and raked a comb through my hair. The air would dry it and evaporate my tears as well. Today I needed to check in with the police station where I'd reported Nova's disappearance and find out if they had anything new.

Perhaps I'd show them more photos or an article of clothing that still carried her scent. I'd taken to sleeping with her Grateful Dead t-shirt. The faint aroma of my daughter relaxed me when no amount of Tylenol PM or even the sedatives from Doc Perkins helped. I stuffed the shirt into my purse.

Outside, the yard rang with the clattering and banging sounds of men at work. Tiny and my Truman, the once shy boy who reconfigured computers but couldn't keep a toothpick sculpture from falling apart, hoisted boards onto sawhorses like seasoned construction workers. My son looked taller and more at ease with himself.

"Measure twice and cut once," Tiny said.

"Sixty-five and three-eighths," Tru said. I couldn't tell whether he smiled at his own math skills or was simply entertained by the loud snap of the metal tape measure. Either way, he looked adorable.

"Okay, then, we're ready to cut."

"Careful, Unc," Tru cautioned. "We can't afford any accidents."

Tiny leaned over with a handsaw and began to rip the board. His trademark red suspenders kept his pants up— pants now baggier than when we'd first met. I understood now what Tru had meant by "accidents."

Since Tiny's coma, Tru had been helping his uncle, reminding him about diet, glucose testing, and injections when they might have been conveniently forgotten. Tru had researched diabetes mellitus on the Internet. No doubt he'd learned how difficult it is for wounds to heal and how diabetics must always protect their extremities. A cut or bruise could be serious, and my son knew it.

I watched them work. They chatted, but Tru didn't prattle; he only asked questions that Tiny answered in a straightforward manner. They made an impressive team, smooth as a machine with all the gears in working order. It was hard to believe the two of them weren't blood relatives.

They both loved tinkering with junk and watching bad TV show reruns, and neither my uncle nor my son was prone to irritability or meanness. I didn't count sibling rivalry; there was nothing extraordinary about his boyish brand of harassment. Tiny and Tru didn't appear to know how to grow bitterness, the way some people do. Lately, I'd teetered on the edge of rancor with Linc and Chaz bugging us again. But each time I looked at Tru I leaned a little more toward letting go and reminded myself I'd carried resentment long and far enough.

Tru held the two-by-fours in place as his uncle hammered. I'd never realized how strong the big man really was; nails almost melted into place with only a few bangs of the hammer. It wasn't long before they'd framed in a wall. I was amazed that it stood upright. I was still admiring their work when the long driveway's gravel crunched under the weight of a massive diesel pickup.

Linc Jackson braked, slammed the truck's king cab door, and strode through the oven-door fence and up the path. His face and neck were redder than usual, and a toothpick bobbed up and down as he worked his jaw muscles. I prayed Rubin hadn't shot any more cows.

"Mornin'," Tiny said, through a mouthful of nails. Sometimes I wished my uncle was as ornery as the rest of us.

"Lutie," he hollered, "bring us some iced tea, please, would ya? Linc's here."

Linc didn't acknowledge the greeting. Instead, he took off his hat and waved it at the newly framed-in wall. "What in the world do you call that?"

"We're building a sun porch," Tru announced importantly.

"That?" Linc laughed, but it was a cold laugh. In the harsh sunlight he looked older than I remembered. He reached out and shook the wall, and it did start to lean a little. Tiny stepped over and laid his hand on Linc's shoulder.

"I think you best back off." My uncle loomed above him and didn't remove his hand until Linc let go of the board.

"That's not why I'm here, anyway," Linc said, stepping back. He stuck his hat back on his head, perhaps to hide the stark white strip of forehead where the sun couldn't reach. He turned to where I stood outside the trailer door. "You," he said, pointing right at me. "This is your fault."

"What are you talking about?"

"None of this would have happened if you hadn't shown up here."

"You're not making sense." I tried to be polite, but my heart banged against my ribs.

"I'll tell you what makes sense," he said, his cheeks turning dark and red. "It makes sense for you to accept my generous offer and go back to where you came from. You and that little harlot of a daughter." You could practically see smoke coming from his ears.

I narrowed my eyes. "My daughter? What's Nova got to do with this? If you know where she is—"

"You tell me. Marvin got this call last night—my caller ID says it came from a pay phone in Portland. Now he's gone, and so is my Caddy. He's run off to meet her in my brand new car. I just drove it home yesterday. I'm holding you responsible."

He was bellowing now, his voice hollow and hoarse. His hat trembled slightly as his finger jabbed the air to punctuate each phrase. I had no idea how far he would go. People get shot every day over even minor issues.

Lutie ran out when the shouting started, gathered Tru, and took him inside. On the way Lutie glared back at Linc, as if to control him with her piercing stare. I tried my best to stay calm, but I felt my insides harden with fury.

"Give me that number," I said in my coolest tone. "My ex-husband lives in Portland. I'll notify him right away. I want my daughter back as much as you want your Cadillac." I blurted out the last part without thinking.

"Think you're pretty cute? You don't know who you're dealing with. I own most of this town. Before long I'll own you and the creek too. Jonto's not the only one with a shotgun around here." By now he was in my face, and he hadn't stopped shouting.

"You don't scare me," I yelled, tasting the angry words. "You couldn't rip off my father, so now you're trying to destroy us. I say Marvin better watch himself, because my daughter is underage." My voice quivered. "Anything happens, and I'll shoot you myself."

Linc shook his head. "That's it. I've been holding back, but you leave me no choice. I'm going to see the water rights judge and settle this once and for all."

I stuck out my chin and looked him right in the eyes, even though I was scared spitless. I'd never been a violent person, but he had just called my daughter a harlot. I lunged forward and wanted to pummel Linc Jackson, but Tiny held me back.

My uncle had been standing next to me throughout my tirade, still toting a load of boards under one massive arm.

"I said, back off, Jackson." Uncle Tiny firmly pushed Linc away from me. My knees shook and threatened to give out but I stood my ground. "Get off my place." This time Tiny sounded dead serious.

"Pretty soon this won't be your place, you big ox." Linc shoved back, and Tiny tripped backwards over one of the tire planters, dropping the heavy wood onto one of his feet. My uncle grabbed his foot and sagged against the side of the trailer as Linc Jackson swaggered past the oven-door fence to his truck, knocking over a stack of bicycle parts as he went. The gravel sprayed like spittle under the tires as he backed up and drove away.

Tiny unlaced his boot as Lutie and Tru flew out the door to help him. His foot was bleeding, where a nail had punctured the top of his big toe. My son's fears about Uncle Tiny injuring himself had come true, but it had been no accident.

Joseph's Journal
October 1999

Most days I remember too much. I remember how the Ponds—Desmond and Geraldine—took Lutie and me in. They taught us to love God. I married and had a beautiful daughter, but your mother left because I couldn't stay away from the drink. The company putting up the dam paid me to go away after concrete claimed two of my fingers.

I bought a home out in the Oregon desert, near the Warm Springs reservation. By then it was too late. I already had liver problems that could kill a man. I couldn't turn my back on God no matter what was taken from me, except for you. Losing you put a sinkhole in the middle of my soul.

Finding you never quite leaves my mind, and the liver disease is taking its toll. But lately I've been fighting another battle too. The neighbor wants me to sell the place to him—strange for a man who owns most of the town.

The neighbor—Linc is his name—says even the creek belongs to him.

I have my own theory; he knows as much about artifacts as I do. I'm sure he's been out here digging. I photographed the items. And then I left the important pieces—the Warm Springs root stick and that arrowhead—where Linc couldn't miss them. Sure enough, now they're gone. Fat cats and collectors pay thousands for these things, and I've seen the glint of covetousness in Linc's eyes. I've watched him go from friendly to fury in a heartbeat.

I sacrificed the artifacts to bait him, but Lutie begs me to stand clear of the trouble. Live and let live, she says. I've never been one to stay quiet. I'll tell anyone who'll listen. These days that's mostly no one. Someday they'll say we should have taken heed of that drunken Indian. Then it'll be too late. The burial site—whether it's really ancient pre-Clovis or just sacred to Native Americans—will disappear. If that happens, a piece of our heritage is lost. The mound will fall silent.

Muri, when I close my eyes I wonder where you are today. I pray you're strong, and I hold your name up to heaven. I hope you take this small but holy land and stream and protect them as I tried to protect them. Sadness washes over me when I think of how little I know you.

I know Linc Jackson well enough. He says he's interested in the good of the community, but some kind of craving possesses the man. Linc calls me Chief. Things have gone downhill since then, but maybe it's fitting. A good chief protects and leads his people. That's all I've tried to do.

18

"Sweet Jesus," was once again all Lutie could say. Questions raced through my head, like ants running in all directions when the nest has been disturbed. Even after Linc's departure, I could still feel the fine hairs on my neck raised.

Tru and I helped Tiny hobble inside. Lutie followed her husband to where we made him lie on the old sofa, and she sat with his foot propped on her lap. I tended to his wound with the disinfectant and some sterile pads, and Lutie fussed and fretted as if he were the prodigal son. Tru got out the literature we'd brought home from the hospital and read me the parts about treating diabetic foot injuries.

"This is quite a puncture," I said, knowing full well he'd need a tetanus shot. You know Dr. Perkins will want to see you, don't you?"

"We don't need to bother Perkins," Tiny said with a grimace. "Just smarted, that's all. Surprised the daylights out of me." He smiled, but I thought he looked pale.

"You old goat," Lutie said, smiling through deep worry lines. "Now you'll just have another excuse to lie around and watch that darn TV." Her eyes glistened with unshed tears.

Everything had happened so fast that I only now wondered why she hadn't gotten into the fray with me. At the Fourth of July barbecue, she'd hauled off and socked Linc without hesitation. But today she had gone inside with Tru, perhaps thinking more of his protection than I had.

"'Green Acres,' here we come," Tiny said to Jim, who lay on the floor next to his master.

Tru gave me an anxious look. "He going to be okay?"

"I'll be fine," Tiny said.

"How do you know?"

"You worry too much," Tiny answered.

I stroked Tru's head and noticed that my hands trembled. "Let Uncle Tiny alone, will you? We'll make sure the doctor sees him soon."

My son ducked away from my attempt to console him. "That Jackson guy stinks," he said, walking back toward the door. "This whole thing stinks!" He stormed outside and I could hear sounds, as if he was knocking the stuffing out of something. I thought I should go after him to address appropriate displays of anger, but then I laughed at myself. I was the she-bear who had been ready to take on Linc Jackson after he insulted my cub.

The delayed rush of adrenaline rattled me inside and out. I shook so uncontrollably that my teeth chattered, and when it subsided, fatigue took over. I felt limp and wished I could crawl off someplace and just blend in with the walls.

"We *will* go to the clinic as soon as we get in touch with the doctor," I promised, when I was less jittery. After Tiny's last episode we couldn't take any chances.

"It's just a scratch—really," Tiny said. "I'll have that sun porch done in no time, my Pearl."

Lutie glared at him and wagged her finger. "Oh, now hush up and take a rest." She picked up his foot and examined it.

"And if I see one red streak—" She leaned her head against the serape on the back of the couch and closed her eyes.

"Hand me the remote," he said.

Rubin's truck is a bumpy ride, I thought all the way over to the highway. I'd decided to go to Portland and hunt down Nova, and now Rubin was driving us there. If Tiny's pickup hadn't quit running and my van hadn't burned, I would have gone by myself. Yet, I had other motives—the arrowhead and heart-shaped rock were safe in my bag, along with Dad's photos and notes.

I knew almost nothing about Native American artifacts and desperately needed a professional opinion. Rubin's friend had mentioned his work during the Fourth of July bash. *Darrin? Davey?* I couldn't remember the guy's name, but he was an archaeologist for Portland State. What were the odds? Rubin had called ahead and after stopping in at Chaz's, we would be meeting with the professor and his wife.

The barren terrain surrounded us mile after mile until we drove over the mountains. We were almost to the interstate before Rubin coaxed his truck up to fifty-five. I sat quiet most of the way, as a Nova-shaped pain ate its way through my heart, but as we drove into the metro area, I tried to act sociable. The old GMC pickup's vibrations tickled my throat when I spoke.

"Thanks for convincing your friend to meet with me. What was his name again?" I leaned against the passenger side door.

Rubin had rolled down his window, so he had to shout above the wind. "Denny. Dr. Dennis Moses. He said he'd love to help out. He's part of the Warm Springs tribe, remember?"

"Okay, it's all coming back now." Since July, I'd learned a lot about Northwest tribes. "How incredible is it that you know a real archaeologist! I looked on the Internet, and amateurs and kooks are everywhere."

"Denny's the real deal. He likes to joke that he's the only Indian he knows with tenure. He's been in the news lately, too, for his work in finding pre-Clovis coprolites."

I sat up straighter. "You're kidding?" My mouth hung open at the mention of pre-Clovis, and a chunk of the guilt that sat on my shoulders suddenly lifted. Stopping the burial mound investigation to look for Nova had felt like a no-win situation, but perhaps luck—I hoped Lutie would forgive me for calling it that—was on my side.

Rubin smiled. "You *do* know what a coprolite is, don't you?"

I nodded. "I'm a librarian, aren't I? A coprolite is petrified poop." It sounded silly, but finding coprolites proved where people settled, what their diet had been, and offered other information vital to the study of ancient peoples. Pre-Clovis? I hadn't mentioned that part of my father's notes to Rubin. For a moment I felt as if something better than luck had fallen my way. "I brought along the rock I found out by the creek," I told him, patting my handbag, "in case it's more than just a rock."

"Of course," Rubin said. "If not, I'm always glad to visit Denny and his wife and kid. I'm the baby's godfather, but it's always so hard to get away. Good thing I found someone to take care of my place while we're gone."

He'd hired this know-nothing kid named Art Fuchs with a preppy haircut and an overbite. Art was thrilled about the emus. Rubin warned him that they could be a handful. I thought it was weird to be thrilled over five-foot birds.

As we crossed into the Portland city limits, I listened to the traffic's white noise. It was good to see real green again; the lushness of the landscape felt like a cool drink: *a watered garden.*

"Ah, Portland," Rubin said. "Some days I'm so tempted to move back up here. Except for the rain, I mean. That reminds me. You find out anything new about the business with Linc?"

I wasn't quite ready to tell Rubin everything. Not yet. I shook my head. "The minute we find Nova," I said, "I'm all over it."

Today was sunny—brilliant, really—and we concentrated on the dark blue-greens of the trees, lighter-hued ferns and mosses, and splashes of yellow scotch broom. Had this been a vacation trip, the ripples in the Willamette River might not have reminded me of tears.

By lunch hour, the city buzzed with neon and traffic. I hadn't heard sirens for months now, I realized, and their distant wails upset me the way a crying baby does. I was glad I wasn't driving. I'd lived away from Portland for only a few months, but negotiating freeways now seemed frightening.

Rubin eased the truck into the flow on another freeway, and I turned my face toward the air rushing through the window, listening. "Show me," I whispered, "please tell me where to look for Nova." There was only a deep wide hole in the sky where I'd rubbed it raw with my thoughts, and I closed my eyes. Finally, I numbed myself against its silence. No one answered.

"Up in the hills, right?" Rubin said, negotiating the tricky twists and turns of Oregon's largest city. Finally, he asked me for the house number again and turned up the street. We climbed a steep road leading to a gated driveway.

"Wow," he said. "Your ex must not be doing too bad."

"It's got more to do with Victoria, his sugar mama—I mean, girlfriend. It's her house. Maybe we should call first?"

"Getting cold feet?"

"I'm scared to death."

"I could turn around."

"No, I have to do this. I loathe that woman." I yanked on the truck's rearview mirror, surveyed myself, and groaned. Just like Muriel in *The Accidental Tourist*, I felt like saying, "I look like the wrath of God." I didn't, though. I was nothing like that character. Geena Davis had been much too attractive for that movie role.

"You look marvelous," he said, maybe picking up my thought waves or maybe just my grimace. "Mah-velous."

"Right."

"Don't worry. I've got your back. Take a deep breath."

"Let's get this over with."

The house was *dank*, as Nova would say. That meant it was fancy, not moldy. Victoria had cleaned up in real estate a few years back and could afford to dabble in hobbies such as art and my ex-husband. I wasn't sure if I disliked her more for the two face-lifts she bragged about—the last one made her eyes appear catlike—or because she treated Chaz as if he had no brain.

My ex looked a little smarter today, even though he was obviously surprised that I showed up at the house. I drew in my breath when he opened the door. He was dressed in a sleeveless undershirt and Nike jogging shorts. His hair was rumpled, even at five in the evening. Chaz Devereaux was still good-looking in an artsy sort of way.

"Muri." His voice came out froggy, and he coughed. I'd never liked that sound. Even now his constant throat clearing irritated me. He couldn't really help it, I knew, but it annoyed me all the same.

"I've come about Nova."

He rubbed his eyes with the heels of his hands and blinked. "I figured," he said, now realizing I wasn't alone. "Who's this?"

Rubin stepped forward and introduced himself as my neighbor. I began to hear a slight edge in my voice, one that longed to slice to bits any fool who came too close. I needed Chaz's help, so I stayed calm. "Has she contacted you?" My eye twitch was acting up.

"Haven't heard a word," Chaz said, stroking his graying goatee.

"It's for real this time," I continued. "I'm worried sick. I've already reported her as a runaway and phoned all her friends."

Inside I was less diplomatic. *Let's hear it, idiot. What's your big plan?*

"Chaz?" Victoria appeared wearing a royal purple pants outfit. Not a bleached hair was out of place. She was taller than Chaz. "Oh, it's you," she said to me.

Later Rubin would comment on the "big ice" dangling from Victoria's finger. I noticed it, too, but as we sat on creamy Italian leather sofas, I kept quiet. I wanted to keep this meeting short and to the point.

Still, I couldn't help thinking about the strangeness of the whole thing: I'd been willing to sell our home, just to be rid of Chaz, and now I'd ended up in a trailer out in the desert. He was living the high life, a kept man. I made a mental pledge to make sure he paid all the capital gains tax on our house, which would be coming due soon. And I vowed never to give Chaz a cent toward the loan with my stepfather, Benjamin.

"I thought she would show up here for sure," I began, after politely accepting Victoria's offer of cappuccino. "She hasn't at least called?"

"You don't think I'd know if my daughter called?" Chaz said. He acted as if being an artist gave you license to offend people. He had put on a pair of ratty jeans but no shirt.

"This is the longest she's ever been gone," I said, after he tried to change the subject. "Get serious, will you? I'll call all her friends, alert the Portland PD. You—"

"Remember, we're flying to New York tomorrow," Victoria said, returning with a tray bearing steaming coffee cups. She turned to me, waggling her fingers, that ridiculous ring bobbing up and down. "Everyone will be there. It'll launch our gallery into the upper atmosphere."

We. Our. I sat there, split in two. One side of me had seen Chaz for who he was and knew beyond a doubt that we didn't love each other. I'd moved on with my life, which in no small way included Rubin Jonto. The other part of me clung to the ghost of a family unit that no longer existed.

Rubin spoke for me. "What Muri's saying is we need to work together. You want to see your daughter end up working the street or worse?"

"Don't go there, buddy." Chaz was paying attention now.

"Get the point then," I said. "How about you help out by providing the missing kids networks a recent picture? And call the cops. The last contact was made from a pay phone in Portland."

"She called?" Chaz stared at me, surprised.

I tried to explain. "Her friend, the grandson of another neighbor of *ours*, is missing as well. He called a couple of days ago." I could play the game too.

"He? She's with a guy? I'll kill him." He added an expletive.

"All I care about is getting her back safely." My throat constricted. "And stop swearing at me."

Victoria broke in. "We'll do what we can." You could practically hear her wondering how soon they'd be rid of us.

Chaz was even more disgusting. "I know some people."

I gave him my best stern librarian look. "Yeah? Well, I know some 'people' too; by the end of the day they'll have flyers made and a phone chain going. You think you can manage to tack up a few of them before you fly to New York?"

"You know I will."

"Really?"

"You're still as big a nag as ever." Chaz stood and paced the off-white carpet in his bare feet. "If you get this ridiculous loan with Benjamin figured out, I might be able to keep my head above water. Sell that crummy property, and we'll both be happy."

The whole room turned glacial, and time stood still. Nobody moved or breathed for about three seconds long. Finally, somebody sighed.

I stood up. "Come on, Rubin. We have work to do." I narrowed my eyes and steeled my jaw and didn't say so much as good-bye to Victoria.

19

"I'm so sorry, Rubin," I said. "This mess is getting worse every minute." I felt selfish after my scene with Chaz and hadn't meant for Rubin to get caught in the cross fire.

I rubbed my temples where they ached. Here I was, tangled in a bunch of trouble I hadn't counted on, dragging people I hardly knew into the web too. Would Murkee hold me responsible for bringing calamity upon their little community? And what about Rubin?

In spite of Nova's disappearance, the artifacts inside my bag stole my attention. I could almost hear my father whispering, urging me to uncover the truth before it was too late. "Let's get over to your friend's place," I said. We piled back into Rubin's truck.

Until today Nova's disappearance hadn't seemed real. Lutie always reminded me that it was fine to feel awful if you had a reason. "Just don't let it rule your life," she'd say. "And giving up your problems to the Lord never hurts, neither." In the truck I bowed my head and pictured myself launching a ton of troubles heavenward as we made our way through the maze of Portland neighborhoods that were no longer home to me.

Twenty minutes later we pulled up to a yellow two-story house trimmed in various hues of lilac, hunter green, and red. "This could be Eugene," I said, referring to the Oregon college town still stuck in the sixties. "I didn't know they were hippies."

"Professors," Rubin corrected. He banged on the door, solid oak with an oval of etched glass in its center. An enormous cat wound its way in and out of our legs.

Dr. Denny opened the door, his black hair in two neat braids reaching almost to his waist. "Ya-hey," he said to Rubin.

"Denny!" Rubin said, and they clapped each other's backs. Rubin turned to me. "Remember Muri?" Denny nodded, and we went inside. Delicate blown-glass sculptures crowded the surface of a vintage treadle sewing machine in the entryway. One glass piece, a milky peach color, reminded me of an angel. After a few moments, Denny's wife, Gwen, descended the staircase on one side of the foyer.

She hugged Rubin. "You promised you'd come sooner," she said, laughing and tugging on his ponytail. "The baby's nearly a year old now, and her godfather has only seen her a few times."

Rubin grinned. "You got me, Mama. Leila won't even recognize me."

Gwen hugged me too. "Rubin told us about what's been going on with your neighbor." She shook her head. "Guy sounds like a mean old cuss."

"Mean's an understatement." I took my bag from my shoulder and unzipped the main compartment. "If Denny can help us, we might get the best of Linc." I dug around the purse's bottom.

"Of course Denny will help you," Gwen said. "But I've got supper on the stove, and it's just about ready."

I inhaled. "Smells wonderful."

Before Gwen could say more, a child's cry floated down from upstairs. "Just let me get her," Gwen said and trotted upstairs. Soon a giggling Leila appeared in her arms. I felt at home.

Gwen balanced the baby on one hip and gently touched my arm. "This must be awful for you," she whispered. "I can't imagine. We've been praying."

I thanked her and sat down at the table. She supplied me with hope, while stew simmering on the stove hissed a cloud of steam against the darkened windows.

After supper, Gwen put the baby to bed and we sat around the living room coffee table. The walls were decorated with Native American art. Something in me recognized the Indian flute and ceremonial drum that sat in one corner. I thought of the burial mound where my father had spent so much time.

Denny was eager to examine the items I'd brought. He was taller and wider than Rubin, but his voice was gentle and his eyes deep and black. His braids fell forward as he leaned over the low table. He examined the arrowhead and turned the rock over in his hands and then studied the photos. He scanned my father's notes, and I told him about the mound. For what felt like hours, he didn't say three words. I was so full of questions that I thought I'd burst. Rubin smiled at me and patted my hand.

Gwen went to the kitchen and brought out coffee while her husband deliberated over the items. After a while, Denny settled back in his chair, gazing at the ceiling as if he were choosing his words carefully. "Pretty impressive, I have to admit."

I couldn't hold back anymore. "What's impressive? What kind of stuff is this?" I sounded like Tru, even to myself. I jammed my shaking hands into my jeans' pockets.

Denny shifted toward me. "Rubin's told me some about the neighbor. He's trying to buy you both out?"

Rubin and I nodded. Rubin added, "Linc Jackson has never cared a whit for that land or the creek. For a while we thought he planned to build a golf course or a resort, but then he took off. Just like that. He was gone for years."

"Four years, eleven months to be exact," I said. "Just shy of the time when his water rights would have expired." Gwen's coffee was delicious, but I'd already drunk too much that day. I could barely control my jitters. "Only Linc wasn't intent on taking water."

Denny looked directly at me. "Your dad—he was half Nez Perce, right?" He didn't wait for me to answer. "From what he wrote in here, I think he knew what he'd found. A Warm Springs burial site, that's definite."

I pointed to the heart-shaped stone. "What about this? I'm not sure if it's an implement or just a funny-looking rock."

Dennis held the rock. "We'd have to date it, but I can tell you that this is more than just 'funny-looking.' The stone has marks that tell me they didn't occur naturally. Maybe some type of hoe or ax."

Rubin glanced at me. "You've got a good eye," he said. "I'll have to take you prospecting."

Denny held up the arrowhead. "This piece, especially," he said. "See the way it's made?"

Prickles rose on my neck. "Is it obsidian?"

Denny shook his head. "This piece is a burgundy chert blade."

"Chert?"

"It's a form of silica," Denny explained patiently. "See how fine the flakes are knapped?" We all took turns examining the arrowhead. Denny ran his fingers across its base. "Nice basal thinning," he said. "A fine specimen."

Gwen laughed. "You lost me. I'll stick to glassblowing."

I could have listened all night. "No wonder my father was so protective of the creek."

Rubin leaned back on the sofa. "And why Linc's bent on taking over the area."

Denny smiled faintly. "Like I said, it'll need testing, but it may pre-date the Northwest tribes altogether—might even be Solutrean or pre-Clovis."

Rubin stared at me. "Pre-Clovis?"

My heart nearly pounded out of my chest.

It was one of the saddest good-byes I'd ever faced. I hadn't located my runaway daughter, and I'd rediscovered some ugly things about my ex-husband. But I'd also found Denny and Gwen, who sent us off with a hamper of fruits and multi-grain bread for the trip home.

They hugged us both, and then Gwen pulled a small object wrapped in tissue paper from her jacket pocket. She held it out to me.

"For you, Muri," she said, unwrapping a small figurine. The same peach-colored blown glass angel I'd noticed in the foyer glittered in her hand.

I took it from her carefully. The angel's spun glass wings caught the glint from the porch light. "Thank you," I said, unable to think of anything else to say.

"We thought you needed an angel." Gwen said. "I'll wrap it so it doesn't break." She went inside and quickly returned with some of that plastic bubble wrap the kids love to pop. She gently packed the angel, and I tucked it into my bag, careful not to let it rest against the heart stone. We said our good-byes, and the couple stayed on the porch until we rounded the corner. If there really were angels running around on earth, I could say I'd met some pretty awesome examples.

20

The tires hummed on the grooved pavement as we headed back to Murkee. The freeways were packed with travelers, and Rubin's truck was swept along like a can of tuna on a crowded conveyor belt. All I could think about was how alone I felt.

Loss has such a curious way of turning things upside down. One moment I believed Nova would return safely; the next I was sure my heart wouldn't last another minute unless she appeared. I rested my head on the back of the seat and counted what blessings I could think of.

We left the rain far behind, and the desert sunshine felt welcome. The sky was that dazzling fall blue, with only a few distant clouds, the kind of spectacular panorama they photograph for travel magazines. The juniper, sage, and scrubby pines looked as comforting and familiar as the red earth that surrounded us. Even the wind wasn't blowing as fiercely as I remembered. As we drew closer to Murkee a hawk swooped out of the late afternoon shadows and plummeted out of the sky. Its talons grabbed at something but missed.

I imagined my father whispering to me, dispensing hope as he reminded me how much he loved me. The father I'd once foolishly believed was a real angel now seemed to reach out to me, assuring me that an everlasting and loving Father awaited me, if only I'd allow Him in. I'd teetered on the edge of falling apart since Nova's disappearance. I couldn't tell if this daydream was a genuine invitation from God or another slice of craziness from a despairing mother. I looked over at Rubin and smiled.

"Thanks for going to Portland with me," I said. It was the first thing I'd said in a while.

Rubin rested his arm on the top of the bench seat. "I'm sorry we didn't find Nova."

I shrugged, holding back tears. "She'll come back. I've got to believe that."

"Anything I can do, just name it."

I smiled. "Friends like you and Denny and Gwen help."

"Friends, sure," he said, "but I've said before I wish we could be more than just friends." He squeezed my hand.

"And I said I'll let you know." I smiled to take away the sting of my words.

I was more determined than ever to find my daughter. I wasn't giving up on Nova or anyone else I loved. I think Joseph Pond would have wanted it that way.

As we drove across the creek the oven-door fence grinned like a Halloween pumpkin, and my life tumbled back at me. Lutie and Tiny and Tru and Jim spilled out the trailer door to greet us.

When I got out of the truck Tru's hug warmed me all over. "Mom!" he cried. I broke down at the sound of Tru's still child-pitched voice. He looked up at me through his glasses. He needed a haircut; I'd meant to take care of it before we left. A wordless sob held my throat. I tousled his hair, which he usually hated; but today he didn't complain. Then he looked into the cab. "You didn't find her?" His expression turned to disappointment. He leaned down to stroke Jim's ears.

"Not yet, but we're still on it, guy." Rubin stood beside me.

I felt as if I were Jack, explaining how I'd sold the cow for a handful of magic beans.

Tru had questions. "Is Nova going to get on *America's Most Wanted*?"

"She's not a criminal, honey. But don't worry, we'll find her."

"Mom, school starts next week, I don't even have gym shoes."

"I'm sure she'll be back before that," I said, hoping all of this would be history by then.

"I really, really, really need new Nikes." Tru was nine, all right.

"Oh, Lord, child," Lutie said, coming out of the screen door. She wore navy blue slacks and a pocketed smock today, as well as one of the crocheted baseball caps. Her wiry arms enfolded each of us in one of her sweet-smelling hugs. Tiny stepped up next, still limping a bit, and hugged us both too.

"Doc, your place has been hopping since you left," Tiny said, leaning against the hood of Rubin's truck. If not for those red suspenders his pants surely would have fallen down by now. "Them emus are mean as junkyard dogs. That's what that kid you hired says." Tiny laughed, a deep rumbling sound that made me feel secure. "He told me he definitely he will *not* specialize in birds." Tiny explained that several emus had escaped their pen.

"I believe it," Rubin said. "I'd better get over there to see what the damage is. No telling what else has gone wrong." He turned to me. "You'll be okay?"

"Of course, she will," Lutie said. "Tiny and Tru here will bring your bags. C'mon honey, we'll get you some iced tea."

"I'll check in with you later," Rubin said.

But he didn't come around much over the next few days, saying he had a lot of things to catch up on. I believed him, but it felt like someone had taken away my safety net, especially late at night when I needed support. Perhaps I'd become too quickly accustomed to having a man around again. Either way, it was unnerving.

No word came from Nova, but I received plenty of calls from the neighbors, passing along rumors and unsolicited advice. I even got a call from Dove down at the Mucky-Muck.

"Good grief, Muri, I'm sorry," she said. Here and there her scratchy voice was broken by a smoker's cough, but her words were soft. "Haven't held a town meeting in a blue moon until this past weekend. When I opened this morning, the back room was an awful mess."

"A mess? What happened?" I imagined that people had left the periodicals strewn about again or that kids had tipped over the book cart.

She coughed a long spell. I thought it sounded like bronchitis. "Excuse me. Got to quit those cancer sticks. I mean everything is just about ruined in there. Somebody threw books and magazines all over the floor, and half of it's wet. Smells like a brewery too. I'm just sick about it."

"I'll be over right away."

I got Tiny to drive me into town. The clutch on that heap was perpetually cranky, and his sore foot must have hurt to work the pedal. But he was glad to help, he said, and didn't complain.

"In fact," he said, grinding the gearshift into third, "it might be a good thing if I go down with you to Dove's place. After what's gone on with Linc, I worry about you a little." He stared straight ahead as we jounced along the road.

"Thanks," I said. I wanted to say something about how wonderful it was to have a family. Nobody had ever fussed over me this way. "That sun porch is looking so good, Uncle Tiny."

"You think?"

"I think."

He smiled at me through the black shock of hair that had fallen across one eye. Tiny had tuned into a Mexican station, and the mariachis rang out of the static-filled radio. I understood little but sensed it was a song full of life.

When we walked into the Mucky-Muck, the place was nearly empty. The after-church crowd had emptied out, and Dove was stuffing napkin dispensers. I'd been here long enough to learn her system by now. Next she would work on refilling the condiment bottles unless she had a customer. You could hear clattering in the kitchen, but I'd never seen the restaurant so deserted.

"Where is everybody?" I asked, dreading the answer. If Linc had been shooting off his mouth about me again, the regulars might be avoiding the café on account of me.

"Oh, most everyone's over at the rodeo in Prineville," Dove said. "Little Crystal Campbell's a ranked barrel racer, and half the town went out to see her." She looked away from me and coughed into her elbow. "Come on, and I'll show you the damage."

The stench of stale beer rushed out when she opened the door to the back room. The Murkee Library was in shambles. Dove laid a hand on my shoulder.

"I'm real sorry about this, Muri. You worked your behind off getting all this together."

Tiny walked up behind me. "Hoo-wee, smells like a beer bust in here."

Dove frowned. "Like I said, they held a town meeting last night—first one in six months."

I held my hand across my nose and mouth and fanned the air. "Town meetings always this rowdy around here?" I asked. Muddy cowboy boot prints crisscrossed the room.

Dove stared at the floor. "Linc had a lot to say about you and Doc Rubin last night," she said. Her voice dropped to a whisper. "You wouldn't really keep folks from using that creek, would you?"

I kneeled to pick up a soggy copy of *National Geographic*. "Of course not," I said. "In fact, my father offered to let Linc build a slough over to his place. Linc's not happy because Rubin and I won't sell out to him."

"That's not how Linc sees it, honey."

"So he gets people worked up about something he started?" I said.

"I'll get a mop." Dove left me alone with the footprints and ruined books.

I was tempted to sit down and do nothing. Instead, I picked up a droopy edition of *David Copperfield*. I'd bought this book in college. It still had my name written in the corner of the title page. In addition to being soaked through with beer, the pages had been slashed and gouged with something sharp. The entire scene reminded me of the morning after a college keg party.

Dove returned, hauling a mop and bucket, and scooted the trash barrel closer to me. "Toss the ones you can't save in here, and then we'll clean up this floor. Ugh, I hate walking on sticky stuff, don't you?" She pushed the wet mop across the linoleum.

"Think someone's sending me a message?" I asked.

She stopped the mop in midstroke and looked at me. "Linc Jackson owns this place," she said. "And what Linc says, goes. That's all I can tell you." She scrubbed at a stubborn spot, and her upper arms swished against her uniform. "Listen, honey,

I might as well be honest here. The library idea was great. It really brought in the customers."

"People seemed so excited. Rhonda Gaye has even started some kind of 'romance of the week' group."

Dove gave me a pitiful look, one that reminded me of the expression she wore the first time she met Nova. All that seemed like a hundred years ago now.

"I know," she continued. "Like I said, the library idea was great. But if you're going head-to-head with Linc Jackson, let's put it this way . . . he might run me out, too, for hiring you. And I'm too old to start over."

"Are you asking me to leave?" I tossed a stack of sodden magazines that thudded into the trash barrel.

"Wish I could say different," Dove said. "I can probably give you a few hours in the cafe. You can work the counter. I know you got a family to support." She leaned the mop against the sign on the door that said WELCOME TO MURKEE PUBLIC LIBRARY. "Got to get back out front," she said. "Lock up when you're done, will you?" The crepe soles of her white waitress shoes squeaked as she headed back to her salt-shakers and squeeze bottles.

I gathered what I could from the floor and draped some of the less damaged books and magazines over the backs of chairs. It would take hours to straighten out the mess, if it could be salvaged at all. Despite the fact that I'd been ordered to leave, I arranged the 1979 World Book Encyclopedias in alphabetical order and returned them to their shelf, all except for the "M" volume, which had several pages ripped from its middle. Later I would mend it with tape, glue its spine back in place, and it might function again. I wasn't as sure if I would be so lucky.

21

Luck wasn't something I'd come to treasure. At the high school where I'd kept watch over the library, there were always kids who had no place to go, or else what they called home was choked off with abuse of one sort or another. You tried to help the ones you could. Those students, whose names I couldn't remember, still haunted me with faces I could never forget. So-called luck had dealt me the roles of mother of missing children, protector of a Native burial site, and librarian of unreadable books.

What luck didn't know about me was that I wouldn't give up. Lutie said the devil ruled luck, that there was really no such thing, and it was just old Beelzebub dancing on your soul. I didn't know about that, but I was fed up with everything.

The next day was Labor Day. Since the café was closed, Lutie and I came back to clean up the library and save what was possible. The stink of the spilled beer no longer overwhelmed us, but the comic books that the kids loved were a pulpy mess. *Spiderman, Batman,* and *The Hulk* were totaled, so we tossed them all in the trash. But I refused to part with my C. S. Lewis books; I didn't care how badly *The Chronicles of Narnia* reeked of hops and yeast.

Lutie pitched another magazine toward the trash. "A person who'd do this is sick, just downright sick." She stopped for a moment, held her rubber-gloved hands up in fists. "And I'd punch that old coot again, as God is my witness."

"I'm sure you would," I said. I went over the floor with the mop again, this time with pine cleaner. "But then he might do something worse." I scrubbed harder, and my hair snaked loose from where I'd twisted it up.

"Well I know one thing," she said, "Joseph wouldn't have stood still for any of this. He didn't care if Linc needed our water to refill the oceans, which he didn't. My brother wasn't letting the likes of that mean old mule sell us all down the river. I wish he were here for you too."

I stopped mopping and stared at Lutie. My heart thudded against my chest like a load of those ancient encyclopedias hitting the floor, and I could barely speak. Before I knew it, I'd crumpled.

"All my life I dreamed about finding him, but I'm too late. And now I don't know what to do," I sobbed.

Instead of handing out a simple answer, Lutie turned over an empty five-gallon bucket and sat down. Her scrawny legs stuck out from her long denim skirt like a schoolgirl's, and she hiked the skirt up to her knees before she pulled me down and folded me into her arms. "Sh, now," Lutie whispered. "Sweet Jesus, comfort your baby girl."

I pulled away and stood up, swiping at my tears. "Jesus never helped me when I used to cry for my daddy, and he isn't going to help me now."

"I know you're hurting." Lutie stood up and closed the door to the room, then sat and arranged herself on the bucket once more. She leaned toward me. "Won't you let him ease your burden?"

I paced back and forth, leaving my footprints on the damp floor. "Aunt Lutie, I'm sure you mean well. But religion won't solve these problems with Linc. Prayers can't bring my father back. How can God help bring my daughter home?"

"Have you given him a chance?"

"I'm out of chances."

Lutie sighed. "Maybe you're not ready. But don't count the good Lord out."

"I'd make a lousy church person."

"I don't give a frosted belly button if you go to church," she said. "I'm sorry if you think that's all there is to it." She clasped her hands together, and I was afraid she'd start praying right then and there. "I shouldn't have brought it up."

"I shouldn't have bit your head off. Sorry."

Lutie got up and engulfed me in a hug. "Joseph loved you more than anything, sweet pea. And he wanted you to know God loves you too." She looked away. "But maybe you have to find that out for yourself."

"Oh, Aunt Lutie, I'm sorry about all of this. Maybe I shouldn't have come to Murkee." I wiped away tears. "I guess I'm stubborn."

"Just like your daddy." She smiled.

I rolled the chair into a corner; it belonged to Dove. Then I carefully peeled the Murkee Public Library sign from the door and tucked it beneath my arm.

On Tuesday I didn't tell anyone where I was going, not even Rubin. This time I wore my own rubber boots to the mound down by the creek and brought along an old stadium pillow to keep my jeans and favorite blue sweater from getting muddy. The heart rock and arrowhead were tucked into my pocket. I loved this spot as much as anybody now, and I justified the time I spent there by thinking of myself as shepherd-ess of the stream, or guardian angel of the stream, depending on how spiritual I felt. Any cow that wandered in here would regret it.

Dr. Denny had photographed and cataloged the artifacts, just as Dad had done. Now it was time to set the bait. I picked my way among the rounded stones and reeds at the water's edge and dug a shallow bed in an eddy, settled the arrowhead firmly in the silt, and pushed my special stone next to it, making sure the arrowhead caught the light. It was the per-fect spot for an amateur archaeologist to look.

"There," I said, "You can't miss it." I hoped no cows would uproot my trap, before Linc took the bait.

I thought about what Aunt Lutie had said about prayer and tried not to be irritated at her. Lately, she'd been more forth-right with her religion, like I'd have to agree with her brand of it now that I had so many thorny problems.

I hoped Dad hadn't been quite so melodramatic about his faith, but I suspected he was a "holy roller," as my mother had claimed. At least he wasn't ashamed of his beliefs or his heri-tage. Had it been hard for him to separate his Native spiritual leanings from his Christian ones? How had he managed to embrace his ethnic heritage and still hang onto faith that had come from the very people who had robbed Indians of their lands? Had he been like me, undecided in what—or whom—to believe?

I didn't really want to give up on God, although I wasn't sure whether he cared to help humans or let them stew in their own juices.

"Our Father, *my* father," I said to heaven or the air, "that's all I ever wanted to find." I sat there and listened for answers among the sounds around me. Were there whispers of my ancient relatives in the creek?

The water fell over the rocks where Rubin had submerged old tires for a fish habitat, but the burbling sounded more like a child's rhyme than profound wisdom from above. Golden leaves from the cottonwood silently parachuted to the water's surface like manna, and here and there a silvery fish broke through with a splat.

Behind me the so-called cattle-proof fence creaked in the breeze. A new metal sign read, No Grazing Allowed—for literate cows, I supposed. It swayed at the same tempo as the fence. It sounded like, "What if? What if?" That got me wondering if enticing Linc to steal my artifacts would be enough.

"What if," I asked a small frog perched on a rock near the bank, "what if I located one of Linc's buyers? There must be some sort of paper trail." That first day I'd seen him in the café, he'd acted like he owned the world. The thought of him standing a pickle upright in the middle of his sandwich still disgusted me. "Linc must know there's no way to keep supplying his sources without taking ownership of the whole area." The frog didn't smile. His throat only inflated and deflated, but he blinked as if he understood so I kept talking. "How'd he fake the certificates?"

The frog blinked again. To prove Linc stole the things I'd hidden, I'd either have to pose as a buyer or find the artifacts in his house. It was unlikely he'd invited me to his house for tea anytime soon. The frog didn't acknowledge my wit or my revelation and kerplunked into the water. I looked at my watch and realized I'd been talking to amphibians for half an hour. I wouldn't even have time to change before I went to town. I jogged back across the hill to the trailer, aware that these days the exercise didn't leave me short of breath.

My attorney George Kutzmore looked surprised. "You got here fast."

I smoothed back my hair. "Thanks for seeing me on such short notice," I said. "I've been frantic since Nova left."

"I'm so sorry about your daughter. Any word?"

"Not yet. But that's not why I'm here."

He offered me a seat, but I declined. "My father, as you probably know, was half Nez Perce."

He nodded. "Your aunt too."

"Yes. When I got here, I couldn't see why he'd spend so much time out at that creek, since it's not a Nez Perce area. It's more likely traditional Warm Springs or Paiute. But after I found some of Dad's old photos, I'm convinced."

George raised his snowy eyebrows. "Convinced?"

I could hardly explain fast enough. "Linc's told the whole town about his 'need' for the water in that creek, right?" I stepped closer to the desk. "Remember how we talked the first time we met that maybe water isn't all he's interested in after all?" I resisted the urge to pace and plunked down both Dad's photos and the ones Dr. Denny had taken.

George examined the pictures as deliberately as Denny had. Finally, he laid the pictures down like a winning poker hand and leaned back in his chair. He steepled his fingers and smiled at me.

"What?" I was not amused.

"You remind me of Erin Brockovich from that movie about nuclear waste, that's all."

"This is a serious matter, George. That area around the creek is an Indian burial site. We were right. My father was protecting it." I grabbed the photos and held them up. "This site is old—ancient, even. Dad knew it. I've consulted an archaeologist who dated two artifacts I found in the creek as possibly pre-Clovis. Do you know what that means?" I told myself to calm down and give George a break. I didn't understand everything, either.

But George was patient. "I've heard about pre-Clovis. There was a debate about it when they found Kennewick Man in Washington State," he said. "That would make these items more than ten thousand years old. But news travels so fast around here. How could Joe—or you, for that matter—dig up this stuff without somebody finding out?"

"We couldn't." I folded my arms and waited.

George's eyes lit up. "Somebody found out. Somebody named Linc Jackson?"

"Just call me Ms. Brockovich." I sat down and crossed my legs. "People thought Dad was seeing things, but he wasn't that far gone. One night he heard Linc's truck pulling away from the creek, and the next morning he found fresh excavations and tire tracks."

"How do you know all that?"

"I read it in his journal."

"Joe kept a journal?"

I nodded and leaned across the desk. "And some of the things Dad had cataloged and left at the site came up missing later—items that had been photographed, identified, and logged. An arrowhead, a stick for digging roots, and something else he didn't name."

"You think Linc's selling it on the black market?" George pulled out a legal pad, flipped to a clean page, and began taking notes.

I nodded. "Money . . . the root of all evil."

"Indeed," George murmured. "Lutie would correct us. The Bible says the root of all evil is the *love* of money."

"Linc must love money enough to pillage First Nation burial sites," I said. "He means to sell to the highest bidder."

George looked me in the eyes. "What did your research turn up?"

I stood up again and paced. "The Tribal Council told me that to legally sell Indian artifacts they must be accompanied by a properly notarized statement. Tribes must approve before a proof-of-ownership document can be issued. I haven't been to the county records department yet, but if Linc sold Indian artifacts, there must be notarized records. All I have to do is track them down."

"Linc's got some nerve."

"You've got that right," I muttered. I hadn't mentioned the vandalism at the library, nor Uncle Tiny's injury.

"I'm sorry about the tormenting you and Tiny have been taking lately."

"You know about the library?" Suddenly, I was aware that I was still dressed for mud, not for the library. I smoothed my ratty blue sweater as best I could, resisting the urge to pick at the pills.

He shrugged. "News travels fast around here. Sorry."

I shrugged. "I can't afford to worry about that right now. I also researched Native American grave laws."

"NAGPRA."

I nodded. "If we could prove he's faked papers in order to sell the artifacts, wouldn't he be in trouble?"

"Big trouble." George's enormous mahogany desk was littered with stacks of files and papers, but he apparently had a system. He plucked the Pond case file from the middle of a pile and opened it, mumbling portions aloud to himself. It struck me that my attorney had no secretary or legal assistant to help him wade through the mountain of documents. I glanced over at his framed credentials to reassure myself that George was a member of the Oregon Bar in good standing.

Yet Linc had tons of influence in Murkee. What kind of chance would we have? It sounded as if it came straight from a grade B movie, but Dove claimed Linc even had the sheriff in his back pocket.

"Linc managed to get his water rights using that four-years and eleven-months technicality. He's no dummy," George said. "His water rights document looks in order right down to the judge's signature."

"But what if he faked the documentation? Or what if he's hoarding the items Dad photographed and cataloged?"

Sunlight poked through the blinds and glinted on George's gray-blue eyes and silver hair. "Robbery? Hm. That might be best—to prove he stole from you or your dad. Linc must know Native American investigations are slow and hard to prosecute. He's a smart cookie." For all his small town ways, the attorney appeared capable and distinguished.

I blew out my breath with a huff. "That's what I'm saying . . . one giant *dishonest* cookie. I set a trap for him to see if he'll bite." If there were a shred of proof for what my father claimed, I'd find it.

George agreed that hiring a documents expert to prove forgery would be a lengthy and expensive process. "Sometimes it takes months to get a document analyzed," he said, "even when it's a priority, and I doubt we'd be at the head of the line. If you try to prove Linc stole artifacts, we need to guard against entrapment."

"What else can I do?" I said.

"Give it a try," he said. "But it won't be easy."

I smiled. "Things that matter are hardly ever easy."

George sighed. "If Linc is dealing Native artifacts on the black market, it'll shake this town to the core. In fact, if the ranchers around here believed it, well, I think they'd say

Linc ought to be hanged." George chuckled. "The law of the West."

"The law of the West? Rubin Jonto says if the people really cared about the land they wouldn't be so quick to let their livestock graze and trample it to death." I couldn't believe how political my statements sounded, even to me.

"Linc must know what he's up against," he said, shuffling the papers into an irregular stack. "We're too close to the Warm Springs reservation for sympathy with grave robbers. Nobody around here wants anything to do with stolen goods."

I resisted the urge to straighten the papers myself. "Do people around here truly believe Linc's on their side?"

"His name may be Jackson, but Linc's got Murkee in his veins. He keeps folks working, not to mention what he does for the ranchers. Folks trust him all right."

"And what about my father? Everybody think he was nothing but an old drunk who was seeing things?"

"Must be hard on you, coming out here after his passing."

"What you're saying is nobody took Joseph Pond seriously."

"Your father was a gentle, honest person who'd rather pray than cast aspersions. But he was in the last stages of alcoholism. I don't know what he saw."

A tear slid down my cheek, and I brushed it away. George offered me a tissue. "Maybe that's why I came here," I said, "—to prove everybody wrong. Tomorrow I'm going to the county seat to look for anything that smells fishy. I'll be in touch." I turned toward the door.

George stood up. "Wait. I have an old friend—former FBI man. He might have access to an expert, someone who'll do a rush job."

I could have hugged the man.

He smiled, and his eyes twinkled. "I'll get hold of my old pal today. Let me know if you need anything."

"Thanks, George. I owe you."

I smiled and breathed deeply on my way out of the office. Outside, a light autumn wind kicked dead leaves and red dust around at my feet. It occurred to me that I'd stared at the ground a lot lately. Maybe Lutie was right . . . maybe I should be looking up, waiting for an answer to our prayers.

Joseph's Journal
December 2005

They're all saying it now: Old Chief Joseph's got a couple of loose screws. A real nutcase. The old sot has gone 'round the bend. The spring of the year is when new life comes aboard, when the earth and God hand out second chances. But this year is so cold, so dry. Maybe the land and the good Lord are trying to tell me something. I know this much . . . change is in the air.

The creek is sacred. On both sides of the banks, all the way to the fence, the earth holds remains of the people who were here before all others. Some say the old ones are Nez Perce, but they don't know our story. Before the white man, we hunted a vast land, from the Blue to the Bitterroot Mountains. But this land was not ours.

I could show you, Muri. You must be old enough to carry so heavy a secret. The creek's bed and banks glitter with potsherds and dark lumps of charcoal from fire pits long ago: a kap'n, a stick worn to a dull point, used for digging roots; arrowheads; shreds of a camas basket; and a coprolite. I hid some of the treasure. A man at the university says they might pre-date the Clovis people. Tell no one about this.

Half of Murkee and your Aunt Lutie think your daddy's gotten carried away again. Can't say I blame them. "What you doing by that creek, anyway?" folks ask me. "Chasing off crows, steers?" I smile and pray they don't see what I see, don't learn what I know.

Nobody believes I saw anything, just like most of the folks aren't sure you ever existed, Muri. I've shown them the photo—you standing on a chair, smiling—but even the church ladies are tired of looking at it. They smile with compassion or pity; I'm never sure which. They say they'll pray I find you. I won't mind if all they remember is to bring another casserole out to the house.

The evening I moved the artifacts, I smelled diesel and dust and heard a truck engine's chatter and whine, going too fast on that rutted old road. How did Jackson learn this place is sacred? Did he watch as I hid the sacred things? I'm glad I recorded what I found. It may be what saves us.

These days, I'm also glad that Rubin, the only guy around Murkee who doesn't call me Chief Joseph, is on our side. Rubin is all about preserving what was and what is, and he has the proper reverence for the First Nations. He's a little gung-ho on eco stuff, but he's a fine vet.

Every day I pray, studying the scars and missing digits of my hands. The half moons on my fingernails grin back at me. Some days I wish I'd never found this place or the creek and its heritage. Whether I'm a scarecrow or an elder, I drink too much out here, and it's killing me. Muri, I'm holding on for you.

Someday soon, I'll tell you more about our ancestors and what I found and I'll tell you about love. Love boiling over for a daughter I lost long ago. Love from a father who's running out of time. I hope God forgives me for moving these sacred things to keep them out of the collectors' hands. The task of protecting them has fallen to me. I must not fail. Livers don't hand out second chances, no matter if it's summer or spring.

Before I go, you must understand the things we must protect. I want you to meet the God I've tried to serve. I hope Jesus will touch you the way he has touched an old sinner like me.

22

Nova had been missing two full weeks, and neither she nor Linc's grandson had been in touch. Tru got the shoes he wanted thanks to a last-minute appeal to Chaz, who had returned from New York but who, in my humble opinion, still wasn't doing enough to find our daughter. I had to wait for Tiny to get his truck running again in order to go to the county offices.

I phoned Denny and Gwen every night, and you would have thought Nova belonged to them. Gwen Moses knew a lot of artists who kept studios in areas where Nova might turn up. The couple had distributed her picture and even made up more flyers at their own expense.

Lutie loved my glass angel, which she promptly named "Nova" and set in a place of honor amidst the family photos. I had trouble looking at it though. It sliced my insides like shards from a broken window, reminding me that she was still gone.

Tru rode the ancient yellow bus to the school that three nearby communities shared. Grades one through eight numbered exactly twenty-seven children, and the high school was only about half that. Some of the students commuted fifty miles each way. Tru only had to ride about twenty miles, but he had no illusions that it was going to be fun. It was the first time I'd been without both kids since Portland, and my separation anxiety showed.

"Think positive, Muri," Tiny said when he noticed my glum mood. It was early afternoon, and he stretched out the full length of the bowed sofa with his huge sock-covered feet hanging over one edge. He pulled down the serape draped across the back of the couch to cover his torso. Siesta time.

"And keep praying," Lutie said from the recliner, where she sat thumbing through her worn New Testament. "Warrior praying, that's what's called for." She looked up and her stare pierced me. "Ponds don't give up, you know."

Jim snuffled from his place on the rug next to Tiny. All my life I'd wished and even prayed at times to find my real family, and here they were, although they were far stranger than any relatives I could have imagined. The only things missing were a cozy fire and a bag of marshmallows. And the two children I held dear.

"Busy hands ward off worry," Lutie said.

I'm not the sort who likes to sit around much, so when she asked me to help crochet soda-can hats for the bazaar, I agreed. It had been decades since I'd done any type of handwork, so I got my aunt's crash course in basic crochet stitches, which I kept confusing with knitting.

"You work the hook in and out like this, easy as pie," she said. "No honey, there's no purling. That's right, wrap around and pull back through. The secret is to keep the tension even all the time." She showed me a cat's cradle type of configuration on one hand.

I felt enough tension for everybody. It was all I could do to keep from screaming at the pigs and anyone else who crossed my path. I railed at inanimate objects and kicked a metal table leg that jumped into my way. I imagined the portrait of Jesus on the living room wall had taken on the same sort of disapproving glare I once used to quiet unruly library patrons. With my nerves crackling like live wires, I could barely be civil to my own reflection. Tiny finally got up and went outside to work on his truck so I could drive to the county seat.

Lutie had to demonstrate the crochet techniques more times than I liked to admit. After she thought I'd finally gotten the hang of it, she handed me a blue metal hook and three skeins of acrylic worsted in hot pink, olive green, and rusty orange. The sight of a finished hat was enough to make me think of a busload of senior citizens on their way to Vegas.

I was being pulled in too many directions at once. I sat there with the basket of yarn, wishing I could unravel the events of the last few months. I imagined having a second chance where Linc wouldn't have turned out to be full of malice and Nova would have stayed home and joined 4-H. I should have left hours ago for the courthouse. I was also aware that I despised crocheting.

Lutie's efforts looked the same every time—tidy little rows of stitches standing at attention. Mine looked like a rat's nest, but she was always patient with me. "The nice thing about crochet is that it's so forgiving."

It might be hard to forgive anything this ugly. When I heard how much business last year's hats had brought in, I prayed we'd break even this time. We'd need every cent we could get to pay all the legal fees we were racking up.

As friendly as he'd been, Mr. Kutzmore was still a lawyer, one who probably charged a lot more than I had. Yet, besides his FBI friend, he also knew a couple of senior staffers at the National Clearinghouse for Missing Children and said he'd put in a personal word to them about Nova. Lutie wasn't surprised that George would do so much for me. When she said this her eyes sparkled.

I struggled with the stitches. Tru, home for a teacher work day, asked what made Mr. Kutzmore so special. Aunt Lutie said, "Like I told you, honey, we go back a long way. That's all there is to it. Just a long, long way."

"Like on the Oregon Trail? Are you really that old?" Tru asked. I thought Lutie looked embarrassed.

"Truman Charles Devereaux!" I snapped. "Apologize to your aunt this minute or you'll copy the definition of *courtesy* a few hundred times, plus be grounded." I hadn't meant to overreact; I just wanted everyone to know I wasn't going to make the same parenting mistakes twice. Later I would realize how ridiculous grounding a kid was when you're stranded in the middle of nowhere.

I ripped out an entire section of gaudy tri-colored yarn where I'd doubled instead of single-crocheted. My mind continued to wander.

Truman looked wounded, mumbled an apology, and then slunk away to his computer screen. Lutie's mouth opened as if she were about to say something, but then abruptly closed it again. I took her silence as an admonition no less important than the one from the Lord himself. My aunt stared at me, and her eyes softened, reminding me that I could be strong and not punitive, firm yet loving. I closed my eyes and tried to calm down.

After a respectable few moments I went over to my son, still surfing away on the Web. Thankfully, he wasn't downloading the "How to Get Revenge on Mean Moms Homepage," if there was such a thing. I peeked over his shoulder. He was looking at pictures of missing children.

"How can we get Nova's picture on this page?" I said.

He turned around and glanced at me, then shrugged. He was still sulking, I could tell.

"Sorry to bark so hard," I said, adding, "Okay, you're not grounded." I hugged him, and he allowed it. Without a word he nodded and hugged me back briefly, the way pre-adolescent kids do. The nice thing about Tru was that he could be so forgiving.

After pulling out my umpteenth stitch, I finally gave up and put away my yarns and hook, which was probably the best thing to happen to those awful hats. Lutie smiled, perhaps from relief more than anything.

"We all have our talents," my aunt said gently, and gave me Tru's job of punching the sides of the aluminum can strips. Maybe Lutie knew that I needed to punch something. It did make me feel calmer, as if worry was a luxury to be indulged only after all the chores were done.

Still, I couldn't keep my mind on even this simple task. The holes I punched snaked unevenly down the edges of the flimsy metal rectangles, so I was glad when Tiny came back inside and pronounced his truck drivable.

"Sure you won't take somebody with you to the county, Muri?" He wiped grease from his stocky fingers with a tea towel and then set to work with a pocketknife, digging grime from beneath his fingernails.

"Don't worry, Unc, I'll be fine. Made it all the way out here, didn't I?"

"Well, I'm glad you got a cell phone," he said.

"She's got AAA, anyway," Lutie pointed out. "Great Lord in heaven, will you keep your dirty hands off of my good towels?"

"Sorry, my Pearl," he said, hiding the soiled cloth behind his back like a child caught at the cookie jar. "I just worry about a woman traveling alone over that road, that's all." He grinned at me, looking like a tanned version of the Pillsbury Doughboy. I had to laugh as he cleaned the knife on the dirty towel. Lutie sighed.

"I'll be okay, really," I said. "Rubin said the same thing. But I'll only be gone a few hours." I hugged Tiny's still ample middle as best I could. "Thanks for thinking of me."

I didn't tell them that I wouldn't have taken Tru along if he had been in school. I missed Rubin, too, so I stopped by his place on my way out. We sat on his porch again, drinking iced tea and discussing my plan. Rubin was having as much trouble with Linc Jackson as I was these days, and I was sure he'd say I was brilliant.

But when I gave him my take on the situation, he frowned. "Hold on," he said. "Better get some hard evidence before you accuse Linc of thievery. Around here stealing is serious business."

"I am serious," I said with a tinge of sarcasm in my voice. "And so is Linc. He's made that clear enough. If he controls the creek, aren't we both at his mercy?"

"Not necessarily. I'm not the least bit afraid of his scare tactics, and he's seen what I'll do if he ignores my property rights." He crossed his arms.

"You won't gun down any more of his livestock, will you? He said he'd press charges." I felt a clawing in my stomach and realized I was holding my breath.

"He can press all the charges he wants. His cows stray onto my land, they're fair game." He had said this with so much conviction that I got the feeling he'd be a tree-hugging pro-tester if he thought it would help.

Then he turned and stared past me toward the creek. I always took these opportunities to study his face. There was a kind of clarity in him that I admired, and I hoped he would understand.

"I've got to do this, Rubin." I set my empty glass on the side table and stood up.

"I know. I just don't want to see you get hurt."

"I'll be careful."

Resolute, I turned my back and strode toward the truck. I refused to get sidetracked. If anyone could locate a forged document, I could. As I started up the truck, it was as though I could feel my father's presence, watching, listening, and waiting.

The more I thought about Dad, the more I was unable to elbow out the God he had worshiped. Holy Roller or not, Joseph Pond's faith had run deep and true, despite his tragic and shortened life. My father's belief in a loving, heavenly Father had bridged the gap between alcoholism and absolution.

On the way to the county seat I decided to act as if God really existed and prayed out all my problems to him. When I ran out of tears and confession, I prayed simple prayers. I wasn't ready to take a full leap of faith yet, but I wasn't closing the door either. I would be sure to thank Tiny for fixing the truck, Rubin for his maps, Lutie and her Tabernacle Ladies for their prayers for travel mercies. When I arrived at the courthouse, I felt for once as if something was going right. Although I had to search until after lunch, I finally made my way to the right department.

A woman, who looked about as old as the ancient microfiche machine in the corner, sat behind a counter, working a cross-stitch pattern. She might have been Native American herself. At least she knew what I was talking about and didn't tell me it wasn't her department. She got up to look through the dusty filing cabinets.

"Let's see, I have one more place to look," she said after a few minutes of small talk and several dead ends. We had both agreed that organization was the key to happiness, and I shared my best record-keeping tips, as if it would do any good. She disappeared into a room marked STAFF ONLY and emerged a few minutes later, toting a large cardboard box. This, I decided, was the extent of her organizational techniques.

"We got all this information on the computer," she said, as if confiding a state secret. "They're switching us over to a new system—*again*. But just try to find what you need on the darn thing. Anyway, it's easier to go haul out the stuff myself."

"Thanks for going to so much trouble," I said. It helped to let her know I was a librarian. "Sometimes I catch myself going to the old card catalog, just to remember what it was like. I could look through the records myself if you're too busy."

The woman plopped herself onto a stool behind the counter. "We're not supposed to do that, you know. Strictly against the rules. But my supervisor is in meetings all day." She paused. "I say, go for it. Not my fault they can't keep the computers up and running."

"If I find what I'm looking for, I'll recommend you for promotion," I said, smiling.

She shrugged and picked up her needlework again, leaving me to wade through a mountain of files. I sorted through old documents and mentally classified them into logical categories. Most of them belonged in the dull and boring pile, but even those were fascinating if you looked hard enough.

Still, a story unfolded. By scanning documents I learned of the struggle between the ranchers and the developers, the conservationists and the families whose survival depended on sustained growth. Much of central and eastern Oregon had faced the same dilemma, apparently, for as far back as the records went. You could opt in favor of the water or people it seemed, but not both. Documents recording Native American artifacts were in short supply, however.

By the time the clerk announced it was quitting time, I had found lists of notarized documents for artifacts located at museums, universities, and held by individuals. But no sign of anything signed by Lincoln Jackson.

23

I trudged out of the county building empty-handed. Still, I was convinced my father was right. Linc had to be involved in the illegal artifacts trade. My search for doctored certificates had fallen short, but George had warned me a paper trail would be hard to follow. I couldn't prove why Linc would lie to everyone about that creek, only that he needed Rubin and me to sell out and leave.

For Tiny and Lutie, leaving was an alien idea. They appeared shocked and lost when Linc threatened to have the judge enforce Linc's water rights and leave us high and dry. Without a source of clean water, we'd be forced out. Lutie had said, "You might as well move us to the moon."

It was true. Tiny's junkyard, Lutie's sun porch: they were a part of them. We might all get along better in the city. Tiny would have access to more consistent medical care. Somehow, though, I doubted my aunt and uncle would thrive anywhere but in Murkee.

Besides, I wanted to walk in the same red dust my father had walked and breathe the same crisp air he breathed. It had taken so long to become the daughter of Joseph Pond. How could I turn my back on him?

I pulled into a small diner before setting out for home. I ordered a grilled cheese sandwich, out of respect for Nova and her vegetarian diet, but my head was stuffed with thoughts of my father. I pictured him, with bowed legs and a cowboy hat, waging war with Linc. My father hadn't vandalized property, and he hadn't bullied anybody. He tried legal avenues; he tried to make the system work. Only so far, it hadn't worked at all. I stared out the window and tried to quench my anger with diet root beer. I was too furious to pray.

When I left the restaurant, the shadows from nearby peaks had already darkened the early evening. The streetlights cast blurry yellow haloes onto the wooden plank sidewalks of the authentic western-style buildings. The effect was eerie. People had already disappeared from the streets, perhaps because the temperature plummeted as soon as the mountains overtook the sun. Only a few hunters dressed in camouflage jackets and orange vests rumbled by in their pickups. It was only September, but the waitress had mentioned the possibility of snow in the passes.

This is the high desert, where winter can come early and hard if it wishes. I didn't want to take a chance getting stuck in the mountains at night, so I phoned Lutie.

"I'll find a motel for the night," I told her. "The truck's running fine, but I still don't trust it in bad weather." Then I said good night to Tru and promised him I'd be home the next day. "Behave for your aunt and uncle," I said, "and do your homework."

I checked into a local mom and pop motel, where ten rooms all faced a gravel parking lot. You could hear the neon vacancy sign sizzle when it flashed. At least they had cable TV, but there wasn't anything on I was interested in, so I turned out the light, stretched out on top of the covers in my clothes. Next door someone played a crackly country radio station.

But that wasn't what kept me awake. In my head Nova and Tru argued over trivial things and laughed about nothing. They jumped on the bed until the springs squeaked and thudded pillows up against each other's heads. I could almost hear my daughter's laughter on her tenth birthday, squealing in delight over that green tutu, only to have the trademark "whatever" and obligatory sighs rush in to overtake her innocence.

I remembered listening for the click of the door when she'd come home late, or the cadence of her breathing when she had pneumonia last year, or the pitch of her voice as she whined about homework, or the distinct stomp of her feet when she was being stubborn.

What I would never remember was the sound of my father's voice. I'd never know if it had been tenor or bass, smooth or raspy, full of animated inflection or more subdued. I'd never know if he said *Carib*bean or Carib*bean*. I knew I would never have tired of the sound of that voice. If blood was indeed thicker than water, then a part of him coursed through me.

Finally, I rolled off the bed, double-checked the door lock, and plumped up the meager motel pillow. Taking off my jeans, I left on my sweatshirt and climbed beneath the thin covers.

Still my mind wouldn't rest. Nova. I ached for her return. I ached for a real home. Would I ever find it? When Rubin talked about Murkee as his home, it sounded so natural. But I still wasn't sure I liked small-town living, especially a small town with no real library.

Then it hit me. Before I returned to Murkee in the morning I'd visit the small public library here. No doubt they had some reference books on water rights and Native artifacts and gravesites. If nothing else, I'd scan the archives. Finally, I slept fitfully.

In the morning, I was the first person in the county library door. I dove into the stack of reference books I piled on a study table and took notes on a yellow legal pad, scanning through chapters on the Oregon desert and histories of different areas in this sparsely settled region. I read about feuds and fights, spanning the twentieth century, and most of them were about the same issue: water. People had even shot each other now and then.

I reread the NAGPRA laws. Besides the FBI, state agencies included the Bureau of Land Management, Bureau of Indian Affairs, and Forestry and Land Use, as well as police. I still couldn't figure out which office kept the document records. I found newspaper accounts of a man in Bend whose entire house had been filled with stolen artifacts. That guy was in jail. Maybe George was right. Accusing Linc of stealing might stick better than trying to trace a document.

I left with an armload of articles about water rights *in perpetuity* and Native American sacred burial sites. The townspeople thought Linc was their benefactor. It wouldn't be simple to change that.

So far, Linc hadn't even flinched. I was the outsider here. Since Nova's disappearance I'd begun to feel even more out of place. The urge to walk away from my father's troubles surfaced once more. What did I know about sacred objects? And was I naïve enough to think Linc would snatch the heart rock and arrowhead and then put his hands in the air in surrender? George said Jackson was a smart cookie.

I climbed into Tiny's pickup and snagged my sweater on a metal coil sticking out from the seat cushion. The truck, cranky in the morning chill, refused to start on the first three tries. Finally, after I stomped on the gas pedal and whispered a quick prayer, the engine turned over.

How could I ever hope to fit into a little one-gas station town like Murkee? I'd be forever running one step ahead of spiteful ranchers like Linc and the inevitable gossips of small-town life. I didn't have the first idea about how to can fruit, and I really didn't care. I certainly hated to crochet. And even if I allowed myself to trust God I doubted if the Red Rock Tabernacle would suit my urban tastes.

Then there was Nova. When I found her, would she return to Murkee? Perhaps if I dangled in front of her the prospect of moving back to the city she might agree to some house rules.

Lost in thought, I made a wrong turn and had to back track five miles to get pointed in the right direction again. My arms ached from gripping the steering wheel.

Suddenly, I craved the familiar—the known. Portland might be a sprawling metropolis, rife with crime and pollution, but it was the only place the kids really knew and called home. For the first time I looked at the situation from their point of view. No wonder Nova had run away. I wouldn't listen.

By the time I pulled into the sheriff's branch office to check on her, my mascara had run from more tears. Maybe we didn't belong in Murkee. I had to find Nova and then I would make some calls to Portland. Running an audio/visual lab part-time had to be better than living in a run-down trailer with Linc Jackson for a neighbor, long-lost father or not. Nova was right. My father was dead and nothing would bring him back.

At the sheriff's department, I retold a female deputy how my daughter had been upset about the divorce, the move to Murkee, and life in general. My voice grew thick as I described her rebellious appearance and her tendency to stomp out in the middle of arguments, only to show up a few days later at a friend's home. The woman looked perplexed, as if she didn't understand how a parent could let these things happen. Or perhaps my guilt was simply as transparent as my attempt to be matter-of-fact.

She wanted to know when I'd last seen her. "A little over two weeks ago," I admitted. "My neighbor's grandson is missing too, and he called once from Portland," I added. "They may be together."

"Uh-huh," she said. The officer shook her head when I explained about Marvin and his grandfather's new Cadillac. I decided to ignore her monotone as well as her indifference.

"My daughter and I had a spat over this boy. She just turned sixteen, and when she left I thought she was just cooling off. You know how kids are—"

"Yes, ma'am, I think I have everything now." Her desk phone rang. "Excuse me, please. We'll let you know if anything turns up."

I tried to smile at the deputy as I stood and nearly ran out of the office.

Driving the rest of the way to Murkee through a cold fog that dimmed the road ahead, I rehearsed how I'd tell Lutie and Tiny I was going back to Portland. Lutie would understand. I imagined her saying something like, "You keep in touch and God bless now." She'd probably be glad to get her sewing room back. Breaking the news to Rubin would be more difficult. I ticked off all the reasons we were better off without each other, from my troubles with Linc to his awful emus, which weren't as cute as I first thought.

I rolled down the window and sang to keep myself awake. My voice cracked as I hummed the lullabies that had put my children to sleep when they were small, until tears choked off the notes. I tried a little "How Great Thou Art," but it was mostly la-la-la because I didn't know the words. When I got desperate I sang jingles from commercials, but only the ones

Nova and Tru liked. By the time the truck pulled into the yard, it was dark, and my throat was scratchy and dry.

Tru didn't understand why I hugged him too long and so fiercely, as if he were the one missing. He wriggled free but looked happy to see me, and I listened to him tell me that the school wasn't so bad after all.

"The bus ride still stinks," he said, "but I sit next to Megan." Megan was a girl he had met, who also loved computers.

I was too tired to explain to Lutie or Tiny about what I'd learned. I tossed my evidence on the table and said I'd explain everything in the morning. Even Jim appeared sympathetic when I said my head throbbed and my throat felt like I'd swallowed ground glass. As I walked down the hall I closed my eyes until I passed Nova's angel, and no one else said anything at all.

24

Rumors percolated through Murkee like contaminated ground water. I wasn't eager to put up with stares and whispers, so I made excuses to stay home. But even out at the trailer I heard the lowdown. Lutie always brought home the latest gossip.

"We're the talk of the town in the Mucky-Muck," she said after returning with the groceries. She set a paper bag next to the kitchen sink and admonished Tiny. "Careful, this one's got eggs." She turned to me. "You'll be interested to know Linc's no longer just picking on us Ponds. He's set on running poor Rubin off too." Aunt Lutie wagged a finger at the air. "Dear Lord Jesus, that man needs his ears boxed."

I sighed and then began to put things away. "I'm not surprised. Linc's been harassing Rubin since we got back from Portland. And Frieda Long won't let go of that emu incident."

Lutie snorted. "Everybody knows Linc is partial to Frieda's hubby. Poor Frieda just can't get through to Fred, even after forty years of marriage. But maybe she looked the other way just to get even with the emus."

"The Longs are always doing Linc Jackson's bidding," Tiny added. He opened a box of saltine crackers and thoughtfully munched one. "If Linc's mad at Rubin it's probably got something to do with us."

Tru had been listening in. Tiny handed him a cracker. "Even over at school all the kids know about it," Tru said. "They say Doc Rubin's no good because he helps us."

This was the first time my son had mentioned rumors at school. "And what's wrong with helping our family?" I asked in my protective mother voice.

He shrugged and looked at the floor. "Don't know."

Uncle Tiny laid a hand on his nephew's shoulder. "What's this about?"

Tru looked up at Tiny's big frame. "We're no good because we won't share the stupid water." He set his jaw. "They say Grandpa Pond was just another drunken Indian."

I froze, with my mouth open and my hand gripping a tall can of spaghetti sauce.

"Think about that," Tiny said, reaching for another saltine. His eyes were patient and kind as he looked down at Tru. "Your granddad *was* half Nez Perce, so I guess those kids are right about him being Native American."

"What about the drunken part?" Tru wanted to know. I braced myself for the answer.

"Alcohol brought him a world of trouble," Tiny said evenly. "There's no denying it."

Lutie's back was turned, so I couldn't see her reaction. Her shoulders sagged a little.

"But Joseph was much more than that," Tiny continued. "Did the best he could. Loved the Lord with everything he had. Loved your mom. Would have loved you too."

I felt the sting of tears but held them back. I silently thanked Tiny for putting things so simply, yet so right. My son smiled, and the two of them went out to hammer nails on Lutie's porch, armed with the rest of the saltines and a jar of peanut butter. Jim trotted after them.

I waited until the screen door closed. "Aunt Lutie, what would Dad have done? What would he say?"

She looked at me and then headed to her recliner to sit down. It seemed like a long time before she spoke. "Don't know if he would have had any answers." She fingered her Bible.

"He'd have done something, wouldn't he?" I stared at his photo on the little table. A breeze fluttered the curtains.

Lutie closed her eyes briefly. "He wanted you to have this place. I know that much for sure. And even though he wasn't a scrapper he didn't hide from trouble, either. I'd say your daddy would stand up to that ornery Linc."

"Linc once accused him of owing him lots of money. Did he?"

"Heavens no, child. If anything Joseph was too honest. It seemed like Linc had something against your daddy from day one. When Joe wouldn't sell out, well, that was it. He was Linc Jackson's number one enemy."

I drew up straighter. "Well, Linc doesn't know it," I said, "but he's got enemies too."

In the morning I drove into town to take George the articles I'd found at the library. Outside, a weak autumn sun tried to burn through a stubborn layer of low clouds. I sighed. The sun and I could both use a break.

"Our expert has agreed to get his findings to us as soon as possible," George said when I told him I hadn't found any artifact certificates.

"As soon as possible? Are we talking days, weeks, what?" We had to hurry.

George held out his hands. "I'm doing all I can."

"I know you are, but I don't trust Linc. When I got here I thought he was a genuine John Wayne type, but now I know better."

George, in typical lawyer fashion, said nothing.

I held up the news article about the Bend artifact thief. "Does this mean anything? If nothing else, it says people do steal and collect and trade this stuff." I tossed the yellowed paper over to him.

Mr. Kutzmore scanned the document. "Convincing," he said, "but proving Linc's been pilfering from the creek area won't be easy. Plus, he's still liable to go after you with that gone-less-than-five-years water argument. How will you get along with no water?" He looked hard at me. "I'll put some more pressure on the documents guy, but keep quiet. The minute Linc gets wind of this he'll go straight to the water judge."

"I'll keep my mouth shut." I stood to leave. "But I know my father was right."

"Sorry he left you with such a big mess. You have my sympathy."

"Sympathy? I don't want sympathy. I want justice." My jaw muscles tightened. "Joseph Pond was more than a crazy Indian. I'm going to prove that, and I don't care how long it takes." The pitch of my voice rose, and I felt my cheeks ignite. "Linc's outright lied about the creek and why he wants our land."

George smiled at me, but it was a lawyer's smile. His poor client was so naive. "Linc will probably lie again too," he said gently. "He's already dragged your dad through the mud. He'll pull out all the stops to discredit you."

I yanked open the door. "We'll see about that."

Fuming mad, I drove back to the trailer. Taking advantage of the nearly deserted road to vent my frustrations in private was becoming a habit. But I wouldn't have cared who heard me. I had been pushed too far. Linc was out to get me, and too many people had already been hurt. This wasn't about eco-systems or water rights or even artifacts anymore. This was about my father's name and the reputation of those I loved.

I rounded the turn in the road. Vehicles lined the access road to Rubin's place. Pickups, four-by-fours, and the Long's dually sat bumper-to-bumper on the dirt road. In the rear windows, hunting rifles and shotguns rested in their racks. Men huddled together, frosty breath billowing from their lips, rubbing their hands together in the cold. One stood with a boot planted on the steps of his rig, gripping a torn piece of brown cardboard that reminded me of a sixties sit-in. Only the sign wasn't about peace and love. The ranchers, it seemed, had declared war.

The slogans weren't original: COW KILLER and JONTO GO HOME. I parked as close as I could, scooped up a pile of papers from the floor of the cab, and ran to where a knot of locals had gathered around Ed Johnson's flatbed truck. The emus paced nervously in their pens, flapping their flightless wings.

Tiny stood next to Rubin's porch. Three of Linc's cows had been found, he told me, shot dead. Linc blamed Rubin. Rubin denied it.

Tru walked over the hill with Lutie. She put her arm around me. "Tiny says they were dead or dying by the time they found them. Rubin had to put down two who were still suffering."

I remembered the day Rubin threatened to shoot more livestock should they stray onto his property. I shuddered. If he had deliberately destroyed healthy animals then I'd never known Rubin Jonto at all.

He stood in the yard, arguing with Linc. I'd dressed as western as I dared, in soft worn jeans and a denim shirt. I was even wearing a hat. Perhaps the crowd wouldn't think of me as an outsider.

"I told you," Rubin said, "one of them was already dead." He sounded exasperated and barely acknowledged me.

Frieda's husband, Fred, turned to Linc and said something I couldn't quite hear.

"Sure, I'll press charges," Linc bellowed. The end of his nose was quite red, his eyes gray as concrete. "And you," he said, jabbing his index finger at Rubin, "you'll be lucky to get a pig for a patient." Linc sneered.

I glared at Linc and felt like kicking dust on his boots. But before I could say anything, he turned and walked away.

He climbed up into the back of the flatbed and got the crowd to quiet down. I'd never noticed before, but Linc Jackson was on the short side for a man. Several of the Tabernacle Ladies' husbands were in the crowd. Ed Johnson, Mr. Mason, and Fred Long shaded their eyes. They all looked upset.

"Jonto here has threatened to shoot cows just for taking a drink of water," he boomed. "And now he's made good on his threats. That sound like a veterinarian to you?" The men grumbled in response. "I like to be as neighborly as the next man, but I won't abide my livestock being picked off deliberately. Might as well be rustling." Linc stared out at where Rubin and I stood. "I ask you, do we need a vet who don't understand what ranching is all about? Do we need this?"

The ranchers roared their displeasure. Asked to choose between their livelihood and a bunch of trout in a small stream, the answer was obvious. To the folks from Murkee, Rubin had betrayed them all.

I had to spill everything, no matter what George said about keeping quiet. I had no choice. I pulled myself up as tall as I could and took a deep breath. "You think Linc wants to help ranchers? I say he wants to help himself."

Rubin grabbed my arm, but I shook him off and climbed up in the truck with Linc. The crowd hushed. Although my insides felt like melted Jell-O, I faced them. "This isn't about Dr. Jonto here," I said in the loudest voice I could muster. "This is about our land and our water. And honesty."

Linc squinted hard at me. For a moment I thought he might shove me out of the truck bed. His mouth hung open. I expected him to interrupt, but for once he was speechless.

I held up a random stack of papers I'd grabbed from the pickup—later I'd find it was a school theme Tru had written about the Oregon desert. I had to make Jackson think I had his forged artifact document in my hand. We couldn't wait for the expert. "Since before my father's death," I said, "Linc's claimed that every drop in that creek belongs to him. Says he was gone one month shy of the five-year limit."

Linc smirked. "And neither you nor Jonto here sees the light."

I stared at him. "I see the light all right," I said. "You may have been gone less than five years, but where were you? What were you doing all that time?"

"None of your business, that's what."

I smiled. "But it is my business. As a Native American, I've looked into federal laws against illegal removal, possession, or sale of sacred objects from burial sites. Forgery, by the way, gets the FBI involved. While you were gone, you just happened to be illegally selling off goods from an archaeological gold mine out at the creek."

He looked stunned. Once more, his expression turned cold. "Smoke and mirrors," Linc said. "A liar—just like your old man. She's desperate, folks."

One man yelled out, "Linc takes care of us. Go back to the city."

"Linc doesn't give a rip about any of you," I shot back. "He needs that creek. But not for ranching." My hand shook as I prayed God would forgive my gamble. "This forged certificate proves it." I waved the papers in the air and hoped no one asked to examine them until the real proof could be found.

"That's a lie," Linc said. He'd found his voice again. "She's lying. I just want what's mine. We've got ranches to run."

"Ranches?" I spoke directly to Linc. "My father saw you digging out there. He was an alcoholic, but he wasn't delusional." I gestured toward the creek. "Before he died Joseph Pond registered items with a noted archaeologist. Then he replaced the actual artifacts—" I paused to point at Linc, "where he knew you'd find them. My father bet you couldn't resist taking them. My evidence shows he was right."

The whole crowd fell silent. The strange part is that standing next to Linc I could hear a slight grinding noise, the working of jaw muscles, the sound of a breath suspended in midair.

When the unexpected occurs, you look back on it and it plays in slow motion. That's the way I remember it: a graceful descent to earth past the sky. My foot slipped off the side of the platform, and I tumbled from Ed Johnson's truck. In reality it only took a second to lose my footing.

I landed on hard ground, unharmed except for a sore backside and wounded dignity. Rubin ran toward me. From the look on his face, I knew he thought I'd been pushed. He helped me up. I dusted the red dirt from my posterior and ignored the rip in the elbow of my shirt. The hat lay crumpled at my feet.

"I'm all right," I said, gasping to regain my breath. "Just lost my balance." I tried to appear unshaken and looked up at Linc once more. "What about it? Tell us about the collector. The one that buys all the artifacts you can supply and is making you a very, very rich man."

Linc acted nonchalant. "I don't know what you're talking about," he said. He leaned over the side of the truck and spat into the dirt. "Drunks and nutcases must run in the family. You're a liar, just like your old man."

Rubin put his arm around me. I wasn't dumb enough to climb back up onto the truck. Instead, I stared at Linc as hard as I could and repeated my challenge. "If my father was a liar, then you won't mind letting the sheriff take a look around your place, will you?" I gathered the fake papers and waved them in the air. "And what about these documents? My expert says they're forged."

The gathering stood frozen as I fell from the truck, unsure perhaps, whether it had been a staged shove or a real one. They murmured now, as if they'd just heard a rancher's version of heresy. Finally, one called out, "What about it, Jackson?" Now it was my turn to smirk.

Tiny and Lutie were at the edge of the crowd, keeping Tru a safe distance away. Their presence strengthened me. I fully expected Linc Jackson to crumble right there on the spot.

But he didn't. Hopping down from the truck bed, with Ed Johnson following, Linc abruptly abandoned the protest. But he stared over my head, refusing to make eye contact.

"I'm not on trial here," he finally said. He turned to the ranchers. "You decide for your sorry selves whether to bring your animals to a vet who murders cattle." He wheeled around once more to point his finger at me. "And you—I'll see you in court." Linc strode off.

Everyone watched him go. The wind picked up and bit into our cheeks, and the sun hid itself altogether. The ranchers hesitated and then fired up their trucks. Some of them shook their heads, as if they knew they'd wasted a perfectly good morning, one better spent on chores.

Even the house and the barn and the emu pens took on a dreariness in the dusty haze. I'd never noticed before, but the boards on Rubin's porch were bowed and splintered in places, and the furniture looked shabbier than ever. Paint had peeled off the window sashes, revealing gray, dead wood. Spots in the chicken wire fences sagged where the emus had pecked unmercifully. The ladies from Red Rock Tabernacle might have said all this was a sign.

As people began to leave, Murkee's illustrious law enforcement showed up: one measly patrol car, with the same female deputy. I wanted to know what she intended to do.

"Linc's terrorizing my family." My breath puffed out in angry clouds. "I'll file charges. The whole crowd thinks I got pushed off that truck." The deputy shrugged and refused to look directly at me. I answered for her. "My word against his? Well, now it's Rubin's word against Linc's. I demand some action."

She looked puzzled and then sighed. "You're welcome to file a complaint. But don't go getting any crazy ideas. This isn't the Wild West. 'Round here we pride ourselves on due process." She eyed both Rubin and me and then climbed back into the patrol car, apparently satisfied that the riot danger had passed. "Shooting cattle is a serious offense in these parts," she said. "If I were you I'd get a good lawyer."

25

I needed to report everything to George. But when I visited his office there still was no word of the expert's findings. Linc had already demanded to see the report, and I didn't have one—unless you counted Tru's school assignment.

"I'm stalling for time," George said. "But Linc's plenty mad. He's already in touch with the judge. What you did out there at Rubin's was, ah, unfortunate."

"I tipped him off," I said. "I admit that. But I know there's a fake deed someplace."

"Our guy contact you?"

"No, but I feel it. And the missing artifacts prove something, don't they?"

George shook his head. "Where are they? How do you know Linc's got them in his possession?"

"I just have a feeling, that's all." I gulped.

George looked upset. "Linc may have already sold the pieces. If he's awarded the water rights, he can do what he wants with the creek. And if that certificate is genuine, Linc will sue you for more than slander."

"I've got photos too," I said. "And a university expert. Besides, Linc won't be able to resist another good find. I'm almost sure of it."

"You're taking a huge risk, Muri. Huge." He smiled. "But I have to admit you've got guts. Good luck."

"Lutie says we've got angels on our side—better than luck." I thought of Nova's angel. "Any leads on my daughter?"

"No," he said. No one had heard anything except rumors that I might be as delusional as my father. "I'll let you know the moment I hear something. Just don't pull any more crazy stunts, okay?" George walked me to the entrance of his office.

"You have my word on it." My shoulders slumped as I walked outside and started Tiny's truck. Sometimes I wished I'd never come here at all.

I drove to the creek to think, to yell, to cry. I knelt at the shallow spot in the creek where I'd buried the arrowhead and heart-shaped rock. I watched for a glint from the arrowhead, but there wasn't a trace. I had to be sure Linc had taken them. Again and again I felt around in the silt and checked up and down the stream, in case the current had carried away the artifacts. Nothing.

I stood alone, my hands and arms dripping with cold mud, and listened to the creek burble. My bait was gone. I only hoped Linc's greed was as big as his ego.

When I got back to the trailer, Rubin was there. He and my uncle discussed the protest scene. Both men shook their heads in disbelief at my speech. Lutie fussed over me and wanted to know if I'd got the proof of Linc's shenanigans yet.

I washed my hands in the outside washtub. I wouldn't say anything about the missing items. Not yet. "No," I said, "but George says our expert's rushing it. We ought to hear something soon."

Rubin said, "If we don't then you'll get blackballed too."

Tru looked defiant. "Don't say that," he said. "You'll show them, Mom. I know it." He pushed up his glasses and then crossed his arms.

Lutie and Tiny were concerned as well. "You watch yourself, honey," Tiny warned. "You never know."

"What do you mean?" My heart banged against my ribs. I still felt the adrenaline of keeping a secret, one that could break Linc or else destroy me.

Rubin answered for him. "He means that in a small town you're either family or you're the enemy. There's no in-between." He sighed. "After what you saw at my place, you might guess we're both the enemy to Linc."

"You didn't do it, did you?" I stared into Rubin's eyes. "Tell me you didn't go out and gun down those cows."

"No, I didn't do it," he said. He raised his hand as if he was taking an oath. "As God is my witness, I only put down the two that were still breathing. Only merciful thing to do."

"I believe you."

"What are you going to do now?" Lutie asked Rubin. "I'll speak to George—"

"Thanks, but I'll handle this myself," Rubin said.

I looked around at the yard, where the truck had mined new gouges into the sepia-toned soil. Already the wind was at work again, lifting and sifting dirt against our faces like a light dusting of face powder. Tiny turned to leave, saying the pigs' feeding time was overdue, and Lutie hauled Tru away on some excuse about his homework. Rubin and I needed to talk and perhaps they sensed it, or maybe they were simply tired of standing in the cold.

I sat down on the tire planter and examined a tear in my shirt. "Linc's got to be worried," I said.

I'd never seen Rubin look so discouraged. "Muri," he said, "I've got to tell you something."

"Don't tell me you shot another pig."

His smiled looked forced. "No. I don't know how to say this, but I've decided to take Linc up on his offer to buy me out." He didn't look at me, just angled his shoulder around a bit as he rested his elbows on a stack of bicycle parts.

"You're kidding. No, you're not kidding." I hoped Tiny and Lutie weren't listening. I stood up and walked farther from the trailer.

Rubin followed. We stopped behind the burned-out shed. "Linc's got too much influence," Rubin said. "I can't survive as a vet if I'm blackballed."

"We're almost home free," I said. "You'll see."

"I can't wait."

"What difference does a day or two make?"

He faced me, his eyes as sad as I'd ever seen them. "You've been here less than six months, not long enough to understand what it's like out here. People don't forget things. People hold grudges."

I had to keep fighting. "I'm sure Linc faked papers to sell the stuff. Once folks know the truth they'll come back. Why can't you trust me?"

Rubin kicked at the ground with his boot heel. "Linc's up to something; you're right. But I'm not the only vet in the county. Those idiotic emus bring in more headaches than cash. And I'm losing the battle to restore the creek."

My arms dropped to my sides. For once I was speechless. I remembered what the real Chief Joseph had said long ago. "Fight no more forever," I said. I braced myself for something terrible and put my fears into the shape of a piece of really bad news.

Rubin's eyes narrowed. "I'm at the end of my rope with Linc, with emus, with everything," he said. "I'm out of here." He slapped the side of the shed so hard I thought it might collapse.

My body grew numb with a tingling that began at the soles of my feet, filling me with a rush of emptiness. Finally I said, "Where will you go?" This was the only thing I could force from my lips. A tornado of images swirled in my mind: the streambed dry and dead and bones of starved emus bleaching in the sun. I pictured myself standing against the wind in the middle of a desert, with all the life sucked out of me—and all because I'd come here to find a family. With Rubin gone I wouldn't only be very lonely but also surrounded.

"I've got this buddy in Bend, another vet who wants to expand his practice." Rubin said.

I placed my hand on Rubin's shoulder. "Please. Give me a little more time."

"I've run out of time." He stroked my hair. "It's not about you. You're the one thing that keeps me going. But I've thought about it a lot. You don't deserve any more problems." He gazed at me with real hurt.

I leaned against his chest. "I've got as many problems as you do, Rubin. Actually, I've been thinking of starting over somewhere else myself."

Rubin held me at arm's length. "Why? You're certain Linc stole the artifacts, right?"

I looked away. "Sort of. Probably." I sighed. "I'm hoping he took the bait."

Rubin whistled softly. "You're as dangerous as I am."

"I feel about as dangerous as a newborn today," I said. "But that's not why I was thinking of leaving."

Rubin held my hands. "Because of me? I swear I'd never shoot an innocent animal."

I shook my head. "No, no, not you. I feel torn, that's all. Torn between you and my father's place and my daughter. If I hadn't hauled us out here, she might never have run away."

"If? That's a big *if*, Muri. Besides, I think Nova just got carried away. She'll be back."

257

"That's what Aunt Lutie says. But it's been weeks. Even when I find her I can't force Nova to live in the middle of nowhere. She was miserable here."

Rubin's eyes took on a hopeful glint. "You could move to Bend. One happy family."

I looked away. "If I relocate, it'll be to Portland. Sorry."

Rubin kissed the top of my head. "I'm sorry too." He sounded defeated. "I guess we'll have to get used to a long-distance relationship."

I looked up. "For now it's the best we can do."

He was suddenly guarded. "Listen, I've got a million things to do. I'd best get going."

"Whatever you need, please let me know." I held back tears.

"Definitely." He ran a hand along my cheek and then quickly turned his back. Over his shoulder, he said, "I'll call you later today." With hunched shoulders and his head down, Rubin walked off. I hoped it wasn't for good.

Staring after him, I watched his breath puff white smoke into the cold air. With so much to worry about, I could hardly breathe at all. I cared about Rubin, and I didn't want to lose him. Stay or go? Portland or Bend? What advice would my father give?

I wished I could sit beneath that cottonwood out by the stream, just stretch out there, commune with leafless branches, and talk to my dad. I wanted to talk all this stuff over with the one who had started it all. The day I'd driven out here, Nova and her brother had sat in the back seat and pelted each other with food. I wished again that my daughter were here. My throat tightened as it did each time her face came into my mind. As time wore on, I thought of her less frequently. Now I was down to missing her just a few thousand times a day.

26

A day later, the phone rang after dinner. Truman picked it up. "Mom, it's for you." I guessed it must be either George or Rubin, but Tru shook his head. "Nope, it's that lady named Gwen."

I had no idea I could move so fast. I sprinted to the phone, and Tru looked at me with surprise. Lutie's mouth gaped for a brief moment, and then she returned to the sink full of dishes, praying out loud. When Tiny came in and banged the screen door, she shushed him, and he grinned as if he was in on some big secret.

"Oh, Lord," I said. "Gwen thinks she knows where Nova is."

Tiny and Tru cheered, and Lutie closed her eyes. I held up my hand for quiet.

"I've had Denny checking on this," Gwen said. "One of our church's outreach guys says he's seen her hanging in the downtown area."

"Is she still with that kid named Marvin?" I don't know why I asked or why I thought it mattered.

"Not sure on that," Gwen said. "But listen, sweetie, here's the tough part: outreach guy says the word on the street is that Nova has checked herself into detox."

A fog of despair paralyzed me. Lutie and the guys fell silent. Detox? "Why on earth would she need—" I stopped before I had to say it out loud.

Gwen's voice stayed even, soothing. "I've got the center's number right here. They won't give Denny or me any information, or we'd have gone down there and talked to her." She paused. "I'm so sorry, Muri."

Tiny took the phone from me because I could barely stand. He wrote down the information and thanked Gwen and Denny for their help. After he hung up the phone he motioned to Tru, who was stroking Jim's ears.

"Come on, son," my uncle said. "We've got some bikes that need fixing." Tiny put his arm around Tru's shoulder and led him outside, with Jim trotting along behind. The screen shut without a sound, restrained by Tiny's hand.

Lutie fixed me some kind of herbal tea while I sobbed. When I could think again, I called the detox center in Portland. It didn't matter that I was Nova's mother. I couldn't get any more information than Denny or Gwen.

The receptionist was friendly but firm. "We can't give out any personal information. HIPPA Privacy Law," she said. "Kids try to get info on their friends and try to sneak in dope. That's why clients go through blackout. Everything's locked down. Wish I could be more helpful."

"Nova, her name's Nova," I whispered into the receiver. "If she's there—if she comes around again, would you please tell her to call home?"

The line clicked off. It had all been too good to be true. Lutie let me alone then, solemnly lowering and raising her yellow-gloved hands in and out of sudsy water, dunking the dishes one by one. The exaggerated quiet told me she felt Nova's loss as keenly as I did.

Tiny and Tru came in and out to fetch tools and once to find the duct tape, which turned up under the serape that blanketed the back of the worn sofa. Tiny pulled off a long strip of tape, the sound ripping the tension apart a little, reminding me that life was still happening. They tracked a little mud in on the rug, too, which Lutie pointed at with a frown.

"I'm going into town for a part," Tiny said. "You want to go, Tru?"

"No, thanks." Tru stood next to me where I sat at the dinette table and placed his small hand on my shoulder.

"Don't worry, Mom," he said. I could have kissed him then for being my son and for being so rock solid. But he slipped away, off to speak the simpler language of sprockets and bicycle gears. I couldn't hold it against him.

I heard the truck engine start, and then Tru let the screen door clap shut once more. The lace curtains fluttered while the family gallery looked on from the rickety side table like a muted cheering section. I stared hard at my father's picture and assured him I was going to find her somehow. Nova's glass angel reflected light and threw a rainbow up on the wall. I felt like the victim of some cosmic cheap trick.

Seconds later, it dawned on me that I didn't hear Tru playing outside in the yard or hammering on wood. My son was certainly old enough to be on his own for some things, but unlike his runaway sister, he always told me where he'd be. Except that this time, he hadn't. Panic rose in my throat.

I threw on my ratty blue sweater and waved to Lutie, crocheting in her chair. "I'm going out to look for Tru. Did he tell you where he was going?"

"What? No." Her face pinched with worry. "And Tiny's gone to town. Lord, Lord, not again."

"If I'm not back in twenty minutes, call the sheriff."

"I'll be warrior praying." She laid down her yarn as I sprinted out the door.

I rounded the curve by the bullet-riddled power company sign. Up ahead, I heard a sound like rocks bouncing off metal. Tru's unmistakable voice floated on the breeze. I looked up and froze. My son was kicking dirt at Linc's shiny monster truck where it sat parked at the edge of our property. Linc was nowhere around.

"I hate you!" Tru yelled. "You pushed my mom. You were mean to my grandpa. I hate you!" Tru picked up a tennis ball-sized rock. Before I could stop him, he hurled it at Linc's truck. The rock clunked into the pickup bed.

I trotted to my son, shouting, "Tru! No!"

By the time I reached him, Tru had managed to climb the side of Linc's truck. He stood on the back bumper, and his feet dangled as he reached into the bed.

"Truman!"

Tru twisted around, pulling a cloth bag the size of a woman's purse with him. A pointed stick protruded from its drawstring. He jumped to the ground, clutching the bag.

I grabbed my son's shoulder. "Did you hear me? You know better than to throw rocks." I could barely keep from shaking him.

Tru started to cry. "I'm sorry, Mom." Still gripping the cloth bag, he took off his glasses and wiped at his tears. "Linc made fun of Grandpa, and he hurt you. I hate him."

He leaned against the bumper and hung his head. I gathered him in my arms and hugged him, the bag in his hands squeezed between us. I stood back and pointed. "What is this?"

Tru shrugged. "I was getting my rock and this was in the back of the truck." He opened the drawstring. "Looks like a bunch of cool stuff."

I took the bag. "The kap'n stick," I whispered, holding out what looked like the root stick from Dad's photo. I rifled through the bag's contents. "Oh, my goodness!" I pulled out the heart-shaped rock. "Do you know what you've done?"

Tru's eyes widened, and his voice shook. "I was only going to look at stuff, Mom. I was going to put it all back. Honest."

"Don't worry; you didn't do anything wrong." I crammed everything back into the bag and pulled the drawstring tight. "You're not a thief. But I know who is."

Tru pushed up his glasses. "Linc?"

I nodded. "Wait until George sees this. C'mon." I took Tru's hand, and we trotted toward our place.

We followed the hill trail. Tru ran ahead by a good hundred yards. As we headed over the rise, the fence I'd come to love would be there, beckoning us home.

Tru ran back toward me, hollering and waving his arms. "Mom! Hurry! There he is! There he is!"

I yanked off my sweater and looped the bag's drawstring around one arm. The bag nestled against my side but the stick poked at my underarm. I threw the sweater back on anyway and picked up my pace until I saw what Tru was yelling about. I stopped. For one instant I couldn't believe what I was seeing.

Linc Jackson, the man who called himself our neighbor, was tearing down the fence my father built.

I wheeled Tru around. "Stay here." I shook my finger at my son. "Promise me you won't move until I say so. Got that?" My hands shook as I buttoned my sweater up to my neck.

"Okay," Tru said. "Promise."

I yelled. I waved my arms and raced toward Linc, running faster than I ever have. "Hey! You can't do that!"

Linc uprooted an aqua oven door from its place in the fence and turned around. "Watch me," he said. He tossed the panel onto a pile of other oven doors that had already been pulled up. "I warned you, Mizz Pond." Linc was breathing hard. He leaned against what was left of the fence. "The water, the creek—and the Chief's place—are mine."

"Not as long as I'm around." I lifted the edge of the aqua door but let it thud in the dust. Those things are heavier than they look.

Linc sneered. "You got no say." He turned and continued dismantling the fence. "You people brought it on yourselves. I haven't done anything wrong."

"What you've done, Mr. Jackson, is more than wrong. It's immoral. My heritage, my father's heritage. You don't give a flying fig what you destroy."

"How do you destroy water?" Linc grunted with every effort. "That's what ticks me off about you city folks. You don't know the first thing about living out here." He tugged on the next oven door, heaving it to one side.

I picked up the edge of the same door. "I know this much," I said between breaths, "you'd run my family off—and anyone else who stands in your way." I dragged the bulky metal door back to where it had been and attempted to replace it. The door teetered but held fast.

Linc tugged on the base of the next door, a pink one. It didn't budge. "Stubborn as your old man," he said and yanked again.

"Yes, I am." I let go of the aqua door.

Linc was undeterred. The oven doors groaned as they were pried from the earth, metal and tempered glass buckling. Tru darted up from behind me. "Tru! Get back!" I cried. Before I could stop him, it was too late.

My son tackled Linc, who looked surprised and then let a sea-green door crash to the ground.

"That's my grandpa's fence!" my son screeched. "Get your stinking hands off my grandpa's fence!" But he was no match for a grown man. Linc shook off Tru. My son went flying, landing on his rear end.

"Out of my way, kid," Linc growled, as if he assaulted children every day. He resumed tearing out fence panels. Tru sat in the dirt, his face the same red as the earth.

I don't know where I got the strength to hoist an oven door; my fingers barely reached around the sides. But before I knew it I'd swung a pink door around and clocked Linc a good one. At least his hat fell off. He doubled over with a loud "oof," then grimaced and staggered over to a part of the fence that still stood upright.

I patted my side, thankful the drawstring bag had stayed under my sweater. Tru cheered like I'd just caught the "hail Mary" pass for a touchdown.

Breathing hard, I stood there not quite sure what I'd done, the bulky pink door still leaning against my thighs. "You won't get away with this," I said. I allowed the pink door to thud to the ground. "This creek is on my property, and you're trespassing."

Linc's stare cut through me until I glanced down. The dream catcher that had hung on the fence lay trampled in the dirt. I picked up the bent circle and dusted off the strings and feathers. I held it against my chest and prayed the bag under my clothing wasn't obvious. "You may own the land temporarily, but the water's mine," he said, holding his side. Linc narrowed his eyes. "You're out of your skull, just like your old man." Linc limped away over the hill.

When Linc had disappeared I said, "Go tell Aunt Lutie what's happened. And tell her to call Rubin. We'll never get this fence repaired by ourselves."

Tru brushed off the seat of his jeans. "Mom," he said, "would Linc really hurt us?"

I pulled him into my arms. He was shaking. "I told you to stay put," I said. "God only knows what Linc might do."

Tru hung his head. I lifted his chin. He was crying. "But you were very brave, son. I'm proud of you."

"For real?"

I nodded. "Your grandfather Joseph would have been proud too."

Tru straightened his shoulders. "I wish he hadn't died," he said. "I wish he was here right now."

"For all we know he's watching us from heaven. Now run home."

Tru jogged toward the trailer.

Linc had only managed to pull down a few sections of the fence, but the man had a lot of nerve. I scanned the edges of the horizon in case Linc decided to finish what he'd started. He was gone, and I was alone. The hills huddled together, dark and silent. I removed the bag from under my sweater.

The stiff breeze grabbed my hat. Over and over it threatened to lift it from my head. Maybe heaven was taunting me, daring me to say I didn't need help. This was the last straw, the way you let go of pent-up tears after you stub your toe. An intense anger welled up in me and exploded. Fears and resentments rushed out. I cursed. I screamed. I screeched and threw pebbles at what was left of the fence. God would have to give up on me now.

I stood with my fists clenched. I hated Linc Jackson for defacing my father's property and for pushing my son around. "This is *your* fault," I yelled at God. My throat felt raw, yet as I ranted, the mystery pressed against me. A dust cloud kicked up, but instead of red, it was bright, like looking into the poet

Mary Oliver's white light. The more I tried to ignore it, the more it felt like a lover's hot breath.

The sun dipped below the skyline. I don't know how long I stayed there, maybe minutes, maybe hours. Finally, I felt a strange calm, and my eye twitch disappeared.

There were no fireworks, no angelic hosts strumming harps, or clouds parting with shafts of light. There was no voice, audible or otherwise. There was only a deep and sure-footed peace. The mysterious presence was something I'd never be able to explain but was real nonetheless. Everlasting arms encircled me. I'd never felt so safe.

My thoughts ran to Lutie with her Bible and Tiny's comforting grin. "I love these people," I said. "They make me feel as if I know you, Dad." When I raised my head I tasted my tears but they weren't bitter as before.

Nova's face sprang into my mind. "Help me find her," I begged. "Please, God." I thought of promising to join a convent or become a missionary if God delivered Nova safely back to me, and then I laughed at my impulse to bargain. The God Lutie talked about seemed absolute and as real as my own heartbeat.

I wanted to kneel down in the red earth, but instead I sat down at the base of the splintered fence and pushed my face up to the wind. I didn't care who saw me speaking to the air. The only thing I knew was that I was in the presence of a Father who loved me. He was there, somewhere. He'd been there all along. I pulled on dry grass and ran my fingers through the reddish earth. My father had worked on this very spot. It was here that I had opened the door to a God I'd rejected. As I brushed away soil from the hole where the pink oven door had stood, shreds of what looked like straw or raffia poked out from the fence line.

With my fingers, I scratched in the dirt. Whatever was buried lay only a few inches below the surface, revealing more of itself with every handful of soil I removed. The same oven door I'd whacked Linc with had sat atop the mystery.

After more digging, I unearthed what resembled a tattered canvas bag. I worked carefully, watching in case Linc made a comeback. After brushing off the dirt, I opened the bag. A woven item lay inside. I cradled what looked to be part of a basket and pulled back one edge. A dark, sausage-shaped rock lay inside the basket. I couldn't say a word. Dad's journal had told about finding something special, about hiding a basket made from camas. My father, lost all these years, helped me to find answers to the questions I didn't know I had.

I carefully folded the basket into its bag, careful not to squash the fragile basket. I brushed the soil from my jeans, hung the crumpled dream catcher on one of the remaining oven doors, and raced home. The pulse of my father's blood pumped through me. In the deepest places of my being, I knew who I was.

27

Furious about my confrontation with Linc, Lutie couldn't stop crying. "Tell George we're pressing any and all charges—from trespassing to destruction of private property to assault. Hand me a tissue, will you?" She blew her nose. "Dear Lord, we can't let that skunk get away with this."

Tiny comforted her. "Don't worry, my sweet Pearl." He set a box of tissues on the recliner arm. "Muri is going to help make things right, aren't you, Muri?"

I sat on the sofa, the artifacts spread over the coffee table like a museum display. "Let's see what George has to say." I held Dad's box on my lap. "I asked him to bring the photos. He'll know if we've got enough to make it stick."

Tru clung to my side. He picked up an arrowhead. It slipped through his fingers and landed, unharmed, on the carpet. He quickly retrieved it and held his hands behind his back.

I smiled at my son. "Tru, don't touch, okay?" He nodded, pushing up his glasses.

The easy part would be showing the bags of artifacts to my attorney. It would be much harder to prove what only Tru and I had seen—the bag with the missing kap'n stick in Linc's truck. And it might be impossible to prove Linc knew where the camas basket was hidden under the oven door.

George arrived a few minutes later and was awed by the collection of ancient items spread before him. He whistled softly. "Joe sure did a fine job," he said. "This is pretty impressive stuff." He ran a hand through his silvery hair.

I glanced up. "That's what Rubin's archaeologist friend said."

Tiny helped Lutie out of her recliner. "George, what do you think? I mean, which angle do we take?" She stood with her hands on her hips.

George frowned. "We aren't home free just yet, but—"

Lutie broke in. "I know that. Are we better off charging Linc with grave desecration or do we go with theft? Or even assault? Good glory, George, he shoved my niece here off the bed of a flatbed truck and could've seriously hurt Tru." Lutie's eyes shone wet again, and my son got up and hugged her.

George held up his hand. "I was going to say, it's not open and shut just yet, but I finally got the search warrant. They're looking for evidence in Linc's place as we speak."

"Thank the Lord," Lutie said.

Tiny nodded, and Tru yelled, "Cool!"

I had to agree. God's love felt almost overwhelming, and I could barely hold back my own tears.

The phone rang again, and I felt a leap of hope. The call wasn't about the search warrant. It was Nova. The moment I heard my daughter's voice I shouted. Tiny and Tru danced around the kitchen table as if we'd won the lottery. Lutie waited until I nodded frantically to her, then she started praising God out loud again, crying harder than before. My newfound faith had just got a boost.

"Nova? Baby, are you all right?" I would have crawled right through the fiber optic cable if I could have.

"Yeah, Mom. It's me."

"Nova."

"I'm fine, Mom. Really."

I detected the small waver in her voice, knowing instantly she was far from okay. "Where are you?"

"With the people who were at Rubin's party. They say you know them."

I interrupted her. "What on earth are you doing at Denny and Gwen's place? Did detox give you my message?" I was afraid she'd hang up on me, but I had to know. Nova didn't answer immediately. "It doesn't matter, honey," I said, trying to mend my words. "I'm just glad to hear your voice."

Nova sounded tired. "I didn't get any message. I wasn't in detox, Mom. It's Marvin. He OD'd. Denny and Gwen found me." She said it as if I ought to have figured that much out.

"Stay put then," I said. "I'll be there right away."

"Denny and Gwen say they're bringing me today."

I was surprised but grateful for these two relative strangers and their generosity. "Don't you just love them?" I asked Nova.

"I love *you*, Mom," she said, something I hadn't heard in a very long time. She put Denny on the line.

Denny explained that he and Gwen had retrieved Nova from the street outside the detox center and taken her to their home.

"We're more than happy to drive over with her," Denny said. "Gwen's mom is watching Leila. We're shoving off in a few minutes. We should make it to your place by late this afternoon."

I was too worn-out to protest. "Thank you so much, Denny. I can't begin to tell you how grateful I am for finding Nova."

"No need," Denny said. "I'm just glad we found her safe. See you in a few hours."

After I hung up, George said, "Rubin's pal is an expert, right?" Lutie had apparently filled George in on Dr. Denny the archaeologist.

"Not to mention an absolute angel," Lutie put in.

George smiled. "We'll have a much better chance in court if an expert witness testifies that the things Tru found in Linc's truck are the same artifacts in the photos. Denny's opinion, combined with the journal and all the rest, might be enough." He shook my hand. "Let me get back to the office and see what the warrant turns up."

I marveled at how complex this issue had become. "Law isn't always an exact science, is it?"

George opened the door and turned. "A good piece of luck helps," he said and grinned at Lutie. "If you believe in luck." He left without banging the screen.

When George was gone, Lutie said, "What we have here isn't luck. It's a miracle. Thank you, Jesus."

Nova was coming home. I sat in a daze, while Lutie stroked my hair in the maternal way I'd grown to love. "God's been looking out for your pretty girl," she said.

I nodded. "I'm sorry for what I said to you about angels," I said. "No offense."

Lutie smiled. "None taken."

I suddenly didn't care who knew about my experience with God. I told my aunt the details. She laughed long and hard when I got to the part where I tried to make a deal with God.

"Folks will say anything when they're desperate," she said. "God knows your heart."

I had to agree. Even if nothing else worked out, my daughter was safe. I hoped God didn't really expect me to join a convent. As for punishment, waiting for Nova felt like torture.

"Mercy, you sure been through the fire." Lutie kissed the top of my head the way I used to do Nova when she was a little girl.

A few hours later, Denny and Gwen met us at the trailer with hearty hellos and hugs. I was already looking past them at my daughter. Nova slouched against the doorway, wearing a tank top and a long flowing skirt adorned with Chinese characters. I couldn't remember when I'd last seen her wear anything but worn-out jeans.

For a long awkward moment I couldn't budge, afraid if I touched her she might evaporate like a desert mirage. Finally, she moved in my direction, so I took that as a signal and swooped over to her like a mother bird.

I hugged my daughter hard enough to make sure she was truly alive until finally, she pushed away. "Mom, I can't breathe."

I stood back, crying. I examined her in the same way mothers of newborns carefully check for adequate numbers of fingers and toes. "It's so good to see you, baby."

She looked away. Crying had never been something she did freely or often. Later, we would both break down and bawl. She couldn't let go just yet—not in front of everyone.

Out of the blue, we all started laughing. Denny and Gwen joked about the freeway congestion, air pollution, and road rage. I thanked them countless times for their prayers and for their aid. They had brought us back together, and I was so thankful I could have melted. After a while they left us alone and headed over to Rubin's for the night.

Tru had gone to bed by the time we heard Nova's story. "He said he was getting into a band that had already been signed," she said, the waver in her voice more like a choked-back sob. "But he didn't tell me how these guys were into needles and stuff. Next thing you know, Marvin's hooked really bad. He passed out, Mom. Somebody called 911."

"What about you? You need help too?" I looked at my fingers. Jesus gazed down from his portrait on the wall. Everything magnified as I awaited her answer.

"No way," she said. "I'm not crazy. I hate needles."

I let my breath out. My Nova, the girl who brought home stray cats and helped injured birds, was still in there. I smiled to myself. "Honey, what are you going to do now?" I forced calm into my voice. "I mean what do you *want* to do?"

She sounded angry. "I hope I never see Marvin again. I've been sleeping outside for two days, and I'm cold, wet, and starved . . . and scared, Mom . . . real scared."

"Oh, Nova."

"I'm so glad to be home with you." She was sobbing now, her voice small and thin.

"Are you sure? You could go stay with your dad." I wanted her to decide without pressure from me.

"Right. Dad really has time. And I detest Victoria. No way, Mom."

Finally, she stopped crying and sighed deeply. Her eyes looked sleepy, and when I tucked her into bed, she fell asleep almost immediately. Her breath was rhythmic, slow, and relaxed. I lay awake, thanking God again and again for returning her to me. His angels had done a good job, I said, and I knew Dad would have been pleased. I drifted off, staring at the ceiling, where Nova's glow-in-the-dark plastic stars still reflected a universe of their own. They had been there all these weeks, faithful as their real counterparts in the central Oregon sky.

28

In the morning, George summoned me to his office. I dressed in that prissy navy skirt again and noticed that instead of binding at the waist, it now hung loosely on my hips. Maybe all that jogging had finally paid off.

I packed Tiny's truck with my father's box, the photos, journal, and the artifacts and slipped Nova's glass angel into my pocket. It felt warm to my touch.

"I don't mind driving you, Muri," Tiny said. "In fact, I'd just blend into the woodwork, like a chauffeur."

"I appreciate that, Uncle Tiny, really. But this is something I need to do alone." I turned to Lutie. "I could use lots of prayers, though." My legs shook uncontrollably.

I thought she might cry then, but she only muttered one of her *glory be's*.

"Why can't I come?" Tru looked angry, something rare for him.

"I'll be back by this afternoon, Tru. Try to understand."

He let out a groan. "Whatever." I could tell that my next teen adventure wasn't far away.

Nova had eaten, showered, and slept for hours and hours. But she awoke long enough to wish me luck. "Mom, I'm sure you're going to win." She hugged me and kissed my cheek and dived back into bed.

On the road to Murkee, I held onto the vibrating steering wheel of Tiny's pickup and weighed the pros and cons. Since Lutie and Tiny were no longer in danger of losing their home, I didn't have to stay. After all, I had found what I'd been looking for. The legacy of Joseph Pond was a part of me now.

Besides, in spite of Dove's offer to get the library started again, I was certain there were more job opportunities in Portland than Murkee. I might have to get certified in elementary education, but my chances of finding a decent job would be higher in a larger town. I squinted hard against the glare of the overcast skies, but today no hawks circled. The clouds had woven themselves together into a heavy blanket.

What about Linc? He might want, no, he would *relish*, any opportunity to make our lives miserable. Tiny and Lutie were part of the community, but we were still outsiders. Leaving would be the safest thing for the kids. In spite of my heroic thoughts about becoming a conservationist and preserving the wilderness, I wasn't exactly a cowgirl.

"But I love it here," I heard myself say. I couldn't make up my mind.

Suddenly, a gleaming SUV with dark tinted windows nearly sideswiped me, and then swerved back into its own lane. I gasped as the guy shook his fist at me. I immediately prayed for some of Lutie's angels to keep me safe. I could almost see my aunt's smile—a smile that was a lot like my father's . . . and a lot like my own.

When I entered George's office he pulled on his suit jacket and looked dashing as the cowboy lawyer in his brown western-style outfit and shiny boots. He also wore an ear-to-ear grin. "Good news."

I gasped and let out a whoop. "Tell me!"

George reached into his coat pocket and pulled out the photos Dad had taken. He pointed to one of the arrowheads. "See this one?" He paused. "Near as we can tell, this is the same artifact that's described in a forged document."

Every citizen in Murkee must have heard. "Fakes," I crowed. "Linc's documents are fakes."

"I was skeptical," George said. "But you were right. Our FBI guy dug up some improper documentation. The articles described were a pre-Clovis arrowhead and some sort of tribal stick for digging roots."

I opened the bag and produced the fragile remnants, gingerly setting them, one by one, on his desk. Now it was George's turn to gasp.

"This one's called a kap'n stick," I told him.

"Hold on, hold on," George said. "The search warrant did its job. An entire room of Linc's house is covered with wall-to-wall artifacts."

George sat down and leaned back in his chair. "More stuff than you can imagine. It'll take weeks to sift through it all." He outlined our next move. "The forged document will be enough to put Linc out of business. But the Feds are interested in the collector. He's the big fish."

"This one," I said, pointing to the camas basket. "In his journal my father wrote about this camas basket. I found it yesterday when Linc tried to pull down the fence."

"We'll get him for that too," George said.

"What matters is that Dad knew this basket was special. When he suspected Linc was stealing from the site, he buried the basket under one of the oven doors." Unexpectedly, loss spread over me like a wet blanket. Would I be able to make the fence as sturdy as before?

Then there was Linc. My neighbor had done terrible things, but now he'd lost everything: his reputation, his grandson to drugs, and his new Cadillac. Maybe he'd lose his freedom too.

"What will they do to Linc?"

George arched his eyebrows. "I'm glad we caught him, but in a way, nobody wins here. He's been a part of this community as long as I can remember. The FBI says they may allow him to plea-bargain in exchange for information on his buyers."

"I don't wish evil on Linc, but he's done a lot of damage."

George nodded. "I didn't think you could beat old Linc Jackson, but here you are. As your aunt would say, 'A man reaps what he sows.'"

I sighed and gently spread open the basket's tattered edges. I lifted out the rock-like plug. "Dr. Denny says this is a real coprolite. It sounds awful, but it may be Dad's most valuable find."

George examined the specimen. "Who would have believed that fossilized waste could be worth anything? But I doubt we can pin this on Jackson directly."

I crossed my arms. "If Dr. Denny dates the site as pre-Clovis, won't everything found out there increase in value?"

George laughed and helped me place the artifacts in their protective bags. "You're as sharp as your Aunt Lutie."

I smiled so hard that my cheeks ached. My father would have agreed. I could have kissed George, but I kept my cool, knowing we'd need to get everything formalized before we could truly relax. I had learned that nothing out in the Oregon desert is a sure thing, especially where water is concerned.

Not that long ago, I would have given anything for a taste of suburbia. A golf course might have been extreme, but how about a movie theater or even a Safeway? Now everything around me had slowed down, just as my life had gentled out from its once frenetic pace. Most of the world had never heard of Murkee Creek or seen the expanses of sagebrush buffeted by wind and the ever-present red soil.

As I left George's office, I nearly knocked over Rubin, who stood leaning against the outside wall.

"Hey," he said.

"Hey."

"Sorry I haven't been around. I can explain. Later, though." He hesitated, perhaps not quite sure what I'd do. Hurt melted away. I hugged him, and he hugged me back.

"I thought you'd bailed on me," I said.

"Wouldn't think of it."

I reached for his hand, but he hesitated. "What's wrong?"

"I can't stay," he said. A painful expression shadowed his eyes. "Come over later, will you?" I nodded, and he walked away.

Back at the trailer, Nova laughed about the coprolite, but no one mentioned Marvin. Had I been with less forgiving people I might have organized a lynch party for that kid. But as Aunt Lutie would later observe, "Just having Linc in your family tree is punishment enough."

"You were right," Nova said. "Denny and Gwen are way cool. Their church's outreach runs a meeting for homeless kids. Even if you aren't sure what you believe, they pray for you. Did you know Gwen designs clothes too? She says I can come and learn glassblowing."

I studied my daughter. She looked thin. Deep shadows encircled her eyes, and her cheekbones protruded. Her hair had grown out some; it was no longer orange or purple or green but a familiar and pleasant brown. The ice blue of her gaze was softer than I remembered. When she first hugged me back, she had smelled like the inside of Gwen and Denny's house.

I smiled at her. "Things will be better now, I promise. We're a real family, just like Lutie said. No more fighting, all right?"

Later, Uncle Tiny told her she needed to fatten up. I could have warned him that any mention of weight would set her off. Like most other girls her age, Nova was convinced she was chubby, even though her jeans were loose.

In true Nova form, she grimaced at the lunch her uncle had cooked and refused to eat it. Tru acknowledged her with a "Hi, geek," and sat down with a plateful of food. Within a minute they were at each other's throats.

"You're such a pig," she said. "Chew with your mouth shut, idiot."

He displayed a half-chewed bite. "I learned it from Jim," he said proudly, and Jim looked up from his bed beside the television set. "Bet you missed us, huh?"

"Gross. You and these disgusting pigs." She shuddered dramatically. "You're such a moron."

"You're totally, what-*ever*." Tru mocked in a higher voice than his normal one.

"You're so immature."

It was a standoff, and they glared at each other, trying to come up with the consummate burn.

Tiny sat down between them and looked at Nova with that ever-present smile of his. His size alone forced an uneasy truce.

"You could always fix yourself something else, Miss Nova," Lutie said from her recliner. She looked up at Jesus with a pleading glance and then went back to her crocheting.

"Fine." Nova scooted her chair back loudly and flounced to the cupboard. Tru made a face at her as she passed him. I smiled. It was just like old times.

Lutie pulled on her yellow gloves. "And don't forget, we got a ton of work to get ready for the bazaar. Rhonda Gaye is coming over this afternoon, so you two can get your entry finished."

"Don't you remember?" Lutie said. "Rhonda's been sewing on that outfit you dreamed up."

"Terrific." Nova said. She turned to make one of her dramatic exits.

"Hold on," I said. "You and Tru pull kitchen duty. Lutie, give Nova your gloves."

Lutie solemnly handed over the gloves, and Nova clucked her tongue. Tru just groaned and the two of them went to the sink and started a name-calling contest. At first I couldn't understand how siblings who said they loved each other so much could bicker like that, but then I decided the put-downs were their way of saying, "Hey, I missed you." At least they didn't throw anything at one another.

When the dishes were finally washed, Nova stripped off the gloves and complained that her freshly painted nails were ruined. "Totally." She put on a pouty look. I summoned her to the bedroom to tell her about my plans, and she trudged along behind me, no doubt convinced I was about to nag her some more.

"This is so not fair!" She yelled when I told her about my idea to move. The look on her face reminded me of the first time she'd tasted broccoli at age three, spit it halfway across the room, and clamped her mouth shut.

"I don't understand." I'd been so certain about this whole thing on my way to Portland. Now I wondered if the girl in front of me was the same Nova I knew.

Defiant, she crossed her arms over her chest. "Did you ask *me* if I wanted to move? How typical!" She clucked her tongue with the same disdain as her "whatevers."

I used my best librarian's voice. "Tru and I like it fine here. You're the one who hates it so much, the one who complains about Murkee being so 'nowhere.'"

"Your idea sounds worse," she said through clenched teeth, "I'd rather die."

Patience rushed out of me, so I took a deeper breath. "I'm doing this for *you*. I thought that's what you wanted."

"You don't get it, Mom."

"What exactly don't I get?" Now *I* felt like throwing something, so I jammed my hands into the pockets of my skirt. I tried not to look at my father's photo, whose eyes pleaded with me to fight no more with my sixteen-year-old rebel.

But instead of attacking, she sat down on the bed and picked at the bumps on the faded chenille spread. "Before I left, I thought this place was like eternal damnation. I'm like, 'Great, I live in a dump with a weird aunt and uncle and a bunch of pigs. Perfect.'" She looked up at me. "But it's different now, okay? In Portland all I thought about was getting back home, and now we're leaving?"

I sat down beside her, stroked her hair, and she didn't pull away. "I thought it would make you happy."

She groaned the way teenagers do when they know they aren't getting through. "And there's something else," she said. She unzipped her battered backpack and took out a small New Testament. "I heard you talking to Aunt Lutie about God. Were you for real?"

I groped for words that didn't sound awkward. "I've had what you might call a spiritual awakening, yes."

"I guess I don't mind too much." She smiled. "Denny and Gwen made God sound pretty cool."

"God thinks you're pretty cool, too," I said, "and so do I."

Nova grimaced. "I'm not a little churchy girl." She held up her Bible. "I said I'd give God a chance." She tossed the Bible onto the bed.

"You're almost a grown-up now," I said. "Nobody's trying to make you do anything."

She sighed and rolled her eyes the familiar way I'd grown to love. "I didn't mean to start a fight," she said, and I thought I saw a tear in her eye. "I'm glad to be home. Really."

I couldn't say anything more. I threw my arms about her.

"Happy?" I managed to say.

"Being home makes me happy," she said.

"Even with a pesky brother and weird relatives and pigs?"

She sighed again loudly but then smiled. "Don't forget a nagging Mom."

"Me? Nag?" I could have kissed her, but she was already out the door.

I sat there awhile longer and smoothed over the wrinkles in the spread where Nova had sat. So much for knowing what my daughter wanted; her mind changed about as often as the color of her hair. Her pleas to stay were not without conditions. She begged me to fix up the house and wondered if Tiny could build her a separate bedroom.

"Can't you homeschool us?" she asked later. "I don't want to be around a bunch of cowboys."

"Out here we're all a bunch of cowboys," Tiny answered.

"Whatever."

Somehow, when Nova explained her reasons for staying in Murkee, they became my own.

29

The pigs were penned up so they would stay out of trouble. They squealed their disapproval at not being allowed to roam all over the yard. Jim was caged with them and stuck his snout through the wire fence and looked woeful.

Tru bent down to scratch Jim's black hairy ears. "Can't we take him with us? I'll watch him, I promise."

"I don't think they let pigs wander around town, son," I said.

My uncle crisscrossed several bungee cords to strap a boy's bike to the bed of the truck, a bike he'd assembled from his stacks of parts. It was for the child of a new family in town. Lutie wanted to know "what on God's green earth" he was doing back there and why we were taking a bicycle along.

"His name is Ryan and he's eight and he needs a bike. That's what Doc Perkins told me," Tiny said, grinning. "There, I believe that'll do it." He jiggled the bike to make sure it was secure.

Nova stormed out of the house, a stack of sewing supplies in her arms. "I told Rhonda I'd be over an hour ago, Mom. Can you drive me?"

"In what? We don't have a car, and Tiny's busy."

Nova stamped her foot. "Whatever."

Tiny and Tru climbed into his truck. Tiny said out the window, "I'd be tickled to give you a ride."

I held up my hand. "You said you were going the other direction, Unc. Nova needs to learn to plan things."

"Mu-ther."

"It's not that far out of my way," Tiny added.

"I give up," I said. Nova clambered into the truck and scooted Tru into the middle. Tiny ground the gears, and the truck bumped down the gravel drive.

Lutie put her arm around me. "You're doing fine," she said, gently brushing strands of hair away from my face. She always smelled fresh and full of life. "I already said more prayers than you could shake a stick at."

Joseph's Journal
March 2008

Today, Lutie grabbed my arm and shook me out of a dream about you, Muri. "I took a slight detour," I told her. Five minutes? An hour? I wasn't sure how long I'd been out. When I tried to move I spilled the last of my iced tea, the only thing I can keep down these days. Lutie helped me to my feet, and I breathed in sharp to steady myself. "Let's get you outside, Joseph," Lutie whispered. "You can watch the sunset."

If you saw me you wouldn't recognize me. I'm a skeleton, shuffling along in the yard. That's what I've become, a suggestion of myself. I hold my hands out in front of me to keep from teetering . . . to be sure I'm still alive. The liver is an unforgiving thing and spiteful as a lot of women I've known.

Lutie guided me to a lawn chair. The yard is just as full of junk as my memory, piled with bicycle parts and flotsam no one will ever want. The fence I built with my own hands leans a little now, but I'm still glad I put those oven doors to good use.

I cling to the only thing left, a loving God, an abiding promise of eternal life. I'm not afraid to die. The Holy Ghost will carry me. When I think about walking through the tunnel I see Jesus standing with outstretched arms, beckoning.

I wish I could package up faith and give it to you and then let it become your own. If I had more time I'd dream my precious Lord into you, Muri, but time is running out. I can't trust this body to keep going.

I don't trust these eyes anymore, either. Seems like the mound's being tampered with again, but I can't catch the thief. Or maybe it's just animals digging for a meal.

I press the edge of my hand against my forehead like a visor, to drive off the summer sun, waiting and listening. If I watch long enough, I'll see a young girl dancing like we used to dance. When I do I won't fight it. I'll run to you and hold you forever.

30

By the end of the week all of Murkee knew Nova was home. We were the only ones, though, who knew that Linc's life had turned "slippery as hog slop," as Tiny said. Linc was gone, supposedly to Portland to fetch his grandson. Before he left, the sheriff brought Linc over. I was suspicious he might have Ed Johnson or Frieda Long's husband waiting to shoot me or torch the trailer.

He came in the evening, looking rumpled, as if he hadn't slept well. His escort wouldn't allow Linc inside, so we both stood in the yard shivering. In late fall the nighttime desert temperature falls below freezing some years. A light dusting of snow clung to the ground and to the junk in the yard, frosting the orbs on top of the posts.

In the semidarkness I couldn't tell if he was sincere, but I wasn't taking any chances. I stood as far away as I could. I shot up an emergency prayer for what to say. I wasn't afraid—only cold. I wrapped my favorite blue sweater tightly around me.

"We've both been through hell with the kids," I said. "I feel awful about Marvin."

"Don't need your sympathy." Linc huffed.

"What do you want then?"

He examined his fingernails perhaps so I wouldn't see his eyes harden. "I come to ask . . . if you ever hear from my grandson, would you . . . oh well, don't bother."

"Look, I won't press charges against Marvin. But he'd best find some sort of help or else he might wind up like his grandfather."

"If you and Jonto had seen things my way, this whole mess could have been avoided," Linc said. He still didn't get it.

I crossed my arms. "Just tell me one thing." I stared him straight in the eye. "Who shot those cows?"

Linc Jackson looked up at the night sky but wouldn't answer.

"I knew it," I whispered and fought to keep from lighting into him again. "You'd probably shoot off your own foot if you thought it would get you what you wanted."

Linc shrugged as if he didn't understand how pathetic he was. "You're just like ol' Chief Joseph."

"You're trespassing," I said. "Now get off my land."

He muttered something under his breath, glanced back at the trailer, and shook his head. He trudged to the waiting patrol car with his hat pulled down and his shoulders hunched forward.

A nudge prompted me to pray for him, although I admit I would rather pray for a rattlesnake. I unclenched my fists and did the best I could, but praying for one's enemies is harder than it sounds.

I watched him go. I'd stood up to Linc with a confidence I had never felt before. My body shook once more, but it wasn't from adrenaline or the cold night air. I could rely on a new strength, one that welled up from someplace deep. My heavenly father had been there all along. I was no longer tormented by the mystery of what kind of man Joseph Pond had been.

The power of God had opened in me a current of peace. I felt loved with every breath I took. When I stopped trembling I pushed open the screen door, which protested more loudly than usual in the cold, and walked into my home.

"Lord have mercy, honey, what's Linc gone and done to you now?" Lutie said, surrounding me with a hug and her sweet smell. Tiny stood at her side with a worried look.

"He didn't do anything to me," I said, hugging her back. "In fact, I think I just socked it to him, as they used to say on *Laugh-In*."

Tru glanced up from his computer screen in the corner and said, "Huh?" and then shook his head and went back to his chess game.

I tousled his hair. "Maybe . . . maybe we're all ready for some changes. Like getting you a haircut."

"Aw, Mom."

Tiny smiled. "I know a good barber."

I smiled. "And let's just say if we're family then maybe we ought to all be sitting in the pew together. It would have made Dad happy."

"Thank you, Jesus," was all Lutie could say.

That's what I loved best about life out here—the way folks just sidestep problems like they do road apples. I felt a little sorry for people like Linc, who thought they could rip into the fabric of their neighbors' lives and still come out on top. As Lutie said, "He's got his just desserts, all right. Lord forgive him." I wasn't sure about the forgiveness part—not yet—but I promised I'd keep trying.

Was it too late to convince Rubin to change his mind and stay? He felt like family too. Next morning, I kept this in mind as I made my way past the emu pens. The birds fluttered their flightless wings at me and then shrunk back against each other in a cowardly clump. Rubin was right. Emus are the weirdest birds on earth.

He was in his office, standing amidst an assortment of books and papers, slightly turned away from me. I didn't announce my presence. I wanted to watch him—the way his fingers curved around the framed certificate he held, the one that said he'd graduated vet school with top honors. I still thought they were capable hands, the hands of a surgeon, even if they operated on cows and sheep and pigs.

I studied his profile, too, for as long as I dared. There was sadness in his face, as well as strength. It was the same quality I'd seen in the photo of my father, and I couldn't look away. Rubin turned and saw me staring.

"I've got so much stuff," he said. He ran his fingers across the frame to wipe off dust. "So much stuff."

"Rubin, I came to tell you—"

"That you're not leaving? I figured it out." He laid the framed certificate on his desk.

"You don't have to go, either," I said. "Linc's in custody."

Rubin shook his head. "I told you before. I'm the local bad boy. My business is history." His words had an edge to them, and he tossed a fat textbook onto a stack of papers. I cringed. He kept his back to me. "Someone's coming out to show the house. Real estate people always want everything neat and tidy."

"Rubin."

He turned around. "You think I'm running away, don't you? I'm desperate. On top of that—"

He paused and stared off into space, and then looked into my eyes. "On top of that I'm falling in love with you." He lifted my chin so I couldn't avoid his gaze. "Marry me, Muri. Please."

I gasped.

"Did you hear me?"

"You don't get it," I said. "You're wonderful, Rubin, but I'm not leaving."

He took my hands. "You telling me no?"

"I'm not telling you anything yet. Give me some time." I pulled away and set an antique novel—a George Eliot—on the stack. "I don't know how to say this. I found—"

"Found what?"

"Something to believe in," I said and pictured Joseph Pond in his cowboy getup. "I didn't get here in time to meet my dad, but he left me his faith. All I know is, from now on things are going to be different."

Rubin smiled. "That's what I love—the way you stand up for what you believe in. I may not make it to church, but I'm not opposed to the idea. Promise you'll at least think it over?"

"I'll think about it," I said. "If you'll think about staying put."

"I'll see what I can work out—for the stream, for the land —for you crazy bunch of Ponds." He hugged me close, and I drank in his now familiar scent.

From Rubin's house I walked the trail to the creek. The power of this land was in the water all right, but I didn't know exactly how I'd keep it from being sucked dry. I thought of the creek, striving to keep cows and fish and people alive. I might never be a rancher or a farmer, but I could be on the side of anyone who wanted to keep this place just a little wild. Maybe I'd even join the land use watchdog group and campaign for their causes. I'd done pretty well up on Ed Johnson's truck.

I leaned against my cottonwood tree. The leaves had all fallen; the stream was iced over where rocks shaded it. Carpets of mosses and lichens—red, greens, and yellows—clung to rocks jutting from the bank. There were no cattle hooves in the muddy spots. Rubin's funny NO GRAZING ALLOWED sign creaked whenever the wind gusted, and its odd rhythm made me feel like dancing. I closed my eyes, waiting, listening.

This was the place Joseph Pond visited most often, the place where I felt I knew him best. Perhaps he'd sat out here reading his Civil War books or drowning out his pain with the birds singing, fingerlings glittering in the shallows. Or perhaps he only came here to pray.

From my spot under the tree I could see the outline of his crazy fence, the windows of the oven doors winking with flashes of sunlight. The fence my father built was odd and uneven, but it was sturdy and able to withstand storms and high winds. It had become the beacon he wrote about in his journal, showing me where to look. The creek he loved really was like a "watered garden." I'd found the reference in Lutie's Bible—in Jeremiah, to be exact.

It won't be that long before the camas on the stream bank will bloom again, and the leaves of the cottonwood will parachute down to the water when the wind coaxes them loose. The toads and frogs will sit on their spots and proclaim their wisdom to anyone who is listening, and I'll be among them. God will teach me how to live and someday I'll be where my father resides. Lutie's got me believing in angels again, and I know for sure Chief Joseph watches over me.

Discussion Questions

1. *The Fence My Father Built* is told mostly in first person through the eyes of Muri Pond, but her deceased father, Joseph, also has a voice through journals he left behind. What picture of Joseph do the journal entries paint? How do these entries help Muri know and understand where she came from? What do you know about your own heritage? How does this knowledge influence you?

2. When Muri arrives at the oven-door fence, the house and her father turn out to be nothing like Muri imagined. What are the invisible walls that Muri erects to shield herself and her family from things she'd rather not face? Have you ever been disappointed when something turned out different than what you expected? How did you deal with your feelings?

3. In Murkee, land and water are integral to the ranchers' survival. Some of the community sees Joseph and Rubin's stream preservation efforts as hurting that survival. Is it possible to have both conservation and progress? Why or why not?

4. Muri initially is standoffish toward her aunt, yet Lutie turns out to be one of Muri's most steady supporters. If Lutie hadn't been there to comfort Muri, do you think Muri would have resolved her problems in the same way? How important are friends? Have your friends helped you through crises? How?

5. Muri likes to sit next to the burial mound and stream, where her father had once sat. There, she feels connected, loved, and at peace. Do you have a favorite place that helps you feel peaceful and connected?

6. Muri's a librarian and can't imagine life without books. What does her start-up library tell you about her as a person? How important are books to your life?

7. Joseph was named after Chief Joseph, the Nez Perce chief who famously said, "I will fight no more forever." Yet Joe's journal entries reveal that he was willing to fight to protect what he loved. Do you see any parallels between his efforts and Muri's struggle to belong? Have you ever felt as if you didn't fit in? How did you handle this?

8. How are Muri and Nova different and yet alike? Do you think both mother and daughter are after some of the same things? Did you ever try to be as different as you could from your parents? How are you alike or different today?

9. Muri's son Truman sees Uncle Tiny as a father figure. Is it a healthy relationship? If you were Muri, how would you approach their friendship?

10. In uncovering Linc's secrets, Muri is also forced to acknowledge her father's odd characteristics and his addiction to alcohol. In what ways does Muri reach toward forgiveness? What does forgiveness mean in this case? How do you react when you discover that someone is not all bad or all good?

11. Why do you think Muri's father built the fence? What does the fence symbolize for Muri? For you as the reader?

12. Muri finally discovers she's found her way home after all. How does her changed attitude help her believe that Murkee, her father's place, and even the oven-door start-up fence are exactly where she belongs? How do you define home?

Want to learn more about author
Linda S. Clare and check out other great
fiction from Abingdon Press?

Sign up for our fiction newletter at
www.AbingdonPress.com
to read interviews with your favorite authors, find tips
for starting a reading group, and stay posted on what
new titles are on the horizon. It's a place to connect
with other fiction readers or post a
comment about this book.

Be sure to visit Linda online!

www.godsonggrace.blogspot.com